"*No Sad Songs* explores the complexities of family, love, and loss, as we follow one young man on a powerful, heartwrenching journey of self-discovery—one that is perfectly balanced with both humor and hope."

> — Amber Smith, *New York Times* bestselling author of *The Way I Used to Be* and *The Last to Let Go*

"In *No Sad Songs*, Frank Morelli has written a beautiful, poignant book about the near-impossible burdens that can be foisted upon us by our unpredictable lives. Gabe LoScuda trudges through the mud in the front lines of his own personal war, and he does it with so much heart you can't help but root for him. Reading Gabe's story, we learn to appreciate, as he does, the people in our lives who can be patient with us as we struggle toward our own awakening—the friends and family who can tell us we're being idiots while still continuing to love us, every muddy step of the way."

> — Jack Cheng, author, *See You in the Cosmos*

"Young meets old in this heartfelt, compelling debut."

> — Jerry Spinelli, author, *The Warden's Daughter* and *Stargirl*

"In *No Sad Songs*, Morelli deftly balances genuinely hilarious moments with gut-punchingly moving ones. A big-hearted, seriously funny read."

> — Lance Rubin, author of *Denton Little's Deathdate* and *Denton Little's Still Not Dead*

"*No Sad Songs* is truly a work of heart! This emotional journey of tough choices is wrapped in the messy but beautiful truth of family obligation and honor. Readers will be rooting for Gabe all the way through."

> — Jennifer Walkup, author, *This Ordinary Life* and *Second Verse*

"With plenty of humor and heart, *No Sad Songs* will have you rooting for its endearing, flawed characters until the very end."

> — Kristin Bartley Lenz, author, *The Art of Holding On and Letting Go*

"An absolutely fantastic read from beginning to end, Frank Morelli's debut novel *No Sad Songs* is at turns hilarious, spirited, and a little bit heartbreaking. What a ride. I'm so glad I took it."

> — Amina Cain, author, *Creature* and *I Go To Some Hollow*

"Relatable on so many levels and to so many ages beyond its YA target, *No Sad Songs* is filled with one amazingly powerful scene after another, with a perfect blend of humor and pathos that will keep you hooked throughout. The YA world is about to have a new king."

— R.J. Fox, author, *Love & Vodka, Tales from the Dork Side,* and *Awaiting Identification*

"When tragedy strikes, Gabe LoScuda's world is quickly turned upside down. Thanks to Frank Morelli's tremendous heart and wit, we laugh through tears as Gabe takes on grief and overwhelming responsibility like a champ."

— Patrick Flores-Scott, author, *Jumped In*

"A story of great loss, sacrifice, and struggle, *No Sad Songs* is a look at resilience and what it means for young and old to come together in life, love, and friendship. A highly recommended read."

— Ann Y.K. Choi, author of the Toronto Book Award finalist, *Kay's Lucky Coin Variety*

"*No Sad Songs* is lovely and funny and heart-aching and true. I didn't want it to end. But the big-hearted story and characters—especially the very real, unforgettable Gabe—will stay with me for a long, long time."

— Jennifer Niven, *New York Times* bestselling author of *All the Bright Places*

"*No Sad Songs* manages to be at once a funny, heartbreaking, and life-affirming coming of age story about the family we love and hate, self-discovery, and the promises we make and which we choose to keep."

— Estelle Laure, author of *This Raging Light* and *But Then I Came Back*

"Frank Morelli's *No Sad Songs* burns bright. With lacerating prose and emotional honesty, Morelli vividly captures the intensity and freedom of young adulthood and the crushing responsibilities of being an adult. The book veers raucously and with wild, teenage abandon from fart jokes to Thoreau and, in between, makes room for me to feel deeply for Gabe LoScuda and to break my heart."

— Bryan Hurt, author, *Everyone Wants to be Ambassador to France*

NO SAD SONGS

Published by Fish Out of Water Books, Ann Arbor, MI, USA.

www.fowbooks.com

© 2018 by Frank Morelli.

ISBN: 978-0-9899087-4-0

Library of Congress Control Number: 2017918452

Pop culture · Coming of age · Travel · Culture shock · Going against the grain · Adversity · Triumph · Extraordinary lives · Ordinary lives

We are all fish out of water.

We publish non-fiction, creative non-fiction, and realistic fiction.

For further information, visit www.fowbooks.com.

Cover design by J. Caleb Clark; www.jcalebdesign.com.

NO SAD SONGS

Frank Morelli

To my grandparents.

Lest we never forget the true
identities of our elders.

1

SNOT, SARDINES, AND OTHER ASSORTED FOLLIES

There's a dried-up booger hanging from his nose. Again.

"Let's wipe it off," I say.

"Get away!" he screams, alerting every customer on the aisle and at least two cute checkout girls to my abuse.

"You gotta keep your nose clean, kid."

"Keep your nose clean," he parrots. "Keep your nose clean."

Grandpa used to be the one to make demands of me. Now he's almost completely gone. His brain is, anyway. His body's as strong as the day he stormed the beach at Normandy. Maybe stronger.

The doctors pegged him with Pick's Disease, a cruel form of Alzheimer's, when I was fourteen. Back then you could barely notice. He'd lose the car keys in his own jacket pocket, forget to send birthday cards—little stuff you could overlook. By the time I was sixteen he couldn't remember his own name. Ernie.

It's like one day he's bringing me lollipops and slipping five-dollar bills in my plastic cowboy holster, and the next he's chucking grenades at me in Mom's spotless kitchen. The grenades are actually hard boiled eggs. He gets things mixed up, and when he does they take the shape of memories from his war days—which is fitting since being around him is like being on a battlefield, even if you're just standing on aisle two at the grocery store.

"Now blow, Grandpa," I say, staying calm and measured like the doctors taught me. Alzheimer's patients hate havoc. Any memories they have are attached to emotion, so I try not to pressure my grandfather because it makes him remember the bad times. I guess that's why it feels like I'm dealing with a four-year-old.

"Come on, Grandpa, you gotta blow into the hanky."

"No!" At least ten heads spin around to gawk at us. Man, I hate rubberneckers.

"Keep your nose clean, kid," I say again. It's the only way I can get him to calm down and it feels weird. I'm eighteen years old and I'm using the same stupid trick my eighty-year-old grandfather used on me when I was three.

"Stop! Get away from me!" he screams, oblivious to his own technique being used against him. The rubber wheels of the courtesy scooter squeak against the floor as he thrashes his arms like a toddler having a tantrum.

The guy from the meat section is walking toward us. You know the guy. The one who wears a bloodstained apron and a shower cap and walks around the store with a cleaver like he's in a slasher film. He has this look on his face that tells me I better get control of the old man. I grab for one of Grandpa's twig-thin wrists. His arm feels slippery. Then I see why. There's a can of sardines cradled in his lap. The lid is peeled back and there's oil and scales and fishy grossness all over Grandpa's arms, pants, his shirt, everything. I catch a whiff of rotten pier as I move in closer for another attempt.

"Excuse me! You'll need to pay for those," the butcher says as I snatch Grandpa by the wrist and squeeze.

"Aaah!" Grandpa has the rubber tires bouncing off the linoleum at this point. You might have thought the store manager installed hydraulics on the damn thing, like some kind of geriatric low-rider.

I squeeze harder. "Release! Dirty Kraut! Combat!" He's shouting random phrases again. That's about all the communication he's capable of these days, which might be encouraging if I didn't get compared to Josef Goebbels every time.

By now, the butcher is a few steps away. His cleaver reflects little sparkles of light. "Hey kid, I'm gonna need you to—"

"Yeah, I get it," I start to say. I'm reaching for the can of sardines when . . . *bam*! Total stars. Like Wile E. Coyote getting crushed by an Acme anvil. I'm reeling a bit. Not sure what happened. I'm on my back. Something trickles from my nose. I look up at the steel girders of a warehouse ceiling. Rows of industrial-sized lights stare down at me like huge Cyclops eyes. A pair of sneakers squeaks across a linoleum floor. And I smell fish. Grandpa. I'm at the grocery store. A man in a bloody smock stands over me. The butcher.

"You okay, kid?" he asks. Suddenly he's not worried about the can of sardines. "Old guy got you good. Right in the nose. He an ex-boxer or something?"

"Ex-army," I manage to say as I smear a trail of blood across my forearm from my upper lip. "I'm his grandson." The butcher offers me his non-cleavered hand and pulls me to my feet. Grandpa is calm. He slides a greasy sardine around in his mouth.

"Jeez," he whispers, "I'd hate to see what he did to his enemies."

I shrug. What can I say? I just got cold-cocked by an octogenarian. It doesn't get more embarrassing than taking a ten count on a grocery store floor after your grandfather jaws you with an uppercut.

The butcher hands me a crisp, white towel. It's the only thing on him that's not covered in red blotches—until I squeeze it against my nose. Ouch. Stars again. My schnoz is probably broken. Great. Like a kid with the last name LoScuda needs an even bigger nose.

"I'll be sure to pay for those," I tell the butcher.

"This can's on me. Keep the towel."

He pats me on the shoulder and gives me this sympathetic look with big eyes and all that junk. I feel like unleashing Grandpa on him, but then I get distracted.

By her.

Marlie McDermott. Homecoming queen. Cheerleader. Goddess of Schuylkill High. Subject of dreams I'd rather not share in public. Or in front of Grandpa, coherent or not.

Oh. Grandpa. Crap. Marlie's staring at me. I start to smile, but then remember it's only because I'm hanging out on aisle two with an old guy in a cart and I'm holding a bloody rag against my face. I see her eyebrows raise and her nose crinkle. She walks toward me like a concerned mother. *Great.* My heart beats so fast I feel like I might puke. Please don't puke on her, I tell myself.

"Oh my God, are you ok?" she asks at roughly the speed of an auctioneer.

"Oh, yeah. I'm fine, thanks. I . . . uh . . . I must have tripped into this display or something." I point to a display of Oreo cookies that is neatly stacked and completely untouched.

"Oh, I thought you got hit," she says, "by that old guy."

"No," I say quickly. "No, no. Definitely not. Get hit by that old guy? Come on." Clearly, I have nothing to tell her that can make this situation any less of a nightmare so I go with, "I don't even know the guy."

"You don't?"

"Of course not. Just trying to help out the elderly." I can hear myself talking and I know I should shut up, but the words spill out against my will. "He couldn't reach a can, you see, and I—"

"Is he here alone?" she asks.

"I guess so. Yes. I mean . . . I'm not sure."

"Shouldn't we get the manager? He looks lost."

A droplet of oily sardine drool rolls down Grandpa's chin. Great timing, old man.

"The manager? Oh, no. That's probably not something—"

"But he's alone. He could be in trouble. I'm getting the manager."

"No, Marlie. I . . . uh . . . just remembered. He's my grandfather."

"Your grandfather? But I thought—"

"Yeah. Just a big misunderstanding. Hit my head, you know. Memory's a bit foggy."

Please shut up now, Gabe. Why are you still talking? It's like my vocal cords fished a dragon roll out of the dumpster behind Ryoshi and gobbled it down in one bite. The result: verbal diarrhea.

"Don't worry," I continue, "we mess around like this all the time. Just a gag. Right, Grandpa?"

If only someone would gag me before another stupid line crosses my lips.

Marlie glances over at the old man. He's holding the tin can upside down and the remaining fishy oil drizzles into his lap.

"Go fish!" he says with a sparkle in his eyes. "You're the Old Maid," he says, pointing toward Marlie.

And he's laughing. Hard. Like he's watching a comedy act—and who can blame him? His only grandson has to be the biggest joke on the planet.

"Ohhhkay," Marlie says at a speed that would never get someone hired as an auctioneer. She's slowly stepping away. Making her escape. I know I have to do something because I've been in love with Marlie since freshman year and our communication has been about as consistent as the Olympics. Once every four years—and I would hardly call it a gold medal performance.

"So, I'll see you around?" I say.

That's it? *I'll see you around?* Really?

But that's all I can manage. My vocal cords must have washed back a dose of Imodium because the flow has stopped. The words are all backed up.

"Yeah," she says. But she doesn't sound so convincing. "I guess."

Ugh. The dagger.

"See you around, Glenn."

I spoke too soon. *That* was the dagger.

Marlie sweeps past me and I catch the soft scent of her golden hair as it swooshes across her slender shoulders. Bubble gum and suntan lotion and cookies baking in the oven. She's intoxicating, and I'm obsessed.

I know I have to give this up. I mean, Christ, she thinks my name is Glenn. Holding out hope for a chance with Marlie carries about the same odds as me winning the Kentucky Derby. And I do mean me. With a pint-sized jockey riding my back as I slog through the mud beside thoroughbreds. Only Grandpa is that jockey, and his riding crop is a nasty can of sardines and a wicked uppercut.

Freaking Grandpa. Why did I get stuck with him?

Gabe LoScuda
English 4A – Personal Essay #1
Mr. Mastrocola
September 19

How To Find Yourself Alone

They were supposed to be gone for one night.

One single night.

But they betrayed me.

It was a Friday. The merciful end to a long week spent forcing my eyelids to flutter open in Dr. Wister's Latin dungeon. I don't know what you have to do to become a doctor of Latin. Is there a Useless Language Hospital somewhere swarming with young Latin scholars who all wear stethoscopes and dissect the fossilized remains of Roman soldiers? Did Dr. Wister have to wear a pager on her belt that beckoned her to the ER of Octavius so she could perform emergency verb conjugation surgeries?

Doctor, we need 20cc of dico. Stat!

Clear! Dicam—I say; Dicas—she says; Dicamus—we say.

Only I haven't said anything in Dr. Wister's class since January of sophomore year. The *volo* incident. *To fly.* Let's just say the correct answers weren't flying out of my mouth that day. But one of those old, dusty chalkboard erasers did fly out of the good doctor's hand and make an impression on my skull. Since then it's been all *sileo* in her class. *Silent.*

My buddy John Chen takes Latin with me. We've been best friends since first grade and have endured a lot of abuse together over the years. But none as sadistic as Dr. Wister.

That night, John and I grabbed a slice and a Coke at Perdomo's. It was our Friday ritual. I think we shared it with the rest of Schuylkill High because the place was always crawling with pimple-faced freshman and you had to lean against the counter and shovel molten cheese down your throat without incinerating the roof of your mouth. Mr. Perdomo was like the ultimate taste bud assassin. He'd sit back behind his pizza counter with the deadliest weapon—an oversized oven peel—and he'd sling pies out of the inferno and on to your plate like flaming Chinese stars. Each slice was equal parts crispy, bubbly, and delicious. If you bit into one too soon—and I always did—it was like drinking napalm. But hey, if you lived in the Philly area like I do—where pizza parlors dot the horizon like freaking tumbleweeds in an old Western—this was a small price to pay for the perfect slice.

After John and I fired off a few straw-paper spitballs at the unsuspecting freshmen that had snaked our usual booth near the pinball machine, we decided to call it a week. We piled into my car—an '81 Trans-Am with 130,000 miles on the clock and t-tops that would leak in the middle of a desert. It had once been my dad's baby—red with silver accents and a grey, cloth interior. He'd wipe it down three times a day with old pairs of tighty-whities that he "couldn't fit his fat ass into anymore."

He gave me the car when I made the baseball team and he got tired of playing chauffeur to all the games and practices. Once I got the damn thing, he stopped coming out to watch me altogether. And I couldn't blame him, because who wants to watch his son collect two butt cheeks full of splinters week in, week out?

I pulled up in John's driveway, careful not to rev the engine a single RPM. John's mom hated loud noises, or neighborhood dogs, or someone breathing or even existing near her rose bushes. Lily's parents had grown up in Chengdu, China where the meanest muscle cars had been men peddling rickshaws, and the neighborhood dogs were strays or chickens. They'd moved to the States in the early fifties and then Lily Chen was born. A first generation American whose parents worked harder than most and, like I've heard Mrs. Chen tell her son from time to time, "had no time for slackers."

John once told me his mom and dad met in college. They were both studying graphic design at Drexel and planned to start a screen printing business together after graduation. They wanted to produce and sell tee shirts with funny sayings on them. Have kids. Live the dream that all Americans hope to live. Then John made his surprise entrance into the world and things didn't seem so funny to the Chens anymore.

"My son never plans ahead," Lily Chen would say. "He didn't even plan to be born." John's lack of planning apparently blew his parents' business model to smithereens. Now Mrs. Chen stayed at home pruning her roses most of the time and his father, Victor, worked a thousand hours a week for the DuPont company. John never talked much about what he did there. Something about space-aged polymers and ballistic nylons and designing flak jackets for law enforcement professionals. It's pretty confusing so I'm not even sure if John truly understood the job description. Probably why he was always so quiet about it.

To the untrained eye, Lily Chen may have looked cute and unassuming in her gardening gear, always outside transforming her yard into a botanical wonderland. But I knew better. I knew she was about five feet of fury. And I knew not to mess with her.

She held the nozzle of her hose in the direction of my car, daring me to make one false step on the gas pedal. The sun, sinking on the horizon, outlined her square shoulders and her floppy garden hat in orange flame. If I didn't know she was John's mom it would have been terrifying. At the same time, I respected Lily Chen for every ounce of tough love she unleashed on her son, because I knew she was the reason he had become John Chen. He didn't complain. Never made excuses. He just woke up every day as the most driven and reliable kid in the entire Delaware Valley. In other words, he didn't turn out like me.

I put the car in park. Let it idle. And I stretched the bill of my Phillies hat down over my eyes so I didn't have to squint.

"You doing anything tonight?" I asked John.

"Promised my mom I'd throw mulch for her," he said as he gathered his books. "Should be done later. Around eight, I guess." Mrs. Chen had her hands on her hips and her head shook slowly, pitifully from side to side. John had about thirty more seconds of chitchat left in him before he'd take a roundhouse kick to the groin.

"Give me a call."

"Why bother?" he asked. "I'll just stop by the house when I'm done. Not like you'll be doing anything."

"Hey, what's that supposed to mean? You never know . . . I might be busy tonight."

"Doing what? Dressing your body pillow up like Marlie? Dude, I've seen her. She's not that lumpy."

I wanted to slug him in the arm out of principle, but Mrs. Chen's shadow loomed over me as she tapped at my window with the blunt steel of the hose nozzle.

"John! That mulch won't spread itself, you know!"

John slung one strap of his backpack over his shoulder. His eyes swirled in their sockets.

"I'll see you around nine," he said. "By then, I'm sure you'll be three games of Madden in the hole."

"We'll see about that," I told him. But he was probably right.

When I got home, Mom was waiting on the front porch. She had forced at least ten more pounds into her black dress than it could handle. I knew something was up. She only wore that dress when Dad got an idea in his head. The last time she wore it, *Garbage Pail Kids* were cool.

"Gabriel! Where. Have. You. Been?" She said it in that voice parents use when they want to make it seem like their words should be a headline in the *Philadelphia Inquirer*.

"I just grabbed a slice at Perdomo's after school like I always do. Is that a problem?" We used to get along great—Mom and I—before she started ragging on me for every little thing. *Is the trash out? Your homework done? Where are you going, Gabriel? How can you sleep until noon, Gabriel?* It was like every time she opened her mouth fireballs shot out. And you can only get your eyebrows singed so many times before you start firing back with pre-emptive strikes.

"Do-not-talk-to-me-like-that-young-man."

I flipped my eyeballs to the sky so hard I thought they'd get lodged in my frontal lobe.

"Or-look-at-me-that-way."

She smelled like jasmine. The perfume Dad had bought her last Christmas. I knew they must have been primping themselves up for a romantic evening. Yuck. Parents should be banned from doing anything that might lead to sex. Once they have their first kid, their sex cards should be shredded on the spot so nobody ever has to have the nasty thoughts I was having at that moment.

"Your father got us a room at Caesar's tonight," she told me. "We're leaving for Atlantic City in fifteen minutes. I called your pager, but you never respond to the damn thing."

She was only partially correct. I did respond to the damn thing. Just not when her or Dad's number popped up in little, pixelated digits. The funny thing was my entire argument for my parents letting me get the damn thing in the first place was: "You can get in touch with me whenever you want. You know, in case of emergency." Only what they saw as an emergency, I didn't happen to see. My emergency: *Gabe, aliens from the planet Gorgon are firing death rays down our chimney!* Mom and Dad's emergency: *Gabe, we're at Macy's. Big sale. What size are your underpants? Check the waist band.*

"Yeah, well, I was busy," I told her.

She didn't respond, which in Mom-speak means don't push it.

Just then, the front door swung open and Dad popped out like a jolly little squirrel that'd found the motherload of acorns. He was wearing his grey business suit. His only suit. There was a goofy grin plastered on his face, which could only mean one thing: Dad was in the mood to gamble.

He loved to gamble, and he'd bet on just about anything. He wasn't particular. Football games, golf matches, poker, how long it would take Mom to make dinner (she didn't like that one). His general rule was: if it happened on this planet, God intended for us to bet on it. Most of the time he'd skip the monetary part of the wager altogether, which was good because teachers don't get paid in gold. But sometimes he'd get himself in trouble. Tonight appeared to be headed in that direction.

"Marie, you look stunning tonight," he said as he took Mom by the hand, spun her in some old geezery type of dance step, and moved in for a big, wet kiss. *Ugh.* The pizza crawled up a little in my throat. "And, Gabe, I must say that you're looking quite useful this evening."

"*Useful?* What's that supposed to mean?"

"It means you're on Grandpa duty," he told me without even pausing on the old man's fandango he was trying to pull off with Mom.

This sucked. Friday night and I was stuck home taking care of the hollow shell that used to be my grandfather. Which is completely different than being stuck home for the sole purpose of sitting in front of the TV.

"No. Uh-uh. I have plans tonight."

"Like what?" Dad said holding back a smile. "A candle lit dinner with your video game controller?" Man, my loser status was really out in the open.

"Not funny," I said. But it was, and suddenly I was having one of those moments where you try to look all pissed and offended but your eyes and the corners of your mouth betray you.

"Come on, Sport." *Sport?* Dad was spreading on the heavy butter now. I was doomed. "You know Grandpa gets freaked out. I can't leave him with a stranger."

He was right. It had been more than two years since they'd hired someone to keep an eye on Gramps. Mom and Dad were only going out to dinner for their anniversary. They were gone two hours. That's all it took. Grandpa locked the caretaker in the bathroom. He was standing sentry with an old Wiffleball bat draped over his shoulder like a rifle when Dad approached him. "Enemy detained, Cap'n," Grandpa said after a full salute.

"Deee-smisssed!" Dad said. What else could he do? His tactic was weird but effective. Grandpa marched off down the hall to his room and Dad slipped the caretaker an extra fifty for her troubles. He vowed never to leave Grandpa with a stranger again. He even went one further. "I'll never put him in one of those places to die alone in an empty hallway," he said, "He's here until the end. Give the man his dignity." And he gave up every waking hour— any spare second away from teaching seventh grade literature at Brandywine Middle—to father the child that had once fathered him.

"Fine," I said. "It's not like I have a choice."

Dad shoved a plastic freezer bag full of pill bottles against my chest.

"You know the drill, Gabe. Keep him on schedule and we'll be back before you know it. Only gone one night."

One night. Right. Just one, single night.

After they left, I sat down at the kitchen table and fumbled through the bag of pills. It was a freaking arsenal of pharmaceutical firepower. Razadyne-this, Aricept-that. It was a damn good thing I was such a Latin scholar or I'd have been struck illiterate on the spot.

There was an index card inside the bag. On it, Dad had scribbled Grandpa's "feeding" schedule like he was a captive in the primate house at the zoo. Two green pills at nine. A red and white at ten. A dose of syrupy, yellow liquid before bed. That was for the cough he'd developed. And a big glass of orange juice spiked with Metamucil at breakfast. I felt like I was back in Mrs. Lockett's kindergarten class and it was my turn to look after Zeke, the classroom hamster. I sure hoped Grandpa wouldn't pee on the wall like Zeke had back then. In fact, if I could keep all bodily fluids off Mom's spotless wallpaper I'd consider the whole matter a success.

John welcomed himself through the door at exactly nine, as he'd predicted. I was in Grandpa's room with a bowl of chocolate pudding. Two green pills were expertly hidden inside the brown goop.

"Have some dessert," I told him. My first attempt—simply handing him the pills with a glass of water—was a miserable failure that resulted in a plastic cup being heaved at my face.

"No! No pills!" he shouted, kicking his afghan off the foot of the bed.

"What pills, Gramps? We're done with those. You already took them, remember?"

It was a dirty trick. I felt guilty pulling one over on a guy with Alzheimer's, especially since he was my own grandfather. But what could I do?

"Come on. This stuff is delicious. I'll eat it myself and there won't be any for you." I skimmed half a spoonful of pudding off the top of the bowl, careful not to uncover the hidden gems I'd placed inside. John had found his way upstairs and stood in the doorway with his eyes wide and his brow wrinkled.

"Don't eat my dessert! Don't. Don't eat!" Grandpa had fallen for my stone cold logic. If it didn't feel like I was feeding a toddler, I might have been proud of myself. I held the bowl for him as he eagerly shoveled pudding in his mouth. He didn't suspect a thing.

John and I headed down to the basement for our weekly Madden marathon. We always fought over who would be the Eagles, our hometown team. Rock, paper, scissors was the decisive vote. John always threw a rock and I'd counter with scissors. Every time. I don't know why I never changed my strategy.

"Be the Giants," John said, "so my beat-down of you will be extra sweet."

"Shut up, John."

"I'm just saying. When I stomp you, you'll be able to enjoy it a little. A productive slaughter."

"Shut up, John."

And you're basically looking at one of our Friday nights. We were a couple of Grade A beefcakes, let me tell you. Rock, paper, scissors. A video game bonanza. Drugged pudding. How were the girls not crashing through the windows?

"You smell something?" John asked as he scored on a last second Hail Mary to push the score to 48-0 and cement a third consecutive beat-down.

"Shut up, John."

"No, I'm serious. It smells like—"

"Shit."

"Yeah, exactly. And we polished off those frozen burritos like two hours ago."

"Well, it wasn't me." I started sniffing around the house. In the kitchen. Near the sink. Maybe something was lodged in the garbage disposal. John fumbled around in the plastic bag of pills just to keep himself busy. The smell grew stronger. It reached down my throat. It threatened to pull all the food I'd eaten that day directly out of my gut and deposit it on the kitchen table.

"Uh, Gabe?"

"Not now. I'm trying to chew this back."

I steadied myself on a kitchen chair and pulled my shirt up over my nose. The stench was so strong I could almost smell it through my tear ducts.

"Gabe, seriously."

"What is it?" I croaked through the thin layer of cotton between my nasal passages and death by odor.

"Did you read the note your dad left in this bag? I mean, the *entire* note?"

"Uh, yeah. Of course. I mean, most of it."

"What about this part?" He flashed the card in front of me with his index finger highlighting a tiny star and an inscription on the bottom line:

No dairy. Grandpa is having trouble with lactose this week.

"Oh, shit," I said. And I meant it literally.

Before I even got to the top of the stairs my senses were on full alert. By the time I pushed through the door at the end of the hall—Grandpa's room— I thought for sure my house had been transformed into a sewage treatment plant. The man's sheets, his pillows, and the majority of the headboard were smeared with a network of brown streaks. It was like my grandfather had done some kind of bizarre, fecal-based finger painting. And then my memories of Mrs. Lockett's class raged through my brain. Only this time they were sullied. Covered in a putrid, brown film. Grandpa was curled up on the very edge of the bed and his eyes were glistening. Tiny sobs wracked his breathing.

"John, I think you should go home," I said.

"No." He didn't blink. His eyes were steely, unmoving. He had no intention of leaving me to deal with the mess alone. It was vintage John. The boy who'd always had my back. When Tony Milletti stole my favorite Matchbox car back in second grade, John reached into his supply box under the guise of snack time to steal it back. When Billy Rasmussen cornered me like a rat in the sixth grade bathroom and threatened to pound the guts out of me, John stood right there beside me and took a rabbit punch himself. And now, with Grandpa's room looking like a stall down at Penn Station, he was willing to don the latex gloves and answer the call. But this time I wasn't sure his help was appropriate. I mean, who wants their best friend standing there when you're changing your grandfather's diaper?

"Go home, John." He didn't respond. He only took another step closer to the bed and removed a soiled pillowcase from one of Grandpa's pillows. No gloves. All heart.

"You'd do it for me," he said. And that was the last we spoke of the matter.

I lifted Grandpa out of bed and half-carried, half-dragged him to the bathtub. You never expect an old man to weigh as much as a mule, but Grandpa didn't make the twenty-foot journey an easy one—especially since I held my breath the whole time. I put the faucet on full blast and hustled back to the bedroom.

John had already stripped the bed and I heard the washing machine filling up with water. He sprayed disinfectant on the headboard and sponged off Grandpa's artwork with a wad of paper towels. Damn. Lily had trained him well.

I grabbed a few paper towels and joined him, but he stopped and looked me in the eyes. "Dude, go take care of Grandpa Ernie. This is under control."

Man, how do you ever return a favor to a friend who rolls up his sleeves and cleans your grandfather's poop fresco off the wall? For a second I just stood there. Visions of a Bruce Lee-style battle between Mrs. Chen and me popped into mind. I could picture John sipping lemonade on his porch and cheering me on as I swung a pair of nunchucks at his mother and she fought me off with kicks, punches, and a pair of garden shears. Even that would fall short.

Grandpa cupped his withered hands and splashed the water around in the bathtub. His pajama bottoms ballooned up on the surface, filled with air bubbles and God knows what else. I squeezed at least half a bottle of Mom's cucumber-melon bubble bath in the mud puddle. Then I started working the buttons on Grandpa's pajama shirt. "Aaah!"

"Don't worry, Gramps. We're gonna get you clean." I tugged at the shirt and heard a few stitches rip. Grandpa thrashed and kicked. Water splashed in my face and down the front of my shirt. It spread across the tile floor. I sponged the sudsy soup over Grandpa's head and tugged at the ankles of his pants.

Ugh. The smell. The sights. The wrinkles. My own grandpa. John with brown globs on paper towels. I wasn't there. I couldn't be.

The images wafted up like ghosts on a silver screen. The world's most heinous silent film. I could almost hear the rat-tat-tat of the spool reeling its way through the projector and I wondered: How did it come to this? How did Mom and Dad endure it?

Thank God my duty was only a one-night thing.

One night. Just one night.

I smacked the plunger and watched the brown sludge whirlpool its way down the drain. The bathroom reeked of melon-scented poop. Not a good candidate for Chanel's fall line of perfume.

I hefted Grandpa out of his swamp and wrapped him in a towel. He just stood there and dripped water on the floor. I'd have to dry him too. Nasty. I started with his white mane. It was shaggy and thin and only partly damp. But it was good enough.

"Aaaah! Unhand me! Urrrghh!"

I didn't respond. Just tried to mop as much moisture off of him as I could before I puked. Dad's robe would do the rest. I wrestled Grandpa out of the bathroom like a prisoner of war and lifted him into bed. John had fitted the mattress with a clean, crisp set of sheets. The only sign that anything out of the ordinary had happened in the room was the faint smell of disinfectant in the air.

I read to Grandpa from Walt Whitman's *Leaves of Grass*. We had studied a few passages in Mrs. Alonzo's eleventh grade English class. Everyone thought it sucked, but they don't appreciate good poetry like I do. Call me weird. My classmates did.

Grandpa's eyelids drooped shut as I read.

"I have heard what the talkers were talking, the talk of the beginning and the end. But I do not talk of the beginning or the end."

John had told his parents he'd probably spend the night, so he was in the basement playing more video games. Kid was an addict.

Hours had passed between our Madden marathon and fumigation time. It had to be maybe two or three in the morning at that point.

And the phone rang.

At two or three in the morning.

Nothing good ever comes from a phone ringing at that hour.

There's never a crazy radio host on the other end offering a cash prize out of the blue. There's never one of your teachers just getting in touch to cancel the homework assignment you forgot was due the next day. It's never, ever good. So my heart did little flip-flops in my chest. And Grandpa's eyes fluttered open. "Urrrgh. Whaaaa?" I placed my hand on his forehead to keep him calm. Maybe to keep me calm.

"John?" I shouted as the shrill bell vibrated through my stomach. "Can you get that?" He either heard me or it was a wrong number because the ringing stopped at once. I continued reading from Whitman: "Will never be any perfection than there is now, nor any more heaven or hell than there is now."

And then I heard footsteps on the stairs. In the hall. Slowly shuffling. Holding back.

"Gabe?" John said with a waver in his voice. "It's the police."

A jolt of electricity shot up from my feet, through my spine, and burned in my ears. I felt the blood in my face. Every red cell. Each tiny molecule bubbling and brewing. I saw a hand reach for the phone. Was it mine? I couldn't tell. I heard the voice on the other end. Very official. Deep. Monotone.

Gambling.

Left early.

Atlantic City Expressway.

Fell asleep.

They were gone.

Not coming back.

Forever?

Yes, forever.

No . . . surely . . . can't be right. This only happens to other people.

Please come to identify the bodies.

Yes, sir.

John's hand on my shoulder.

Warm tears on my cheek.

Alone.

Just me and Gramps.

And no one could protect me. Not even John.

2

THE END OF THE BEGINNING

The next few days are like staring into a kaleidoscope. Only I'm not the one holding it. It's strapped to my face and I don't want it there. An invisible hand squeezes the colors in my eyes until they burn. The brilliant triangles of pink, yellow, and purple—the mosaics of childhood—are replaced by blacks and greys.

Twist. The morgue.

Twist, twist. Lawyers. A will hearing. "You're in charge now, Gabriel. Executor."

Twist. The phone rings. A funeral director. "We'll take care of everything according to the will."

Twist, Twist, Twist.

A knock at the door. It's Mrs. Chen. "Wonton soup, Gabe. You have to eat." *Not hungry. Never hungry again.* The soup spoils on the counter.

I don't remember sliding into my confirmation suit. Kind of short around the ankles, a little too much wrist hangs from each sleeve. Somehow I get Grandpa dressed and now, somehow, he's in the Trans Am with me; and somehow we show up at St. Theresa's to say our goodbyes. Mom and Dad were never all that strict about us going to church. We were always more like satellite Catholics. We did our worship from afar and showed up for major events. Like my confirmation. Or my communion, where I almost gagged on one of those super-dry wafers. I guess today also qualifies as one of those big events.

Most people look around the pews at a funeral and see the faces of their family—people who'd help them through the most drastic situations. There are no faces like that for me. Mom and Dad had met "later in life" as they liked to say. It was basically code for "we're, like, forty years older than our son."

I had never really thought much about it. Most of my relatives had passed on when I was too young to understand or even feel sad about it. I didn't know them. Never had the chance. But, as I sit in a church filled with random neighbors and coworkers, I find myself pining for those same lost relatives I never knew. I have John sitting in the pew behind me, but my own flesh and blood? Didn't I deserve that? And Grandpa didn't count. For all he knew, he could have been sitting in a laundromat waiting for his underwear to dry.

I mop some gunk from the corners of his mouth and I'm careful not to fight him too hard. I don't want him to go into freakout mode, but I figure his face should look somewhat presentable at his son's funeral. And at least Grandpa's was a face I could recognize, even if I was all but a stranger to him. For all I cared, the rest of their faces could have been swallowed by that weird blur effect you see on *Maury Povich* or *Montell Williams* or any of the other idiotic afternoon talk shows.

Just a bunch of outstretched hands and pats on the shoulder and prayers pledged in my honor. Like they'd say some stupid prayer and Mom and Dad would burst out of their caskets, dust off, and head out for an early lunch. Of course, they all mean well. I know that. But it simply makes me hate them and I don't know why. I want to scream as loud as I can. I want to thrash my arms like Grandpa and run through the church and tell them how stupid they all are to have their cozy, normal lives with their families and their suits that fit and their stupid kids who could go to school and come home and never worry.

I hate them all and I want to scream it. Just scream in their stupid faces that I didn't even recognize and would never remember, and then spit at their feet when they got all surprised about what I was telling them. And then I'd ask them why? Why me? And what am I going to do now? What the hell am I supposed to do now? I want to, but I don't. I simply smile an empty smile and say thank you. Over and over and over again.

I can feel the tears singe the corners of my eyes, and I stare through the blurriness at my mom and dad. They are reduced to shiny, rectangular boxes. On display, but closed to the world. Too lifeless for living eyes to bear. And I can feel the muscles in my calves and the backs of my thighs contract, ready to heave me up out of the pew and run me out the doors. But tears always seem to extinguish action. So I just sit there like a good little boy and listen to Grandpa mouth-breath his own nasally melodies. And I try hard—as hard as I can—to wake up from the nightmare.

That's when I feel a heavy paw drop down on my shoulder. The smell of aftershave and last night's whiskey smolders in my nose hairs. I think, nobody better let this dude near the candle offering.

I turn to meet his eyes. They are soft, brown. In them I see the spirit of a boy with skinned knees and fireflies in a mason jar. His face tells a different story. The eyelids are wrinkled and puffy. The lips thin and cracked. Blotches of patchy, dry skin border his hairline from the temples down past his sideburns. The hair had once been dark chocolate, but is now mixed with broad sections of shredded coconut.

"Hey, Gabe. It's me," he whispers as a few last-minute tributeers file into pews. I squint my eyes and try to place him. There's something familiar in the way he tips his chin to the left as he speaks, but I can't quite make the connection.

"Don't you remember me?" His eyes meet the floor when I don't respond. I can tell he's disappointed.

"No, sir," I whisper back a moment later. "I don't. But thanks for coming and—"

"You don't you remember your own godfather? I used to bounce you around on my knee when you were the size of a basketball."

"Uncle Nick!?"

I can't believe it. Nobody has seen the guy in years. I was so young the last time he came around I barely remember meeting him at all. He never called. Never visited. Never once sent a birthday card. He was like a ghost. The closest thing I had to a relationship with the man was listening to Dad make snide remarks about that "drunken, good-for-nothing loser kid brother of mine."

And now he's plopped himself down between Grandpa and me and he's squeezing my bicep like we've been pals all along.

"What are you doing here?" I ask.

"Whaddya mean what am I doing here? Sal was my brother, wasn't he?"

I want to call him a liar right there on the spot. In front of everyone in the church and the priests and the altar boys. In front of God.

A brother?

A brother is someone you can count on. Someone who doesn't run off at age seventeen in search of some asinine destiny that doesn't exist. Someone who picks up the damn telephone once in a while to say hello. I didn't even have a brother and I knew that much. Uncle Nick was no brother.

But I can't say all of that in a whisper so what comes out is, "Yeah. I guess."

The choir director punches a few chords on the pipe organ and the parishioners rise to their feet like toy soldiers. Grandpa's chin is plastered against his chest in the pew next to Uncle Nick. His eyes are closed and a thin string of drool rolls down his chin. Nobody cares that he stays seated. The service is about to begin.

But Uncle Nick hasn't finished his piece. "Your father's not the only reason I'm here. We're family. All that's left."

I stare at him. Not because I'm interested in what he has to say, but because he actually has the balls to pretend he cares about family.

"What's your point?"

"I'm staying," he says. "With you."

My brain almost explodes and spews a shower of grey bits out of my ears like a cognitive fireplug.

"I'm sure you could use the extra help with my father and I'm not tied down to anything at the moment."

Was he *ever* tied down to anything? What a joke.

"I can stay at the house."

No. No. No. No. No. NO!. This is not happening. I am not opening the doors of my parents' house—scratch that, *my* house—to this loser. This ingrate. This absentee uncle.

But it dawns on me that the keyword, after all, is "uncle." A face that I recognize. It may have taken a bit of prodding on Nick's part, but I recognize it. And that means he is *family*. Maybe Uncle Nick doesn't understand what it truly means to be a part of a family, but that doesn't give me the right to abandon him the same way he did us. Does it?

And so, I simply nod my head and whisper, "Thank you. When do you think you might be able to move in?"

"Today. After the service."

Great. Now I have to take care of two sniveling toddlers.

The future looks bright, Gabe. You schmuck.

3

HALF IN THE BAG, NO CRUST

There's no worse sound than the crackle of electricity that surges through the circuits of my clock radio right before the alarm goes off. I'm still half asleep but totally aware of the machinery moving. Then it blares Metallica's "Ride the Lightning" like a six a.m. bugle call—talk about "freedom from the frightening dream"—and I'm forced to swallow my heart before breakfast. Only I haven't eaten breakfast since Mom and Dad deserted me.

It's funny. They left me with a place to live, a small sum of cash to pay bills (a really small sum), and even a pre-paid law guy to help me sign the assorted court orders and powers of attorney and whatever other nonsense lay heaped and awaiting my John Hancock in that towering mound of paperwork. Mom and Dad had spelled it all out for me in their will, like they'd been planning to die all along. And yet they never thought to leave me a box of toaster pastries or some frozen waffles. Maybe that's why I hate wills, because they can never provide you with the most important meal of the day. At least not the way Mom did.

The truth is it's mostly my fault for going hungry every morning. I mean, I do slug the snooze button like I have narcolepsy. I don't even remember doing it half the time. Then I finally wake up and the numeric eyes of the clock glare at me and say, "dude, you have, like, twenty minutes."

I have to run a marathon's-worth of chores through the house, pick up John and break through the prison-camp walls of Schuylkill High before homeroom starts. It's kind of fitting that if you want to pronounce the name of my school in perfect English you'd say, "School – Kill", which in Philadelphianese sounds more like "scookle." Either way something seems to get "kill"ed by the time you reach the end of it.

My bare feet hit the shaggy carpet. It's the color of the creepy moss that bubbles up between cracks in the pavement. I stand on a patch that looks like a putting green floating in a sea of dirty clothes, soda cans, and other assorted crap.

I take the plunge.

Something crinkles under my right foot—a plastic cup—and a sticky stream of flat root beer washes over my left. I'll clean it up later. No time now. If Mom were around she would have said something like, "No son of mine will live in a landfill." But she's not around, and I have bigger things to worry about.

I'm in and out of the shower so fast I barely get wet. Then I pull my daily brush-your-teeth, shave-with-Dad's-disposable-razor combo. You might not think that sounds impressive, but give it a try. It's dexterity at a whole new level. And it's high risk. I mean, who wants to lose an ear lobe getting ready for school?

It's still a little weird using Dad's razor. The first time I did I washed out the blade and a couple flecks of his old salt and pepper were still left in there. I brushed them out completely. I don't know what I'll do when the thing gets dull. Good thing I only have one or two patches of actual hair on my face—one on my chin and another random one on my cheek. Not exactly the kind of mane that'll tear through a razor. That'll give me some time to forget about them. The hairs. Not my parents.

I spit my toothpaste in the sink and rush downstairs to the kitchen to pack a lunch. I know. It's pretty lame. But cafeteria food sucks. I'd rather sidecar up to a gang of vultures and eat road kill on the interstate than endure one of those creepy, greenish hot dogs they serve. Just the smell makes me ill. And the burgers? I caught a puck at a Flyers game that was juicier than one of those things. I'll bet you could skip a few of those burgers off the glassy surface of the Schuylkill River and, like flattened projectiles, they'd sink at least one or two crew teams trying to paddle past the Victorians on Boathouse Row.

There's not much food in my house these days. Only things that won't go bad or you can cook in two minutes or less. It's like Mom's kitchen has been reduced to a fifties-era bomb shelter within the space of a couple of weeks. Not like when she was around and would have both mine and Dad's lunches packed neatly in brown bags and waiting on the kitchen table by 7:30 so we could sweep past, peck her on the cheek, and rush off to our respective schools—Dad to teach and me to learn. Of course, then Mom would pack her own lunch and head to Dr. Harrison's orthodontics office where she'd been the sitting receptionist for the past fifteen years. She never took a vacation day.

I slather some peanut butter and some jelly between the dried-up end pieces of Wonder Bread and toss it and a bruised banana in a plastic shopping bag. We're out of lunch bags too. I add it to the running list of items we constantly need but never have, and then charge back up the steps to Grandpa's room. I put the glass of water down on his nightstand and pop various pills out of their containers. By now, I don't even need to look at my hands as I dispense. I'm like one of those rip-off artists you see flipping cards on street corners. And there's no more pudding. Grandpa and I have reached an understanding: he understands it makes his grandson happy when he takes the pills; I understand that he's a crazy, old fool that's taken the place of my real grandfather.

I shake him and pop most of the pills in his mouth before he realizes he's awake. Then I hand him the glass of water and pray to God he doesn't soak me down with it. I really don't have time to change clothes. I'm lucky I got myself together enough to be wearing the same wrinkled t-shirt and jeans I wore on Monday.

The pills usually put Grandpa back to sleep for a while, so I don't need to count on Uncle Nick for more than a few hours each day. Trust me, I wish he did more to help, but the time he does put in is scary enough. The dude can barely take care of himself. Scratch that. He's basically an infant. Just yesterday I had to throw a freaking load of laundry in for the guy. I got tired of smelling him. He's like a thousand years old and he doesn't even have a job. But he's always out looking. Yes, he'll constantly remind me of that.

"I've been out seeking gainful employment," he says each time I ask him where the hell he's been all night. But how many people go out job hunting after dinner and come home stinking of booze close to breakfast? Seeking employment my ass. So excuse me for slipping past the couch and out the door without saying a word to Uncle Nick, who happened to be sprawled across the cushions like an obese leech—a leech that's sucking every last bit of patience out of me.

I'm left with about five minutes to pick up John and storm to school, which is eight minutes away. These are times when it's good to have an old Trans-Am you can beat the crap out of. The fuel gauge hovers only a few ticks above empty, but I pound the accelerator anyway and ignore the brake the whole six blocks to John's house. John is already bounding off his front porch as I pull in the driveway. He's run this bizarre relay race so many times over the past few weeks he might as well be carrying a baton.

"Looks like we're running on LoScuda time," he blurts out as he slams the door shut. "If I get detention again, you owe me."

"Get a car and then we'll talk about who owes who," I say as I back down the driveway. Then I notice a tiny flash from the window of John's house. I can see the outline of Mrs. Chen silhouetted behind the blinds. Even her shadow looks pissed.

"She hates me, doesn't she?"

"Not hate. Her actual words were 'If Gabe is late today, he'll be early to his own funeral.'"

"Then we'd better get moving." I wink at him. He doesn't look pleased.

"No, Ga—"

I punch the gas pedal and John doesn't finish his sentence until we're three intersections away. When I next look in the rearview I'm pretty sure I see a mushroom cloud rising from John's house. Then I get one of those feelings like I forgot something. And those feelings never lie.

"My lunch," I say under my breath.

"What's that?" John sounds agitated. I guess he's not looking forward to dealing with his mom after my little shenanigans. Whatever. It'll make him stronger.

"Oh. Nothing. Just forgot my lunch."

"Buy some."

He's still pretty pissed. But he can't stay mad. Not John. He cares too much. Not like me.

"No money."

I can feel the tension release as soon as I say it. John loosens his grip on the dashboard. He takes a few breaths and his mouth starts to move like he wants to say something but the words keep stacking up on him like cars on the interstate.

"We'll meet up," he says finally. "I'll take care of it."

I knew it. I told you the kid's aces. Makes me feel kind of bad about leaving an inch of burnt rubber on his driveway. But I don't have time for sympathy because the clock's ticking.

The last few minutes of our morning drive always looks like something from a NASCAR highlight reel. Or like being on a roller coaster run by a deranged circus clown, where it was all too possible to crash into other cars, people, even buildings. Not very pretty. Definitely not legal. And obviously not the best way to start your day—unless you're a professional stunt man or a crash test-dummy.

I bank the Trans-Am hard into a curve and we're somehow in the student parking lot with less than a minute to spare. Lots of cars. Not many people. Probably because they're already inside avoiding detention. The Schuylkill High School student parking lot is probably the closest thing you'll ever get to a full demographic report on all the cozy, suburban developments that crash up against the Philadelphia skyline — and without having to spend half your life in the public library paging through census data. You have your front row parking spots, the ones so close to Franklin Gymnasium you could watch a game of hoops from the back seat of your car. These are always claimed by the late-model Beamer set, wealthy Main Line kids who seemed to get the same perks as their wealthy, Main Line parents — including a sweet deal on a hand-me-down ride. Then there are all the other spots, melted into a sprawling mass of concrete and divided into no less than a hundred rows. It is a no-man's land that bubbles and oozes in one asphalt blob from the crest of the school all the way down to Clarke Football Stadium, home of the mighty Schooners, which oddly enough is built in an old cow pasture that floods out if a deer sneezes in the woods.

When all these spots fill up before the school day, the lot kind of looks like the Island of Misfit Toys. You have old Ford Broncos hand-painted black with single, green fenders. You have your Hyundais, your Datsuns and Gremlins, and your Honda hatchbacks all huddled together on a ten-foot section of cement in solidarity against the bigger, meaner cars. You have your pick-up trucks and your Jeep Wranglers with two hundred thousand miles on the tickers, still raring to go. And then you have your dreamers. Like me and the Trans-Am. The ones that don't really fit comfortably in any of the spaces. Not refined enough to be a front-of-the-lot import, but too fast to park with the punch-buggies. Jeez. I guess that kind of sums it all up for me and John here at Schuylkill High.

I snag a spot in the back of the lot near the stadium, and the relay race commences before the car is in park. John sprints off without more than a grunt. I'm off in the opposite direction since our homerooms are in different corridors of the sprawling building.

I hit the door at exactly eight o'clock, but it's too late. Not because I'm legitimately late. That's debatable. It's because Coach Foley is patrolling the entrance. Just my luck.

"Late again, LoScuda," he says without raising an eyebrow from his clipboard. Suddenly there's a detention slip dangling in front of my nose. "You're showing me a lot so far this year." There's a twinge of sarcasm to everything he says, like he has to hide behind a bullshit armor of authority because he bucked up a fifty-spot for his gym teacher's license. "Your baseball career's looking mighty promising about now." Like he knows anything about baseball. Dude couldn't coach his way out of a paper bag. His teams haven't finished above .500 since I've been at Schuylkill High.

"C'mon, Coach. The bell wasn't—"

"Can it, LoScuda. We don't have time for a one-act play here. Just take the slip."

I grab the slip and stuff it in the pocket of my jeans. There's no sense arguing. Freaking Foley. A detention from him was permanent, like the kind of stuff you'd chisel on stone tablets. Figures. He'd use any excuse to cut my ass at spring tryouts.

"LoScuda." I look over my shoulder and Foley's motioning me back with a discreet wag of his finger. What the hell could he want now? "Give me the slip," he says under his breath as I approach.

"What?"

"The slip, LoScuda. Hand it over."

I'm confused, but I stuff my hand into my jeans pocket and hand him the wrinkled piece of paper.

"Trade me."

He hands me a late pass and I'm sort of stunned.

"I know things are tough right now, LoScuda. But life doesn't make pit stops."

There it is. *The pity.*

"Thanks, Coach," I say, but I'm not all that thrilled about the trade.

The homeroom bell rings and students file into classrooms like fire ants. I'm in no rush. I have the pass in my pocket to prove it, so I hang-dog it to my locker. Students push past me like I'm some first-time concertgoer fighting my way to the stage.

A group of freshman girls sidle up to me like a gang of paparazzi. "How are you today?" says the leader of the group, a pudgy redhead with no less than a million freckles. I've never seen them before, but all of a sudden they want to get close enough to use a rectal thermometer on me.

"We're all very much behind you, Gabe."

The worst. Fake sympathy

I nod politely and walk faster. Nothing bothers me more than having a bunch of people fawn over me just so they can look like the world's greatest missionaries. Like them telling me they're sorry is somehow close to living out Gandhi's hunger strike. Like they know what it feels like to be me. And they're probably the same people who'd pin one of those shitty "kick me" signs to the back of my t-shirt if I wasn't such a charity case. Man, I doubt Gandhi ever pinned anything to anyone's t-shirt. Probably never owned a t-shirt either.

What's worse is the people I want to talk to never say anything, even though we've been going to school together for over a decade. Since way back in elementary school. But I don't care. I'm used to it by now. I guess when you're popular you don't say hello to the weird kid with the dead parents and the mental-case geezer yapping at his heels. It just doesn't happen. I get it. Maybe they're worried that I'm contagious or something.

Then suddenly I'm like Moses and I'm parting the waves with only the power of my mind. That's how things look to me sometimes when I see her. Marlie. Trust me, the three or four barely-visible freckles she has on her nose are enough to give any guy tunnel vision.

So, I push a group of snorting tech geeks against a bay of rusty lockers with the powers of my eyes alone, and I jack another staggered grouping of stoners, in their assorted band t-shirts, into the darkness that is the shop-class hallway. Two perky cheerleaders strut right through the depths of the sea and I catapult them out of my vision because they don't matter. Right now, only she matters. And I could spot her if a school-wide riot broke out around her. If she would have been the character in those stupid *Where's Waldo?* puzzles I used to do with Grandpa—when I was a kid and he wasn't an alien—maybe I wouldn't have thought they were so stupid.

She's walking in my direction, stepping over abandoned textbooks and weaving around open lockers, but she might as well be tiptoeing down a runway or floating on a pillow of clouds. I should say something to her. Not like the crap I piled on her at the grocery store, either. Like something smooth. Something that will make her notice me. But what?

She's only a few feet away now. Better start thinking. *You look nice?* No. *I love you?* Definitely not. Here she comes, Gabe. Maybe I'll go with . . . oh boy . . . it's now or never.

"Hey, sorry about the sardines," I say.

Wow. Really, Gabe? Freaking sardines? When did a sardine ever win a girl's heart? I bet you can search through the annals of history and never find one case.

"Oh. Yeah," she says.

Boy, I've got her now.

"Don't worry about it. It's Gary, right?"

"Yeah," I say, "Thanks."

Wow. Way to go, Gary.

"No problem," she says.

And that's it. I don't even have a chance to respond. She's already half a mile down the hallway, and the waves are crashing in on me again

Since the day is off to such a promising start, I stop screwing around in the halls and grab my books from the old locker. I figure if I spend any more time out here there's no telling how much more humiliation I can inflict on myself. Who knows? I could split my pants, or start involuntarily dancing the Macarena, or end up on an episode of *America's Most Wanted* — or all three at once. My goodness. I could split my pants while dancing the Macarena in an effort to evade police. Trust me. I'm "Gary" LoScuda. It could happen.

But as I push through the door into Mr. Mastrocola's homeroom I think, "That's pretty cynical, Gabe. Don't look at it that way. Maybe you've faced the worst of it for today. I mean, what else could possibly happen?" And that puts a smile on my face. Maybe I can at least hold on to it for the time it takes to get to my seat.

Mastrocola is taking roll when I slip in and try to close the door without it squeaking or bouncing off the jamb. I'd rather not disturb him because I have already heard enough soapbox lectures for the day. But you'd have to be freaking invisible to sneak past old Mastro. Even then I think he'd be able to smell you or something.

"James."

"Here."

"Jenson."

"Here."

"Kinkaid."

"Here."

"LoScuda, so very nice of you to join us today," he says without raising an eye from his roll book. "You actually made it before dusk. That's an achievement."

"I had a rough morning," I start to say, "My grandpa, well—"

"No need to explain, Gabe. We all have lives outside of this classroom. Even me."

There's a twinkle in his eye that tells me he's enjoying this little bull session.

"Sorry to disappoint. I know you guys think they roll me out of a box and switch on my circuits each morning."

There are a few muffled laughs from the back of the room.

"As dark as it is, this is coffee in my cup. Not motor oil."

Good old Mastro. He taught English and served as a bookend, meaning he was the first smiling face you met as a freshman and the one who'd boot your ass out the door as a senior. Kind of cool how it goes full-circle like that, especially since Mastro is the best teacher I've ever had. He's funny. He's not super-old like most English teachers. You know the ones. Not only do they act like they're authorities on guys like Shakespeare, but they may have actually grown up with him. But not Mastro. The dude actually listens to your thoughts and opinions about literature instead of sniping at people because they ask "can" instead of "may" I go to the bathroom. That kind of stuff always pisses me off. But it's not Mastro's style.

He is the reason I like poetry. He is also the reason I'm keeping a diary. He makes a big show of calling it a "personal essay portfolio," which I guess sounds more scholarly—and definitely more manly. But let's be real for a second: it's a freaking diary. And I'm actually kind of into the thing. Don't ask me why. Mastro claims it'll help us make connections between our own experiences and the poetry we are studying and that it might even yield a potential college application essay. I don't know about any of that, but it sure feels good to have someone who will listen to all of my crap—even if that someone, in reality, is me. It's a good thing the portfolio is a pretty painless assignment because Mastro tells us our deadline is in freaking May. Guess he actually wants us to spend some time on it.

"You can sit down now, Gabe," he finishes with a smirk on his face. "Unless you plan to sing for all of us. Whaddyasay?"

I file to my seat before the razzing of my classmates makes me feel obliged to sing freaking "Hot Cross Buns" to them or something. Man, Mr. Mastro. Always pulling that kind of garbage—which is exactly why we love him so much.

I grab the only open seat in the room, a wobbly chair/desk combo the school board probably excavated from an archeological dig. It squeaks like a baby chick each time I shift my weight, but at least I'm sitting. At least nobody's in my face about how crappy a kid I am, and at least I can just sit here for a few minutes and zone out while the A/V geeks read through morning announcements. At least I can have some peace before I have to plunge back out into those hallways and start swimming again.

That's when the door swings open and I realize my peace and quiet had already come and gone. The doorknob crashes against the cinderblock wall and it's like a needle screeching across a vinyl record. Mastro cranes his neck above his newspaper as a disheveled-looking older gentleman half-walks, half-staggers to the front of his desk. His white t-shirt has a hole on the back of the left shoulder and the pit stains are so thick and brown it's like he's been wearing the darn thing since birth. His hands are shaky as he clutches at the handles of a plastic shopping bag.

I slap my palm across my forehead and cover my eyes. It's not that I'm alarmed by the mere sight of a man you could easily mistake for a common hobo. That doesn't bother me. It's just, this particular hobo happens to be Uncle Nick. What the hell is he doing here?

"Can I help you, sir?" Mastro asks with a slight waver in his voice. And who can blame him? A seedy-looking old dude crashes his classroom holding an unidentifiable bag? I'm surprised the bomb-sniffing dogs and the damn SWAT team hasn't dropped through the air ducts yet. All I know is I have to put a stop to this. And fast.

"Yeah, I'm looking for—"

"It's for me, Mr. Mastrocola," I say. I'm already out of my seat and half way to the front of the room before the last word comes out. There's no way I'm about to risk another second with Uncle Nick staggering and running his mouth at the same time. That's a lethal concoction built on strange chemical reactions I doubt even Nick could explain. The toxic byproduct? That's easy: the end of my life at Schuylkill High. Death by embarrassment. I didn't have to live with the guy to learn that lesson—but I had. Learned the lesson. Repeatedly.

I think, maybe I'm not too late to stop him from ruining my life today. But Uncle Nick's eyes are already bulging with recognition and he has the same stupid grin on his face little kids get when you hand them an ice cream cone.

"GAAAAABE!" he shouts before I can hop a stray backpack and spin-kick him out of the classroom. "What up there, broseph?!"

Oh, God. Please stop talking, Nick. You're not cool or hip or whatever your generation of geezers wants to call themselves—and you never will be. Mastro rises from his desk. He takes a few steps toward Nick and I see his mouth start to open. I can tell he's searching for the right words to combat the outburst of a true idiot and save me from embarrassment at the same time. But I know that's just a waste of time.

"Don't worry," I whisper to him. "He's my uncle. I'll take care of it." I mean, I'm already mortified. The last thing I need is for the teacher to step in and save the day for helpless, little Gabey-pooh.

I grab a handful of rancid t-shirt and drag him toward the door. Maybe it's still not too late to save this.

"You forgot yo' lunch, homey!"

Oh, God. We're almost to the door. It's not too late. It's not too late.

"I cut off the crusts for you there, my skillet!" Too late. Much too late. My life is over and now we're finally in the hallway. Nice timing, Gabe. Nice work, Nick.

Freaking Nick. He's still wearing the goofy grin and his eyes are glazed like old-fashioned doughnuts. My stupid, plastic lunch bag is hanging from two of his fingers. He smells like whiskey again and I just stare at him with a look that says, "you're disgusting," "you're a loser," and "I hate you" at the same time. He doesn't notice.

"I even tossed in an old Ho Ho I found in—"

"Nick! Quiet!" The words come out of my mouth in a hush and Nick looks surprised. I still have a hand full of t-shirt, so I lead him off through a set of doors and into the stairwell "What are you doing here? How'd you even get in?"

"I . . . I kinda slipped in with a few maintenance guys."

I can see the resemblance. There's black grease under his fingernails and a thin smudge of it caked in the stubble of his beard. And he seems proud of himself, rocking back and forth like he's waiting for me to congratulate him or something. Like I'm supposed to throw a parade because he realized that, somehow, without even getting off the couch, he looks like a guy who toils in a boiler room all day. He's so excited it almost makes me feel bad to put an end to this and any future visits.

"Nick . . . please . . . don't come here anymore," I say. "I don't care if the whole school disappears into a sinkhole, or if the Earth itself is about to explode. Just stay away."

Nick's eyes flash to the ground. They look soft and sad, like strips of brown velvet.

"I was just trying to—"

"I don't care, Nick. This is embarrassing."

He looks like I punched him in the gut, but I'm not kidding. I really don't care. It's bad enough I have to be responsible for the old, crazy guy. At least he has an excuse. But, besides Grandpa, I don't have room in my life for any other old, crazy guys.

And then something occurs to me.

"Nick, where the hell is Grandpa?"

His brow creases and his eyes lift from their view of my shoes.

"He's at home. Why?"

"At home? At home, Nick? You know he can't be left on his own!"

"He can't?"

"No! Of course not!"

"Then I better get back to the house right away, huh?"

"Yes! You'd better! Before there is no house! Or Grandpa!"

Uncle Nick turns and paces off down the hall.

"And, Nick . . . remember what I said. School is off-limits."

He nods and heads for the double doors.

The idiot. How is any of this ever going to work?

4

STITCHES AND SHOCK THERAPY

"Johnny Cash! Make it louder." I grab Grandpa's wrist as he reaches for the knob. The speakers in the Trans-Am can't take much more of this. Neither can my eardrums.

"I already told you. It's too loud!"

He's still fighting when the traffic light goes red again. "Quit it! It's not even Johnny Cash," I tell him. "It's freaking Ace of Base."

There are simultaneously two things I can't believe. *One:* I'm listening to Ace of Base. I quickly tap the dial. WMMR. Classic Rock. You can never go wrong. *Two:* how is the old guy fighting back like a ninja? He is unbelievable. It reminds me I'm grateful I wasn't his enemy in a war or anything—like the Germans, those poor bastards.

"Here. Take this," I say, and I hand him a green lollipop that's been in my cup holder forever. I think it came with the car—probably installed at the plant in Detroit. Grandpa takes it and shoves it in his mouth with the wrapper still intact. I want to correct him, but I don't have the strength or the patience. It keeps him quiet, so I pretend I don't hear the plastic crinkling back and forth across his teeth.

The light turns green and I nudge the Trans-Am down Main Street toward Dr. Weston's office. I should kick Uncle Nick in the groin for sending me on this hell ride. If he hadn't drowned himself in a bottle of Jack Daniels and left Grandpa alone, none of this would have happened. If he didn't storm into homeroom this morning wearing garbage bags for underwear, looking like he used a pile of stray cats as a pillow the night before and then say, "Yeah, can I talk to Gabe LoScuda? That's Gabe. G-A-B-E. I'm his uncle. He's related to me."

Ugh. Every time I think about it I want to puke.

But I don't even have time to puke, because the second I get home from school I'm greeted by a trail of blood that starts as a few drops on the doorknob, and ends in shaky, red streaks across most of the living room furniture. I half expected some dude to be standing there in a hockey mask waving a cleaver at me. Instead, it was just Nick sitting between bloodstains on the couch.

"Pops broke a glass while I was out," he said without moving his eyes from the television. Some stupid infomercial about the latest and greatest Chia Pet blared from the screen.

"What's with all the blood?"

"Cut himself pretty bad. I washed it off. Put a Band-Aid on it. He'll live."

When I went to check on Grandpa, there was definitely a Band-Aid on his boo-boo. Only it covered less than half of the wound, and there were still a few droplets of watery blood dribbling through his closed fingers.

I called Dr. Weston.

If not for old Doc, I don't know what we'd do. He has an office down at the veteran's hospital, which is good because it's the only way Grandpa's able to afford it—which means it's the only way I can afford it. It's sad, though, because as soon as Gramps gets his pension check for being a damn war hero he has to turn it over to Dr. Weston just so he can continue going on surviving as a human being. I guess it could be worse. Doc let me look at some of the medical bills he pays out once Grandpa's money gets to him and all those pages were filled with very big numbers with lots of little zeroes after them. When I look at it that way, Gramps is getting a bargain for the two cents he's able to rub together off his pension.

"Turn up Johnny Cash!" Grandpa shouts about two centimeters away from my eustachian tubes.

"What the hell, Grandpa?! I'm trying to drive!" I look at him for a split second and notice he needs the corner of his mouth cleaned with a wet wipe again. When I turn back to the road, a pair of bright, red lights stare at me from the tail of a car in front of me.

I jam my foot on the brake pedal. The tires squeal. The rear-end slides left, then swings back to the right like a pendulum. The glowing taillights laugh at me from the Buick's rear panel. I stomp the brakes so hard I think my feet may hit pavement. And then the friction of rubber on asphalt takes hold. The tires lock down. The car bucks forward and the seatbelt tightens on my chest. Grandpa flails in his seat and I see his hand—the hurt one—smack against the dashboard like a dead trout. There's a thin spray of blood on the windshield, and a stain darkens the paper towel bandage I'd wrapped around the wound before we left the house.

We're safe, but I'm stunned. My heart bounces around in my chest and my head feels all foggy like I just woke up from a dream.

"You all right, Grandpa?" I ask as the light changes from green to yellow and back to red for the second time. A car pulls up next to us in the right lane. I'm too shell-shocked to turn my head and acknowledge it. "Gramps," I say when he doesn't answer. "You okay?"

But Grandpa isn't paying attention to me, or the car, or his hand, or the fact that we almost became a pair of June bugs on the windshield. No. The old bastard is too busy trying to pick up girls. I'm serious. Before I can react, he's half out the window and his stupid, grey mane is blowing in the wind. He makes googly eyes at a couple of cute girls who are probably close to my age.

Scratch that. They *are* my age.

Oh God, oh God . . . they're in my class. Justine Klein and Mandy So-and-So. I forget her name, but I know she's friends with Marlie. I better get control of the old guy before they notice. A kid can only face so much embarrassment in one day, and I think I've already surpassed my quota.

I reach for Grandpa's arm, careful not to get blood all over the seats. But it's too late. The door swings open and the dashboard chime rings in my ears—probably the factory-installed warning for "geezer overboard."

I burst out of the car and run a Chinese fire drill over to Grandpa just as he plops his bloody paw on the door panel and leans in the window like Danny freaking Zucco in *Grease*.

Justine is in the driver's seat. Her head snaps back in shock. She looks scared to death. And who can blame her? There's a crazy old guy bleeding all over her car and hanging half in the window.

"Aaaaah!!! Omigod! Make him stop!" Justine has a knuckle-white grasp on the steering wheel and her shrieking approaches the approximate pitch level required to shatter glass. Mandy So-and-So looks like a rigor mortis case, with her back pressed flat against the passenger seat, her lips pursed in tight against her teeth, and two full moons for eyes staring straight ahead, never blinking. I realize this scene has no casual escape. "Help!! Omigod!! Get him off!!"

"I'm so sorry," I start to say as I pull Grandpa out of the car by his shirt. But the old man keeps shouting. "Ladies, cut a rug!" over and over like an insane parrot. Justine can't hear a word I'm saying and Mandy So-and-So makes this motion with her hands that tells me Grandpa and I better get the hell out of the way. The tires chirp and Justine floors it through the intersection just as the light changes again from green to yellow.

Great. Looks like school will be a blast again tomorrow.

I wrestle Grandpa back in the Trans-Am, so we can take this traffic light to round three. I swear, if I didn't care about living up to Dad's wishes I would have thrown in the towel on the whole Grandpa prize fight twenty seconds into the first round. Now it's up to me to be the last man standing.

I park the car in the back lot of the VA hospital so no one can see me wrestle with Grandpa again. He's all tangled up in the seatbelt, which is covered in crusts of dried blood. Thanks, Gramps. When I think about how much grief Dad would have given me for screwing up the car, a familiar sting builds in the corners of my eyes. I take a deep breath and hold back the waterworks. It might sound weird, but I think I'd trade anything to hear Dad hound me about car maintenance one more time—even if it had been Grandpa's fault.

"You can't just wash the damn thing and call it a day," Dad would grumble. "The interior, Gabe. You can't forget the interior. It's top dog." I didn't agree. I never did. I wish I could remind him.

After Grandpa is free from his seatbelt web, I grab his hand and lead him to the entrance. He hums some off-key tune that sounds like the "Star-Spangled Banner" and a New Kids on the Block song mixed together and spun backwards on an Alvin and the Chipmunks record player. But it keeps him occupied. We even look like normal people for a few seconds as I usher him through the elevator doors and up to the third floor. Dr. Weston's office—the only general physician in a building full of ER nurses, orderlies, and cut-rate surgeons. But I trust him, and so does Grandpa's military insurance.

I check-in with the receptionist. "Make your grandfather comfortable in the waiting room," she says, "The doctor will be with you shortly." I've heard that phrase before—it's code for "have fun keeping the old man in check for the next twenty minutes."

I sweep a still-humming Grandpa into the crowded room and we sit down on a pair of rusty folding chairs in the corner. There's a table full of last year's magazines beside us. I scoop up a copy of *Highlights for Children* and skim through a "Goofus and Gallant" comic. I used to love this crap when I was a kid, waiting for the doctor or dentist with Mom, and I can't lie—I still love the stuff. Plus, it provides cover. I can duck behind the wrinkled pages and pretend no one is staring at Grandpa as he continues to hum his tune and dig for earwax.

I'm doing a good job of blending in with the grey walls when something—or rather someone—catches my eyes. But not in the way you're thinking. Not really. More like if you're walking down the street and a man-eating lizard crosses the sidewalk in front of you; like, in a weirded-out, scared, but still kind of fascinated sort of way.

There's at least a dozen metal hoops hanging from her ears and a thick, painful-looking stud pushed through the corner of her eyebrow. Her tight, black jeans are torn to shreds on each thigh. Patches of olive-colored skin and tattoo ink shine through. Her black t-shirt reads "Shock-Therapist" in lime-green, block letters, and there's a cartoony drawing of what looks like Joey Ramone dead center. Her hair is dark and straight, and it hangs in thin wisps over her ears and sections of her forehead. There's a thick, leather bracelet tied around her wrist with a skull and crossbones woven through the basket pattern. A pair of raggedy headphones hangs upside-down from her face. The cord is a tangled mass of frayed rubber and coppery wires that snakes down to a bright yellow Walkman clipped to her pocket. The volume is turned up admirably loud—so loud that I can almost hear the lyrics from across the waiting room. Something hard, fast, and mindless.

Punk music.

I don't know how long I stare at her before she reanimates from a lifeless trance and our eyes meet. I'm so startled I can't even look away real fast and pretend I'd been stretching my neck or something. Her eyes are a deep brown. Almost scary brown. Like swamp water. Or a mud puddle. But there's something inviting about them, too. I can't explain it.

Grandpa's tune suddenly stops and he finishes the digital excavation of his ear canal. He throws his arm around me and shouts, "My grandson!" He then sags back in the folding chair and nods off on his own shoulder. It's annoying, but I'm used to it. At least he knows my identity for once.

The girl seems both surprised and amused. She lifts an eyebrow and raises her pinky finger to her lip like she's simultaneously filthy rich and drinking tea—just like the stuffed shirt in the chair across from me who happened to bear a striking resemblance to the guy on the front of the *Monopoly* game box. I smile. Then I look around for another mark. There are plenty of weirdoes sitting around us, so I take my pick. An older lady with skin so pale she must sleep in a coffin. She's paging through a magazine super hard like the paper itself murdered her children—probably paper cuts. I motion over to the lady with my chin and watch Punk Girl steal a quick glance. Then, I curl my hands up like claws and bare my fangs like a vampire. I let out a little hiss and everyone raises their heads from their reading to stare at me, the psycho. I hear Punk Girl let out a laugh that she tries to stifle. Grandpa starts snoring and drooling a little bit on his own shoulder. I pull out an old tissue and wipe the corner of his mouth without waking him. When I look up, Punk Girl is puckering her lips and making this dainty motion, all proper-like, with her hand as if she's some old nursemaid cleaning gunk off a kid's face. I shake my head, but I can't hold back the smile.

The nurse shuffles in with a bunch of clipboards. She's kind of squatty around the middle and her scalp explodes in a million wiry curls. "Gabe," she says. "You can bring him back now if you can wake him."

"Thanks, Danielle."

I give Grandpa a quick elbow jab, nothing to hurt him, and he snorts a bit. His eyelids flap open and he's back in motion—like a freaking robot with a bunch of blown-out circuits. Makes me want to cry a little sometimes. But I won't, because that's not what Dad would do. And I'd look like a punk—and not in a good way—in front of the only girl in the world who doesn't yet know I'm a moron, even if she's weird as hell and I don't know her name.

Somehow, after all of the insanity of the day, Grandpa is in good spirits. There's never really any pattern to it. He could be humming some wacked-out tune one minute and then be trying to kick me in the groin the next. You never know. So, I'm quick to hustle him past the front desk and into the far recesses of Dr. Weston's offices before his mood changes.

Grandpa's humming away by the time I have him seated at the doctor's table with his shoes tucked underneath and his shirt unbuttoned half way. I wonder if he'll be this happy when the doctor tries to lace him up with a row of stitches?

Gabe LoScuda
English 4A – Personal Essay #2
Mr. Mastrocola
October 3

Leather and Pipe Tobacco

"Put your face in it, Gabe. Really get your nose in there."

Grandpa slid the glove off his weathered hand and dropped down to one knee. There was a twinkle in his eye. The sun sparkled off grey strands that poked out from beneath his brown mane. It was the first time I ever saw him smile. Even then, I had to look pretty hard as he fought to banish it from his face.

Dad stood a few steps behind, silent, a goofy grin plastered on his face. It was like they'd already shared this moment and relished in their chance to relive it. Like they'd been waiting for it to happen every day since the last.

"Go ahead, Gabe. Give it your best stuff."

He pushed the heavy piece of rawhide against my frail chest. I took hold and slipped my left hand inside. It felt slick with Grandpa's sweat. My fingers barely reached the holes they were destined to fill one day. Gramps and Dad had spent most of the morning pounding their fists into the pocket, slathering it with oil, and contorting it into all sorts of painful-looking shapes.

Grandpa pushed the glove up toward my face.

"Go ahead, son. She's yours now."

I inhaled, and my lungs were filled with the rich scent of tanned leather— the defining moment that lures a youngster to the game from the very first time his hand reaches inside a mitt.

My eyes bulged and my mouth puckered into a tiny, three-year-old "O."

"There it is, Dad! You see that?"

Gramps and Dad burst out into proud and joyous laughter.

Grandpa tussled my hair with his aging hand, and the scent of pipe tobacco mingled with the lingering glove leather. He pinched my nose between his knuckles and said, "Don't forget to keep it clean now, kid." It was the first time I ever heard him utter the phrase. "Let's toss the old ball around," Grandpa said once the moment had been thoroughly savored.

Dad and Grandpa pulled their gloves, cracked and scuffed by decades of use, out from the backs of their waistbands. They slipped them on and popped the pockets a few times with clenched fists. "Watch and learn, Gabe," Grandpa said as he flipped a side-arm toss over to Dad, who squeezed it in the pocket and covered it up with his throwing hand. "Always use two hands. Your father learned that lesson a few times." Dad shook his head and kept throwing. "Look the ball into the glove. And, for Pete's sake, stay in front of the damn thing. It's a ball, not a bomb."

Dad shook his head again, but kept throwing and catching.

"Now it's your turn."

Grandpa knelt down and put his hands on my shoulders. He jostled me around a bit until I was in the right position and then he took a few steps back and held the ball out in front of his chest.

"You ready?"

I didn't know what to say, so I just nodded and held my glove in front of my face. My eyes barely peaked over the webbing.

"Here goes."

And Grandpa wound back and tossed the ball. The top half caught the sun and gleamed in white. The bottom half was the dark side of the moon. The laces flipped and twirled, and I fought hard to keep myself from jumping out of the way and disappointing Grandpa.

Then I felt leather make contact with leather. The weight gathered in the pocket. There was a soft SNAP! as my bare hand clamped over the front of the glove.

"Would you look at that?! My grandson's a friggin' natural!"

"The next Willie Mays," Dad said. "The next Willie Mays."

I often think about moments like these—the ones that feel so light and carefree at the time, but that carry with them much heavier insights. It's only in the future, after time has beaten the ever-loving crap out you, that you realize what was actually taking place on a day like that. And it reminds me of one of Roberts Frost's most famous poems, which also happens to appear in one of my favorite books of all time: *The Outsiders*. I may have read S.E. Hinton's most popular book way back in middle school, but I will never forget the sage insight Johnny Cade gives to Ponyboy through Frost's words. They still ring in my ears:

Nature's first green is gold,
Her hardest hue to hold.
Her early leaf's a flower;

But only so an hour.
Then leaf subsides to leaf,
So Eden sank to grief,
So Dawn goes down to day
Nothing gold can stay.

When the ball popped my mitt that day—so many years ago when I could barely see over the shoulders of a cricket—and I squeezed it before it flipped lifelessly to the grass, I had held onto more than just the ball. I had held that gold in my hand—the hardest hue. And Gramps and Dad recognized it immediately, for they had once held the same hue in their own hands. Their appreciation for the gift that had been mysteriously stolen from them—their youth—was the catalyst for all the smiles and laughter these two produced in my honor. But, for them, that first youthful hue was far behind them, just a distant blip that wouldn't even register on a satellite image. For them, dawn had long ago gone down to day, and the only gold they'd see again would exist within the DNA they had passed along to me.

These days, I'm not even sure I possess the hue anymore. I'm eighteen years old and, for me, the light is already starting to fade. But I'm lucky. For Gramps and for Dad, men whose youth and energy once injected jolts of electricity into anything they touched, the flame has already been extinguished—and nothing they or I or even God could do would ever change that fact.

5

THE CLOSER

"I honestly don't know how much longer I can live with him."

I cram a full half of my peanut butter sandwich into my mouth. John looks disgusted.

"Dude, you don't need to inhale it. She's not even here yet. Besides, your pops isn't that bad."

"It's not Grandpa. At least he has an excuse for lying around the house all day and only hitting the toilet with thirty percent accuracy. It's Nick. I'm gonna kill the guy."

I cram the other half of sandwich behind my molars. There's a cool sweat building under my shirt. It's almost time.

"He still out of work?"

"Again. Held the last job for a new record."

"How long?"

"Three days. Then they shot his ass out of a cannon."

"Brutal."

"I mean, how hard is it to make a few phone calls and ask people if they like their cable service?"

"Doesn't sound like surgery."

"But he tells me some crap like, 'It hurts my feelings when people hang up on me.' But you'd actually have to show up to work before anyone has a chance to hang up on you. It's pathetic."

"Pa-thet-tic," John says, but he's barely paying attention. His eyes are busy trolling for Marlie's entrance into the cafeteria. His disinterest reminds me I should be pretty damn nervous right now.

The cafeteria at Schuylkill High smells like a cross between an old subway tunnel and a ballpark, which can only mean one thing: hot dog day. The cavernous, cinderblock walls contain an explosion of laughter and shouting, chairs scraping on linoleum, and plastic utensils tapping on trays. But John and I are stiff and silent—struck by the reality of what we're about to do.

"At least you don't have an Uncle Lily," John says when our tension starts to itch.

"What?"

"My mom. I thought I'd be smart, get a bit of studying in right after school. She told me it doesn't count if she doesn't know about it. Had me holed-up in my room identifying pig parts all night."

"Pig parts?"

"We're dissecting fetal pigs in Honor's Bio next week."

"Wow. Don't forget *that* suave one-liner when prom rolls around. How will the girls resist you?"

"Shut up, Gabe. Besides, shouldn't you be the one worried about smoothness?"

John rolls his eyes over my right shoulder and without looking I know Marlie is approaching—probably flanked by her annoying gaggle of giggling girlfriends. "You remember what to do?"

"Of course," I say. "Wait for Marlie to get her lunch and then it's go-time. Operation: The Closer."

"Worst name ever," John says under his breath.

"Not the worst name ever. I'm trying to keep the closer mentality. Shut her down and don't let her say 'no.' Close the deal at all costs."

"Did you graduate business school last night? Cause you sound like my father's stockbroker. And I doubt Marlie wants to be seen with a bald guy named Barry."

"Shut up, John. Here she comes. Do your thing and take care of the peanut gallery."

"Peanut gallery? Do you hear yourself, Gabe? You sound like the devil child that'd be born if James Bond married Betty Crocker."

"Would you shut up already? I need to concentrate. Got my line picked out and everything. Sonnet 116. William Shakespeare. No chance any girl can resist it. Not even Marlie."

"Great. You're a poet. Only three and a half years at Schuylkill High and you might make it to an actual dance. Impressive stuff, Gabe. Will you be wearing an ascot to the affair?"

I'm about to slug him from across the table when I'm stopped by a shock of blond hair.

"Here she comes," I whisper. "Let's move."

We leave what's left of our lunches in two half-eaten piles and follow Marlie's trail. John and I know her path well by now. I mean, it's not like we've been secretly analyzing her every move for the past two weeks, or anything.

She sits at the big, round table near the snack machine every day. Justine Klein and Mandy So-and-So walk half a step behind her like bodyguards and then they giggle and make small talk for a few seconds before sitting. That's our cue.

I motion to John and he breaks off around the long table usually reserved for the band geeks. Today, it appears to be somewhat abandoned. I'm worried it might not provide enough cover for John to complete his mission. But my friend is stealthy from living with the ever-omniscient Lily Chen all these years and he slips around the table with super-ninja speed and swings in behind Marlie's table unnoticed.

I reach down and check my pockets. Full of paper towels, just like we'd planned. I give John a soft nod, and he taps the bridge of his nose to acknowledge the signal. "Operation: The Closer" is a full go.

Marlie rests her tray against the table, and John springs into action. He moonwalks a few steps in her direction, does a quick Michael Jackson spin, and finishes off with a low kick that flips Marlie's tray no less than four times. A cloud of French fries, mangled hot dog bun, and Jell-O hangs in the air for a single, weightless second before the whole mess splatters on the floor in a chunky heap.

The cafeteria goes silent and Marlie's hands start to shake. Her eyes bulge like when you put a candy Peep in the microwave. John moonwalks a few more steps over to Justine and Mandy So-and-So, and it looks like Marlie's about to have a melt down.

"You . . . hey, you!"

But suddenly I'm there.

Her knight in shining armor. Totally by chance. No signs of a plot afoot at all. And I'm here to save the date. I mean, the day.

"Don't worry," I tell her, pulling the wads of paper towel I'd stolen from the bathroom earlier out of my pockets. They're all wrinkled. One's a little wet for some reason, but I swoop down and wipe a few beads of green Jell-O off her shoes before she can object. I hear John spouting off a bunch of crap to Justine and Mandy So-and-So. Something about "kinetics is what the King of Pop relies on and that's what makes him a scientist . . ." *Blah.*

Blah. Blah. Attaboy, John. Keep them busy.

All at once our classmates lose interest, and the hush of silence in the cafeteria erupts into the usual obnoxious symphony.

"Let me give you a hand," I tell Marlie like a guy who just happened to stumble across her at that very moment with the requisite amount of toilet tissue stuffed in his pants. Man, that doesn't sound right.

"Ok, thanks," she says. She's not shaking and her head doesn't seem to be on the verge of explosion anymore. I figure it's the perfect time to put the final phase of Operation: The Closer in motion.

"You know, we have to stop running into each other this way," I say as I scoop a pile of French fries back on the tray.

Come on, Gabe. Lame line. Don't let this plan unravel. You've come so far.

"What I mean is . . . you know, homecoming is just around the . . ."

She's smiling, Gabe. But is it because you're stuttering and holding a chicken finger in front of your face? Do something, genius!

"What I mean to say is 'If this be error and upon me proved, I never writ, nor no man has ever loved.'"

She watches me wipe up the last bit of green sludge from the floor. I hand her the tray and wait for that one, tiny word. The word that would make the whole damn operation a success. The one word that—

"Later, Gary," she says. And she pats me on the shoulder like some stupid kid brother. Then she walks away. Again.

A second later, that idiot, jock-strap sniffer Brent Corcoran says something and she hands him her tray. I can read the words as they come off her lips. "Thank you Brent. You're so sweet."

The bastard.

6

GOD SAVE THE QUEEN

"I'll go to the doc with you and Gramps," he says over the top of his newspaper—the classifieds, no less. "It's a Saturday. Not the best day for jobs." He's on such a roll I don't mention that it seems, for Nick, no day is a good day for jobs.

"Okay," I say.

Trust me. This was a big deal. Nick was making me think he might have a soul after all. But I didn't want to sound all needy because, in reality, I didn't need him. Like Dad always said, "it was the principle of the matter." Don't ask me which principle I was sticking to here, because Nick had already smashed most of them under his boot like so many of his cigarette butts. But I felt like I was sticking to something.

Still, it was nice escorting the old man across the hospital parking lot with a little back up. Made the whole chore feel a little less like a carnival act. So, when Gramps somehow kicked off one of his shoes and started hobbling across the asphalt like some kind of malfunctioning robot, I didn't have to worry. Nick was there to corral him before he stomped a limp and baggy sock down on a busted-up pile of old Heineken bottles. And I was there to ratchet the flat tire back on the old man's foot. We were like a damn pit crew for demented people, Nick and me.

We're the first appointment of the day. I planned it that way. Got up at the butt crack of dawn to get Grandpa ready. Time to remove the old stitches. The waiting room is empty at eight o'clock on a Saturday morning. Good. The last thing I need is for a studio audience to witness a repeat of what happened when Gramps got laced up the first time.

It's all still a bit of a blur. All I can say is the process started with a lot of screaming. Real high-pitched, blood curdling stuff like you hear in slasher films. There was a whole lot of pulling an old geezer out of his foxhole—the underside of Dr. Weston's examination table. A cascade of tongue depressors washing over the doctor, his nurses, and, of course, the patient, marked the climax of the piece. The scene ended with a dozen stunned faces staring at the red-faced teen and his babbling, and somehow freshly-stitched grandfather as they made a quick escape to the safety of a dark parking lot.

That's why I want to kiss Nick on the lips when he tells the receptionist, "I'll take him back today." *Really Nick? You'll take the crazy circus clown back to his clown car? You will? Well, you're a sucker, buddy, and I love you for it.* I snap a look over at Danielle sitting in her ergonomic receptionist's chair. Her chin hangs a bit slack on her jawline, like she just witnessed some kind of miracle. Good old Uncle Nick—number double-zero on the list of world wonders. I smile and she averts her eyes, pretending to copy a case number off one of the many cardboard file boxes stacked in the narrow cubicle.

Of course, just when I'm about to thank Uncle Nick for pitching in with his own father, he goes and ruins everything. "Yeah, I'll take him back," he says to the nurse, "I don't want it to be like last time."

Like last time? Are you serious, Nick? You think I wanted Grandpa to have the National Guard called in because he got four stitches? You think I wanted to sprint out of the waiting room like I just tied up Dr. Weston and all of his nurses in a back closet and was leaving with their jewels? Like freaking last time?

"You know what? Thanks, Nick. But I usually take him—"

"Yeah," he said. "I know." And he has this smug look on his face all of a sudden. I want to punch him.

"I'll take him back," I say, and I grab Grandpa by one of his sleeves.

Nick shuffles to his left to block our way. One of his flabby arms brushes against a basket full of lollipops on the reception desk and they cascade over the edge like a candy waterfall. Nick drops to one knee and scoops up a pile of them in one of his bear claws. The cellophane crinkles between his fingers as he drops them back in the basket. "He's my father, Gabe. I can handle it."

"He's used to me, Nick. It's better if—"

"I said I'll take care of it. Hey, don't forget your place."

My place? Did he really think I wanted my place to be under the drool rag of an old man who barely remembered me? Get serious, Nick.

"Ok, have it your way," I grumble just as Dr. Weston approaches with his clipboard.

"Everything all right this morning, gentlemen?

"Fine," I tell him.

"Just fine," Nick parrots. Then he leads Grandpa back to the examining room with the doctor a few steps behind. Out of the corner of my eye I see Gramps peel a laminated poster depicting the Heimlich maneuver off the wall. It had been stuck up there with that weird, blue putty-looking stuff they use in classrooms. Nick grabs it from him and reapplies the adhesive to the cold cinderblock. I look away before he notices I'm watching. This is his battle now.

I pull my English notebook out of my backpack and sit on a folding chair in the empty waiting room. I'm happy I can get a little homework done while I wait. It's pretty sad when homework is the most entertaining thing you do all day. At least we're not memorizing a bunch of presidents or dates or crap like that. All that stuff only sticks in my brain until I take the test. Then, I guess, my brain pukes it all up and refills with more important stuff, like song lyrics and pizza toppings and baseball statistics—stuff that matters. Or, at least they used to matter before my brain became Grandpa's brain and Uncle Nick's brain, and gets filled up with crap from the prescription bottles, child safety instructions, and dead-end leads to non-existent jobs.

At least in Mastro's class we're looking at how literature made an impact on our nation's beginnings. So we're talking about guys like Ralph Waldo Emerson and Henry David Thoreau. I love that stuff—how these guys were so important they had to have three names instead of two. I'm gonna have that one day, if I ever get my life back for a few seconds. They'll call me Gabe Freaking LoScuda, or something of that sort, and everything I say or write will swing the course of human history like the tides to a ship. And Uncle Nick and Grandpa won't bother me for a second because they'll be dead and—

It startles me. The thought. You know, of them being . . . gone. And I look down at my notebook. And a line or two of Thoreau stares back at me through all the other scribbles on the page. They're from a piece called "I am the Autumnal Sun," a poem Bernard Tiller in my class called "I am the Hemmorhoidal Bum." He's British, but mostly he's obnoxious, and he spends every spare moment between classes in the bathroom puffing a one-hitter. But I can't think about Tiller right now. I can only think about Grandpa and Nick and the lines from the poem: "And the rattling of the withered leaf/is the constant music of my grief." And I'm not sure why.

Then the doorknob rattles and a bell rings. It startles me half way to hell. She walks in by herself. Her eyes are black buttons set against heavy blotches of dark eye shadow. Her hair reaches down to her waist in silky, black snakes. A heavy stream of shouting and some recognizable guitar chords leak from her headphones and pollute the air. She brushes past me like I'm a piece of office furniture and she parks herself in front of the receptionist. They exchange a few words I can't make out, but I do hear her say something like, "She's not awake? Then I'll wait."

She spins around and heads for a chair facing mine. My eyes instantly shoot down onto my notebook. She smells kind of nice when she walks past. Kind of like warm tortillas and lavender. I keep my eyes on the notebook, jotting fake notes in the margins and underlining things like a madman just to make myself look scholarly. Before I know it, there's a border so thick and black around the lines of Thoreau's poem that it looks like a picture frame, and the notebook paper is flimsy and full of all these tiny holes that make it look perforated. I try to cover it up with my hand but she's already turning down the volume on her Walkman. She's already pulling one earpiece and then the other from her ears. She's already taking a deep breath and getting ready to say something.

"So . . . I bet you think you're pretty deep," she says.

She speaks like a statue, her eyes still and her lips thin and barely moving. I'm not sure if she's talking to me or if she's just floating her words out there on the stale hospital air—maybe to get trapped in the thumb of a latex glove or under the plunger of a syringe.

"Me?" I ask. I look around to make sure I'm still the only other person in the waiting room.

"No, I'm talking to that guy." She points to the table where a stack of magazines is topped with a Mr. Potato Head figurine. Poor guy is faceless and only has one ear. I feel a little sorry for him, to tell you the truth.

"Yeah," I say. "That guy's been chatting me up all morning. Doesn't even have a damn mouth, just that one lonely ear." She pops off the ear and slips it in a tiny pocket on the sleeve of her leather jacket. She smiles without showing her teeth—just a few sly wrinkles at the corners of her mouth.

"That better?" I nod. "Good," she says. She continues to stare at the crinkled page of my notebook.

"I'm not that deep, if that's what you're thinking."

"That's not what I'm thinking."

"Oh, well I saw—"

"Not exactly. It's complicated. And you're not . . . deep, that is. Nothing about you really suggests it. Plain t-shirt, blue jeans, a pair of sturdy track shoes. Nope. Not deep."

"Thanks a lot."

"So now you want to be deep?"

"No, I don't want to be deep."

"Oh please," she says, and it's the most emotion I've seen out of her in two waiting room visits. "The withered red leeeeaaaaves," she cries in some ghostly, Cockney-sounding moan. "Does that sound like a guy not trying to be deep?"

"It sounds kind of like a drunken ogre if you want to know the truth," I tell her.

"I sound like a drunken ogre?"

"A little bit."

"Well, I like it."

"Sounding like an ogre?"

"No, the poem. Even if it does sound all fancy and full of shit."

She smiles again. This time she flashes teeth and a twinkle in her eyes—like a mannequin that's suddenly come to life.

"If it's shit, how can you like it?"

"It's not shit exactly. It's just that it's full of shit. It takes a simple idea and makes it complicated so the d-bag who wrote it can blow smoke up his own arse."

"Arse?"

She smiles. "It seemed to fit the moment. I like the message though. Like we're all sitting around just getting older and getting more and more bothered by it every day . . . and still we do nothing about it." The words trickle from her mouth in a continuous stream. She takes a deep breath to replenish herself. "No future," she says.

"What?"

"No future. Like the song."

"I don't get it."

"Your poem. It's just a long, annoying, hoighty-toighty way of saying the same thing the Sex Pistols say at the end of 'God Save the Queen.' Listen." She pushes her Walkman across the table to me.

I give her a look and then hold the phones to my ears and press "play." There's a splash and a clatter of drums, a rash of guitar, and some maniac screaming "No future! No future! No future for you!" over and over again.

"So, you're into punk?" I ask as I slide the Walkman back to her.

"Boy, you really are deep. What gave it away?"

"Well, the—"

"Oh God. Please don't answer. Just tell me if you liked it."

"Yeah it was great. Couple of aspirin and it would have been perfect."

"Lame," she says, but for some reason it doesn't feel like a dagger through my heart like it would have if someone like Marlie had said it to me.

"Are you sick?" I ask.

"What? Because I like punk music?"

"Uhh, no. Because you're in a hospital."

"Oh. No. It's my mom. Cancer."

I'm staring down at my notebook again and trying to remove one of my giant-ass shoes from my mouth. *Idiot, Gabe.* "I'm, uhh . . . I'm sor—"

"You don't have to apologize or anything. It's not like it's contagious and you gave it to her or something."

"Yeah," I say, trying to play off my twitchiness as stone-cold aloofness, "of course not." *She's not buying it, Gabe. Time to change the direction of this conversation.* "I'm not sick either. I'm here because my grandfather—"

"I know. I was here last time . . . for the escape from Alcatraz."

"Oh, that's right," I say rubbing my eyes, "you saw that?" That feeling is rushing in again. The Marlie feeling. The one where I'm this tiny, little ant crawling around on the kitchen floor and she's towering above me ready to crush me without even knowing it.

"I'm Sofia," she says. *Wait. What? She's actually a witness to me dragging Grandpa out of there like some abusive prison warden from Hell . . . and then she tells me her name? Maybe I do like punk music.*

"I'm Gabe," I say before any drool can roll down my chin. Right at that moment, a door slams in the bowels of Dr. Weston's offices and I hear someone shout, "Hold him there!" It's a low, gruff voice like the one that demands things from a perch on my couch every morning. Uncle Nick. Two sets of footsteps clomp down the back hallway, clearly gaining on the waiting room.

I glance over at Sofia. Her eyes are dark circles and her face is vampire pale, like she's been avoiding sun her whole life. She looks over my shoulder at Nick and Dr. Weston, who's standing in the doorway with his clipboard in one hand and a paper towel pressed to his nose in the other. The paper towel is wet, and a red stain spreads slowly through its fibers.

"What the hell happened, Nick? You were supposed to be watching Grandpa."

"I was doing everything but strangling him."

"I don't want to hear it! I knew I should have—"

"Gabe," Dr. Weston says in a low growl that evaporates the rest of my statement. "He did all he could. It was an accident and I assure you, I'm not going to die. But I would like to have a word with the two of you in my office. My nurses will attend to your grandfather and keep him busy."

"Yeah, I've seen him in there," Nick says. His voice is all strained now, like he just competed in a full decathlon. The guy can put on quite a show. "We better make our chat quick," he says, "before my father terrorizes those poor ladies." Then—right on cue—there's a loud crash and the recognizable scuffle of nurse's shoes on linoleum. We all look in the direction of the examining rooms. The battle has apparently begun.

"I agree," says Dr. Weston. He motions to us with a jerky head movement—since both his hands, and probably his nose, are full. The folding chair squeals on the tile floor as I rise to my feet. There's a plastic sheen of total and unmistakable disinterest on Sofia's face, which reminds me: I have shitty luck.

"It was nice meeting you," I say to her over my shoulder—all suave and manly, like I meet girls in waiting rooms and parking lots out of habit.

"Yeah," she says, still in a trance from the commotion and Doc's bloody nose. "It was cool. Even if you're a lame, poet geek."

She smiles and I'm about to come back with something all casual and flirtatious, something you'd hear in one of those romantic comedies where the man and woman pretend they're total enemies but then end up in bed together. I hate those movies, because stuff like that never happens to guys like me, but I'm about to say something all mysterious and drenched in irony—something perfect like, "I'd agree . . . if lame, poet geeks were into labels." I don't know. Maybe not that, but I would have thought of something.

Instead, I hear, "Look at my nephew go, Doc! Hitting on broads right here in your waiting room. Takes stones."

"Shut up, Nick," I say in place of my line.

"You read poetry to her already? He works quick, that nephew of mine—"

"Nick!" I grab my notebook and start the long walk from the waiting room to the hallway. I can feel her eyes on me. Her cheeks are probably puffed out like a blowfish and her chest is probably heaving with the laugh she's saving until she hears Doc's door slam shut. And I can't take it anymore. Something about this crazy girl with the dark makeup, leather jacket, and pierced everything forces me to do it.

I turn around.

There's no laugh, but she's smiling. Not a teeth-showing smile, but I can tell she's amused. I guess amused is better than mortified. Something tells me this girl doesn't do mortified. And I like it. Scratch that, I admire it.

Dr. Weston's office is the typical medical chamber. Carved panels encase the room in dark-stained oak. An oppressive-looking desk takes up most of the room and any open areas are covered by shelves with rows of leather-bound medical books stacked on them. There are a bunch of picture frames on the desk, all facing Dr. Weston—presumably his wife and kids.

I snag a starlight mint from a small bowl next to the picture frames and slump down next to Nick on a brown, leather chair facing the doctor. He squeezes a tissue around his nose, so when he talks his voice comes out sounding like what you'd expect to hear if someone tried to smother the Keebler elf.

"Gentlemen, I brought you back here for obvious reasons," he says, and immediately I can tell this little conversation is not going in a positive direction. "The incident last week putting in Ernest's stitches was a pretty clear indicator. Today's boxing match was confirmation."

The doctor pauses for a moment and looks down at the page of notes on his desk. I know this move. It didn't work on Sofia and it's not about to work on me.

"What are you saying?" I ask before he drags this out any longer.

"I'm saying I don't think you and Nick are capable of taking care of your grandfather. I'm saying it might be time to seek professional help."

"Now wait just a minute," Uncle Nick says, and I can't believe it. He might literally have the eye of the tiger right now—wide and full of fire. He sits on the edge of the couch cushion, like he could spring forward and attack the doctor at any moment. A few veins bulge out from beneath the stained neckline of his t-shirt. "My nephew and I take good care of my father. He might be difficult at times, but no one is going to—"

"Nick, Nick," Dr. Weston says in a soothing voice—he's trying to diffuse the land mine currently perched on his new couch. "No one is trying to say you don't know how to care for Ernest. That's not the point. But, did you see what he did to us in there? He's not himself. He's still strong as an ox, but his brain, Nick. It's not the same."

"We understand that, Doctor," I say, and I can't believe I said *we* as if Nick and I were somehow a team. "But there's no way we'll give up on him."

"You wouldn't be giving up on him. Patients like your grandfather are unpredictable. They can become disoriented and their fears often result in violence. They can become a danger to themselves and to anyone they come in contact with. It's purely a matter of safety."

"You heard my nephew. There's no chance. My father stays with us."

Good, old Nick—the number two in our one-two LoScuda punch. Suddenly, I'm bolstered. "And I can never break the promise my father made to him," I add. "That man will die with dignity. He's a damn war hero."

"That's your decision," Dr. Weston says, "and I will do my best to support you both. But please know I'll be writing my recommendations here in my notes. I need you to understand they could become relevant if anything were to happen in the future."

"The future," I whisper.

"Son, you need to face it. He has no future."

"Well, if he has no future," Nick says, "he's sure as hell gonna spend it with us. Come on, Gabe. Let's get Grandpa."

And, for once, Uncle Nick and I agree on something.

7

It Sings of Freedom

Each day I spend as a teenage nursemaid makes me realize Mom and Dad were complete badasses. They were like a pair of crazy street jugglers you'd find in Baltimore Harbor. A mortgage, two jobs, a marriage, Grandpa—all shiny, enameled bowling pins to be flipped through the air and never allowed to touch the ground. And then there was me, the flaming baton—only to be tossed in at the precise moment every pin dangled in its most perilous position. How my parents kept the act in business for all those years, I'll never know. But at least they had each other. Here I am trying to figure it out on my own.

I woke up this morning at six, emptied the garbage, washed Nick's dishes from last night, caught up on a late homework assignment for Mastro's class (we're studying modern poets these days), ate a peanut butter and banana sandwich, and force-fed Grandpa his morning meds. Did I mention it's Saturday? Apparently none of this matters to Nick, who's currently wedged between the couch cushions like a sloppy helping of cellulite taco. He's out cold and the classifieds section is nowhere in sight. But he's trying. I have to give him that. Putting his foot down in Doc's office showed me that somewhere, beneath the neck rolls and the ever-questionable blood alcohol content, Nick cares about what happens to Grandpa. I can work with that, which is actually what I plan to do. Get a job. It'll be some tough-juggling when baseball season rolls around—what with school and Grandpa still shaking me down every day—but that won't even come close to the type of act Mom and Dad pulled off for almost two decades putting up with my garbage. Besides, it's kind of hard to expect Nick to join the ranks of the employed if I'm not there with him.

It's still early, so I figure I'll get a jump on next week's reading for Mastro's class—and actually know what people are talking about for a change. It's from Maya Angelou's *I Know Why the Caged Bird Sings*. She's the National Poet Laureate. She even read her poetry at President Clinton's inauguration. I guess anyone who gets recognized for poetry needs a little respect. I mean, I write my own poetry but it's not like I'll ever let another soul read it. Good old Maya's out there sharing her deepest and darkest thoughts with the world. Even the freaking president knows them. That's a pretty heavy weight to carry, don't you think?

I figure I might as well read the stuff out loud to Grandpa. Doc says patients like him are soothed by the human voice—so I'll learn some crap and mellow out the old man at the same time. How's that for juggling?

I read a bio piece from the front jacket that says Angelou's writing was pretty influential during the height of the Civil Rights Movement. She was even pals with Dr. Martin Luther King, Jr. I didn't think Gramps was all that much into civil rights. At least he never mentioned anything about them, or the fact that he lived through the era, but he didn't seem to mind. He just lounges back against the headboard—shoes off, eyes half shut—and listens to me read.

Thing is, the more I read the more charged up I start to feel. The more Angelou's words begin, like all good poetry, to speak directly to me. The more I want to chirp them loudly from my swinging perch. The more I want to peck my way out of the cage.

But a bird that stalks
down his narrow cage
can seldom see through
his bars of rage

And I think about it. Not too many months ago my biggest worries were passing my driving test and learning how to hit a curveball. Now people's lives, including my own, are nothing more than products of the decisions I'll make. An invisible cage, maybe. But still a cage. One that's been holding me hostage from the man, no the kid, I want to be. I knew what had to be done. Even if my new life had completely obliterated the old one, at least I could take small trips back in time—like little vacations from reality.

his wings are clipped
and his feet are tied
so he opens his throat to sing.

I pull Grandpa's afghan up over his chest. He's only half awake, so I figure I have a good hour of freedom before he needs my services again. Nick is sitting up on the couch when I pass through the living room. Progress. He shovels palms full of Cocoa Puffs into his mouth straight from the box. His watery eyes are glued to the television where bugle calls and gunfire tell me the cavalry has arrived in whatever matinee western he is watching.

"I'm going out," I say as I pass. He grunts something unintelligible, so I know he hears me.

I creep into the garage and untangle the old Mongoose from its cobwebby tomb. Haven't been on the damn thing since I got my license. Standing here, with the garage light reflecting off its chrome frame and the smell of cracked rubber wafting off a thin tread on the blue tires, it seems strange I traded it in for the Trans-Am so quickly. There wasn't much thought to it, I guess. But it feels nice to perch on the pedals and hop a few curbs like the old days—so nice I decide to pedal it over to Perdomo's for an early slice.

Perdomo's is only a few blocks into town, but the scenery is like a trail back in time through the trials and tribulations of Gabe's life. Seriously. The sign read "Maple Street," but it could probably be changed to "LoScuda's Shameful Way" and no one would notice. I could see it now:

An old, married couple reaches the street corner. They look up at the sign. She says, "Oh yes, honey, that's the boy who crashed his bike into the hydrant near the dry cleaners."

"Are you sure, Dolores?"

"Oh yes. Don't you remember? He skinned his knee. Left the bike there and everything. Ran screaming all the way down the street. Scared my girlfriend Mabel half to death."

"Over a skinned knee?"

"Yep. All over a skinned knee."

I'll spare you any more horror stories, this being a tame one. My exploits are known far and wide along the Maple Street corridor. Just another bullet point to tack on my list titled: *Reasons Why I'm at Home Playing Video Games on Friday Nights*. Only, I'd give just about anything to abandon the juggling and get back to weekend Madden marathons as soon as possible. Since that won't be happening, a slice of pizza might ease the pain.

I lean my bike up against the brick façade at Perdomo's like I've done since I learned to ride a bike and eat a slice at the same time. It's kind of early for lunch, but there are already a few patrons inside. Kind of an odd mix. There's a middle-aged guy in a business suit sitting at a table for two near the front window. His briefcase sits on the empty chair and he's craning his neck back to suck in a glob of cheese before it lands on his tie.

There's a couple about my age sitting on the same bench seat of a booth near the counter. She makes creepy little cooing noises—like a wacked out pigeon with a speech impediment—and feeds him pieces of pizza crust like I'd do to the seagulls in Wildwood, NJ. He seems to like it. Mr. Perdomo does not. He leans on his broom and stares at them over the register. He catches me watching him and passes along his most solemn and judgmental nod.

"Gabey-boy!" he says. "I was starting to think you and Johnny don't like my pizza no more. I never see you guys."

"The pizza's great," I tell him. "It's the rest of my life that's kind of shitty." Perdomo looks at me weird and I realize all this acting like an adult is making me forget how to talk to them as a kid. "I mean crappy, sir. That's a little better."

"Not much," he says. "But I'll take it." He ruffles the front of my hair like he's done since I was maybe three years old. Then there's another weird look, but this is one I recognize. It's *pity*. The eyes. The soft tones. The dramatic silence. Ugh. The same crud I get at school. "So, son," he says in the voice of a guidance counselor, "how ya holding up? Ya know, if you need me for anything you can always ask, cause I know how hard it is to—"

"Things are good," I say before he can make this scene any more grotesque. I'm lying but I don't need Perdomo thinking I'm a charity case too. I decide to lay it on extra thick. "My Uncle Nick and I, we're taking care of my grandfather. I'm acing all my classes, and I'm gonna start second base on the baseball team."

"Second base, eh? That was my position when I was at Schuylkill. I trust you with it."

"It's in good hands, sir."

"And your Uncle Nick? He's you mother's brother?"

"My dad's."

"I didn't know he had one."

"Sometimes I felt that way too. But he's back now and we're moving forward."

"That's good to hear, Gabey-boy."

"Yep. I'm even thinking about getting myself out there in the job market."

Job market? Do you hear yourself, Gabe? You didn't graduate Harvard Business School. You're looking for minimum wage.

Perdomo smiles. Apparently he's amused by my stockbroker talk.

"Job market, eh? Well, I'm proud of you. Hard work's important. In fact, I'm actually looking for a little help at the moment."

"You mean me? You think I'm capable of flipping pizzas?"

"No, son. I don't. But we got other things to do around here. We'll work our way up to the flipping." I don't know what to say, so I just hold out my hand and we shake. In the same motion, Mr. Perdomo slides a slice across the counter to me.

"On the house," he says. Amazing what you can get with a little youthful energy. A few curb jumps on the Mongoose turned into a free lunch and a new job. I'm so shocked, happy, and relieved at the same time I decide to take the slice on the road. Eat it on the Mongoose. Hands on pizza only. "You can start after school on Monday!" I hear Perdomo shout as I hit the doors. I give him a quick thumbs-up and then hop on my bike for a final joy ride.

All that's left of the pizza as I pedal into the driveway is a grease-covered plate that I roll into a spyglass and attempt to use as my view-finder for the final ten feet or so of the ride. I toss it in the garbage can (I gotta remember to put that damn thing away), and head for the door.

But I notice something. At first I think it might be just a trick of the light, but as I get closer it's confirmed. A scratch—or rather a series of scratches and a dent—on the front, passenger-side fender of the Trans-Am. It's freaking mangled. Little flakes of paint cling like curly banana peels in places where something—presumably a giant cheese grater—rubbed them raw from the colorless steel below. A quarter-sized dimple sits in the middle of the collage like a lifeless eye.

It was driveable. Sure. But I could almost feel the pull of Dad's eyes on the back of my skull, like he was standing there on the porch, as always, shaking his head and doubting my abilities as a motorist. "But how could this have happened?" he would say. "WHERE would this have happened?" would be the follow-up.

"I don't know," I'd tell him. "The only place I've driven it is to school."

School. The maniacal, dog-eat-dog world that is the Schuylkill High School parking lot. That had to be where it happened. Someone must have clipped her before I got out of there yesterday. All I'd have to do is find the car in the lot on Monday with red streaks down its side and I'll know the identity of the classmate who will be purchasing my new fender. The son of a bitch. I'll worry about it on Monday. I'm in too good of a mood to let it screw me today. Time for a Madden marathon. Maybe I'll call John.

When I push through the front door, Nick is still drooling in front of his Western. Grandpa staggers out of the bathroom and shuffles a couple of feet back to his bedroom.

"I'm back," I say in Nick's general direction.

"I know. I heard you. Not like you were trying to be quiet."

"Whatever. Everything alright?"

"Look around. The place is still here." He's still glued to the Western and his words come out like he's communicating through a zombie translator—so I let him get back to his busy schedule.

I pick up the phone and dial John. As it rings, I notice I'm clearing a bunch of crap off the hall table that should have been put away—a box of toothpicks, an old tissue, a beer can, Nick's wallet, my spare set of keys.

Ugh. I feel like Mom. Always juggling.

Never Leave a Debt

Robert Frost provided me with perhaps my very first taste of poetry, way back when I thought verse could only exist in neat, little rhyming packages with sing-songy refrains. My mom used to recite "Stopping By Woods on a Snowy Evening" every year around Thanksgiving, when the temperatures in the Philly area started to nip at the ears and bite at the hands. I guess maybe she thought her reading would summon up a snow day so that we'd skip school and work and spend the day drinking cocoa and sitting in front of the fireplace between rounds of sledding. Her recitations rarely worked, but the poem did leave its impression on me.

In it, Frost writes, "These woods are lovely, dark and deep, but I have promises to keep, and miles to go before I sleep" which always made me think, "Wow, this dude is trekking across an arctic freaking landscape and he's still worried about keeping some dumb promise, probably to some girl he likes."

Hey, I was a little kid, but I still got the feeling that promises were not just something you threw out there to be polite. So, Frost is probably to blame for my borderline psychotic obsession with maintaining Dad's promise to Grandpa. Then again, maybe it wasn't Frost at all. Maybe it was actually Gramps who'd created the impression for me—on a pleasant afternoon way back when he was still able to hoist me up off the ground and lift me over his head in a single swoop.

The shadows of oak leaves flickered around me on that day. They made me feel like an undersea diver searching for daggers of light in a darkened world. My darkened world was a mass of gnarled roots that jutted up through the lawn under the canopy of Grandpa's prized shade tree.

Mom and Dad had a wedding to attend. Someone from Dad's work, I remember. Another teacher. They'd left me with Gramps in the morning and I was all too happy to grab my G.I. Joe action figures and have Joe himself stake military claim to a small chunk of my grandfather's yard. The tree roots provided the perfect base, a network of hardwood highways that twisted and turned in impossible directions. Natural depressions between the moist soil and the roadways were dream locations to arrange mine fields and build trenches and set traps to ambush Cobra and his evil cronies.

As I shot down plastic helicopters with imaginary surface-to-air missiles, Grandpa worked his way up and down the ladder like a mechanized monkey. He slathered brick-red paint on his ancient shutters with the bristles of a five-inch horsehair brush, never once leaving a speckle of the red on his brilliant, white shingles.

There was a sting in the air that morning, the kind of chill that surprises you in early October. The kind that gives meddling moms all the reason they need to force their sons into winter coats against their wills. With the warmth of the midday sun came the absence of my winter coat, which I'd left sprawled-out across the lawn—a sort of munitions dump to stash spare propeller blades and headless figurines.

"Didn't your mother tell you to keep that coat on your body?"

His voice was gruff and heavy and it startled me out of my fantasy army world. He smelled like some kind of spicy aftershave. Probably Aqua Velva. He always kept a bottle of that blue stuff on his bathroom sink. And I always fought the urge to slug it down like a bottle of Gatorade. Don't ask.

I looked up at him from under a dense shadow. "She told me to wear it this morning," I said with the stone-cold logic of a seven-year-old. "Now it's afternoon."

"That does seem to be the case." A slight grin rose on his face and he wiped it away with the back of his hand. "Well, seeing as you've finally burst out of that cocoon your mother packed you in—and seeing as I'm out of paint—what do you say we take a ride to the hardware store in your granddaddy's Caddy?"

It didn't take much to sell me on a ride in his Coupe Deville. In the same way my father saw the Trans-Am as a living entity, Gramps provided for his Deville like he would a spouse. Even gave the damn thing a name. An old lady's name—Rita.

"Rita told me she's itching to take a few sweeping turns today," he told me as he hoisted me up on the camel-colored passenger seat. "And who am I to keep old Rita from her joy?"

Gramps hopped into the driver's seat and cranked the engine. He popped a white tape in the cassette player and pushed the "play" button until it held fast. A few soft guitar chords flirted with the rising hush of a live audience. Grandpa patted my knee with a weather-beaten hand. "Nothing like a little

Johnny Cash to get you over that midday hump," he said. "Now hold on tight." He tugged a bit on my seatbelt, nodded his approval, then slapped both hands on the leather steering wheel and stomped on the gas. We shot out of the driveway like one of those racecars that has to fire a freaking parachute out its backside just to stop.

All the skin on my face stretched tight against my skull and my spine nestled firmly against the seat. The corners of Grandpa's mouth creased upward, his eyelids relaxed, and the usually taught lines in his forehead seemed washed away. His face bore an expression of pure serenity that matched the rolling deepness of Mr. Cash's lyrics.

We pushed past the boundary lines of his neighborhood and sped down a straight stretch of highway sewn through a patch of forest like a concrete artery. Gramps steadied the wheel and guided the Deville with only the slightest flick and twitch of his bony wrists. The car glided around curves the way Olympic skaters carve figure eights into sheets of pristine ice. And good old Johnny just sat in the back seat and strummed his guitar and grunted out lyrics about a beautiful girl in a long, black veil in a rawhide, Cowboy cadence.

Gramps rolled down the volume a few notches and careened around another curve with only his left hand on the wheel. Then he pointed deep into a clearing as we approached it on the left side. "Take a look over there, Gabe," he said. Three fat, Jersey cows munched on dandelions beside a rotted-out barn. They stared at us, eyes gleaming with innocence, as we roared past in the Deville. Then, suddenly, we pulled up at an intersection and we were in town. A long strip of traffic lights, strip malls, and cement moseyed off into the sunset beyond. Mabel's Hardware store was a quick left after the first light.

"I'll just be a few minutes," Grandpa said as he pulled up in the empty lot. "Wait here for me and don't get out of the car."

I nodded, because what boy in his right mind would ever want to leave a vehicle like this? All the levers and buttons and ashtray covers to open? All the windows to crank and seats to reposition? All the treasure to be found under the floor mats or, better yet, in the glove box?

The glove box.

My curiosity was burning. I waited until Grandpa was safely inside the store, then I popped open the little compartment in front of my seat as if I were a secret agent cracking a safe in Saddam Hussein's palace. A wad of crinkled napkins flipped out first, followed by a vinyl-covered booklet of sorts that had the same symbol raised on its cover that Grandpa had displayed as an ornament on his hood. Weird. I tossed it in the back seat and kept digging.

A box of fuses, three dried-up cigars, a tire gauge, and a few pairs of out-of-style glasses later and I found the mother lode. Some kind of medal. It was dark bronze with signs of weathering on the surface. A few pieces of lint from the glove box had collected on its face. I wiped them clear to reveal a small, misshapen heart with a few odd words and an eagle transcribed around it. It was attached to some kind of ribbon with a pin, probably so you could hook it on your shirt or something.

I flipped it over and over again, allowing the smooth finish to play against the palm of my hand. I tried to imagine any of the variety of ways Grandpa could have won the medal. It was a heart, so maybe Grandma had given it to him? There was an eagle on it, so maybe he won it playing football or maybe for spotting the most birds through his binoculars? Or, maybe he'd won it in a spelling bee or something? There were a bunch of words on it I didn't understand, so Gramps had to be a pretty good speller to figure them out.

Whatever it was Gramps had achieved I was about to find out, because suddenly I heard the driver's side door unlatch and a shadow loomed over me. I looked up, the medal still sitting in the middle of my palm, and Grandpa's eyes were glued to it, unmoving. His lips were thin and tight, and his hand a bit shaky as he propped himself against the wheel.

"Looks like you found yourself a relic," he said.

"What's a relish?" I asked. "Is it something you win for doing cool stuff?"

Grandpa's eyes softened and he sat down in the seat beside me. He let out an almost silent chuckle before speaking. "Not a relish, Gabe. A relic. It's a keepsake. Something to help you remember an important moment in time."

"How'd you get it?"

"Well, you were right about one thing. I won it . . . for doing some pretty cool stuff." He flicked the ignition on the Deville and stretched his arm into the back seat to deposit his new can of paint on the floor.

"I think this may be a time for some ice cream, Gabe. Every story deserves a cone of vanilla. Don't you think?"

"Chocolate," I said.

"Okay, chocolate it is." And Gramps pulled out of that parking lot with the same grace as Mario Andretti. He hugged the dotted lines on the road like a surgeon making an incision. He was in complete control of the Deville, and I'd never felt safer in my life.

We pulled up at the Dairy Queen for our frozen treats and lapped up the long ribbons of chocolate soft serve in the empty parking lot.

"This medal is called a Purple Heart," Grandpa said as he cradled it in his hand like a trapped ladybug. "Given to me by the President of the United States, Mr. Harry S. Truman. Most of the boys in my unit got one."

"Why?"

"Because we happened to step in the wrong place at the wrong time."

"They gave you an award for screwing up?" I asked.

"Not exactly, Gabe. But then again, I guess you might be on to something. See, we were coming up over this ridge and the Germans had us pinned between them and a thick bramble of trees. Kind of a thicket, I guess. We didn't have the ammunition to fire on them, so we took the only choice they gave us. We retreated into the woods. It was exactly what they wanted us to do."

He paused to take a big bite of his ice cream and another glance at the medal.

"Why would they want you to do that? Wouldn't you be able to escape?"

"That's what we thought. Boy, were we wrong. See, the Germans had filled up that whole darn thicket with bouncing Bettys."

"They tried to attack you with a bunch of . . . gymnasts?"

Grandpa lost it for some reason when I asked the question. Melted ice cream sprayed from his mouth as he laughed, and he handed me the medal while he mopped it off the dashboard and its various instruments.

"Bouncing Bettys are land mines," he said after a few breaths. "They bury the devils in a secluded place and when you walk on them they get tripped—meaning they blow up. Only these suckers bounce up from the ground and blow up at chest level. They shoot little bits of sharpened metal all over the battlefield when they do. It's how most of us were wounded that day."

"You got wounded in battle?"

"Yep. Just a small wound. Here." He lifted up his pant leg and pushed down his sock to reveal a jagged scar that ran across his ankle and half way up the back of his calf. "Most of the muscle was hanging out like a batch of giblet gravy, and you could see the bone in a few places. But it wasn't half as bad as what happened to Private Gus Bradley."

"What happened to him?"

"One of those Bettys blew his arm clean off his body. We found it a good thirty yards away hanging from a willow tree. Well, we did after reinforcements arrived and we cleaned the Krauts out of the area."

"What happened to Private Bradley?"

"I did the only thing I could think of at the time. I hoisted myself up on one leg, grabbed a downed branch to use as a crutch, and hobbled over to him as fast as I could. He wasn't moving, just breathing real heavy and sweat was rolling down his face in little beads. I carried him as far as I could. Got him off the battlefield and delivered him to the MPs."

"You're a hero, Grandpa."

"I guess some people would say that, Gabe. Not me. See, Private Bradley didn't make it. Died right there on the gurney before they even got him to the field hospital."

He looked off into the distance for a few seconds. I could see the muscles twitching along his jawline. He scooped up a napkin and dabbed it over his eyes a few times. "Must have got a bit of ice cream in there when you made me laugh," he said with a wink. "Now, Gabe, where's the rest of the stuff? The glasses?"

"I put them in the back seat."

I quickly dove behind the seat like a little jackrabbit and snagged the old glasses.

"Ah," Grandpa said. "These." He held up a pair of black-rimmed reading glasses. They were pretty basic, but he stared at them like he was looking at one of the Seven Wonders of the World.

"What's so special about those things?" I asked.

"They're his," he said. "Private Bradley's. It's the only one of his possessions that made it out intact that day."

"Why do you have them, Grandpa?"

"Always thought I'd deliver them to his widowed wife one day. You know, as a keepsake. But I never had the courage."

"Were you afraid of her?"

"In a way, Gabe, she scared me more than the German army. I was afraid to face her. To explain to her why I couldn't save her husband. Why I was still alive and her husband was dead. I couldn't do it, but I always thought she should have them."

"Can't you bring them to her now?"

"It's too late, Gabe. She's gone. Had a funeral a few years back and I was too much of a coward to even show up for that."

He slid the last bite of cone between his lips and chewed it slowly, still staring far off into the distance as if Private Bradley would somehow reemerge on the horizon.

"Let me tell you one thing, Gabe, and please remember this for all of your days. Do you promise to remember it?"

"I do, Grandpa," I told him through a mouth full of ice cream. "I'll never forget."

"Good. Now here it is. *Never leave a debt, Gabe. Never.* If you owe something to another—if you've made them any sort of promise whatsoever—stand by it. Because the only thing worse than debt is the regret of never having repaid it."

I'm not sure I knew what he was talking about that day, more than a decade ago, but I do now.

And Dad knew.

So maybe Grandpa's advice is somehow more important now than it's ever been.

8

HIT AND RUN

"Just one time I want you to be a team other than the Cowboys," I say. "Just once."

"I would if you didn't call the Eagles for eternity," John snaps back. He cocks the controller like he's actually on the field. So annoying. Then he wheels Troy Aikman to the right sideline, waits for my defender to be close enough to see remnants of powdered donut from the quarterback's breakfast, and then fires a bullet to freaking Michael Irvin in the back of the end zone. No one's covering. I strangle my plastic Big Gulp cup until little, fizzy droplets of Mountain Dew surge to the top and dribble down the sides.

"Unbelievable."

"I don't think it matters which team I pick," John boasts. "Same result." John elects to attempt an onside kick on the ensuing kickoff. Who does that? I'm not prepared, so I watch helplessly as his kicker—his freaking kicker—pounces on the football while three of my heftiest lineman stand around and count their fingers. I don't say anything. Just take a sip of Dew and place the cup back on the coffee table.

"It's getting pretty silent over there, LoScuda," John says as we select plays for the next snap. "Nothing for me? No excuses about my team selection, or my choice in uniforms, or the sun glare out there on the animated gridiron? Nothing?"

"Shut up, John."

"Okay, I'm just checking because you seem a little—"

"It doesn't help when you pick a team with a Super Bowl MVP, a rushing champ, and a reception machine, and—"

"Oh, I see." He calls timeout and pauses the game. Mid snap. What's with this guy?

"What are you doing?"

He doesn't respond. Just keeps toggling through his depth chart, moving guys from first string to third string and back again at warp speed.

I swear this kid's faster on the controls than Giordi on freaking *Star Trek: The Next Generation.*

"John, let's play already," I tell him when the shuffling takes its toll. He hits "start" and we're back to selecting plays.

"That's better," he says.

"What'd you do? Take out half your starting lineup?" I notice some schmoe named Burroughs is lined up under center. "Jesus Christ." John snaps the ball and maneuvers his scrub quarterback around the left end, dodges two or three tackles, throws a damn stiff arm, and then disappears into the sunset. A scrub touchdown. The bastard.

"Same result," he says, but I'm already up out of my chair and I'm bounding for the power button.

"Don't do that," I hear John screech from behind me. Then I hear some magazines ruffle and flip off the coffee table, and John has me in a headlock.

"You don't want to do that, Gabe. Finish it out! Finish it out!"

"Beat me with the Redskins and we'll talk," I tell him as I drive the legs and break free. He tugs at the collar of my t-shirt and I hear the stitches tighten and snap, but it's too late. My finger is already on the trigger. The picture on the screen is already wavy, and the evening news report is already shining through the game.

"Protest!" John shouts, but there's something happening on the news. Something important. "Protest!"

"John," I say. The word "breaking" is plastered in bold, red letters on the screen.

"This game's under pro—"

"John, will you shut the hell up!?"

I give him a look that says *I'm sorry* and *pay attention* at the same time. Like a tin soldier, he's about-face and in his chair with eyes and ears glued to the set.

Police are looking for an aggressive driver who almost took the life of a five-year-old child this morning. Shortly before noon, residents on the 400 block of Montgomery Street were shocked to find their sleepy, suburban street blocked off by an active crime scene.

Witnesses reportedly heard a loud collision and saw a late model sports car speed away heading East. The young child was struck as he pedaled out of a driveway in front of his own home. He sustained multiple injuries and is recovering tonight at Children's Hospital as a search for the driver intensifies across the Philadelphia suburbs. A squadron of plainclothes officers combed the neighborhood for additional witnesses who may be able to confirm the identity of the hit-and-run driver, but none emerged.

"At this time, we are unable to produce a reliable sketch of the alleged assailant," said Detective Michael Patterson, the lead investigator on the case, "but we are determined to build on the existing evidence until justice is served."

Concerned neighbors like Mary Wolnick, who lives two blocks away on Spruce Drive, plan to keep a sharp eye on the roadways outside their homes until the driver is found. "It's just terrible," Wolnick said. "In a small town we deserve to cross the street without fear. I know I won't feel safe until this criminal is behind bars."

If you have information regarding the incident on Montgomery Street, please call our Crime Stopper hotline at . . .

I can't watch any more, so I hit the power button on the remote and stare at the blank screen.

"So what?" John says. "A kid got hit by a car. Happens all the time."

"That's right around the corner from here," I say. I haven't blinked or moved my eyes from the blank screen. It's like I'm frozen in this moment before reality becomes reality.

"Yeah, so?"

I don't know if my gut is telling me the truth or making me paranoid, but if anyone can help me make the determination it's John.

"Let me show you something."

Out on the driveway, I crouch down next to the front fender of the Trans-Am and motion John over like I'm in one of those old detective movies. I don't want anyone taking notice of us assessing of the damage.

"See for yourself," I say.

John kneels down and runs two fingers over the scratches and the giant pockmark at its epicenter.

"What happened?"

I motion him over to the garage and he looks at me funny, like I'm the nutjob for trying to be subtle.

"You're acting weird," he says.

When we're safely inside the garage I say, "Well, I thought maybe some idiot sideswiped me in the Schuylkill lot Friday afternoon. Thought maybe I didn't notice at the time since it's on the passenger side."

"It wasn't there, Gabe. I got in this side. I would have noticed something like that. You would have been pissed and annoying on the ride home, but I would have taken my chances and told you about it anyway."

"John, do you know what this means?"

John stares down at his feet, thinks for a second. Then his eyes get all wide and he takes a deep breath.

"It doesn't necessarily mean—"

"I found my spare keys sitting out on the hall table when I got back from Perdomo's."

"But he couldn't have—"

"Nick said he heard me come home. Said I was loud. Tell me, John, how loud is my Mongoose?"

"Not very loud."

We stare at each other with masks on our faces—masks of shock that block away all other thoughts and feelings. We have no other thoughts at the moment—only flashes of catastrophe, of all the unpleasant possibilities we could land on because of one moment of misguided judgment. All because I wanted to be the me I used to be for a just a few hours.

"Maybe it's just a coincidence," John says. But he doesn't seem so sure of himself.

"There's another way to check," I say, and I lead him to Grandpa's room to assist in a surprise inspection. If all goes well Grandpa won't even know it happened.

"Time for pajamas!" I shout out of nowhere. John almost launches out of his shoes, but Gramps knows the drill. Like a robot, he's programmed to inch himself off the bed, drop his drawers and await further instructions. John looks on. He seems amazed at the swami-like powers I have over Grandpa in the pajama-changing department. One day I'll tell him the whole routine is but a small win—especially since the grand prize happens to be a personal and rather intimate viewing of the wrinkled madness that is my grandfather without clothes—but it's a win I'll take.

I grab Grandpa's flannels off the top of his dresser and John helps me roll the legs up over his feet. When we get to about thigh level, I feel a tap on my shoulder. John is doing this weird squinty thing with his right eye. Then I see what he sees. A purple, snakelike bruise on the old man's upper thigh—the type of bruise he might get if, say, he jammed the brakes without a seatbelt on and took a dead-leg from the underside of a steering wheel. It was *that* kind of bruise.

So it was confirmed.

Somehow, Grandpa had escaped the house undetected (freaking Nick). Somehow, he was able to take the Trans-Am out for a geezerly drive (freaking Nick). Somehow, Grandpa was the hit-and-run driver—and my car was the weapon of choice.

We put the finishing touches on Grandpa's pajama party. "Take a rest in bed," I tell him. "I'll be back in a few minutes to read you a story." Thankfully, Gramps is in good spirits. He climbs into bed and pulls the covers up over himself. John rolls the shades so Grandpa doesn't realize it's barely twilight outside.

When John and I are back outside I say, "What the hell am I going to do?" I pace back and forth through Mom's dais+ies. She would have flipped out, but I can't worry about that right now.

"You should call the police, Gabe. I know he's—"

"Yeah. I'm not calling the police."

"But you can—"

"Look, John. No police! If they find out he did what I think he did, they'll toss him in jail, or worse . . . one of those homes where the orderlies harvest organs and perform senior citizen sacrifices."

"Dude, you've been watching too much *60 Minutes* or something."

"You know what I mean." I look him in the eyes really hard—like, criminally hard—and he nods. John gets it. He always gets it.

"Then I guess we only have one choice," he says.

"And what's that?"

"I hope you paid attention in auto shop."

"John, Schuylkill High doesn't offer auto shop."

"Well then we're probably screwed. But it's worth a try, right?"

I look at him like he's an idiot, because his idea is one that an idiot and only an idiot could ever dream up.

"Unless you have any better ideas."

I don't, so I pop the Trans-Am in neutral and John helps me push her into the garage—away from prying eyes.

"See you in the morning," I say as he scuttles off down the driveway.

"First thing."

9

SMOOTH AS SHE'LL EVER BE

I'm in the garage by six o'clock the next morning. I have my AC/DC shirt on and there's a bandana on my head in the style of freaking Blackbeard's ghost. It took me twenty minutes to tie the damn thing and I still look a bit like Aunt Jemima. I flip on the radio to Philly's number one rock station: 94.1 WYSP. Kurt Cobain is singing "All Apologies" and, for once, it's not the crappy acoustic version.

All of this prep work is just so we can look like we know what we're doing—even if my last attempt at mechanics was building a tree house in the apple tree next to Mom's garden . . . out of papier-mâché. Apparently, I didn't take the lessons learned by the first two pigs very seriously when Dad would read me all those bedtime stories. Anyway, it rained that night and my paper house ended up looking like the victim of a fratboy prank by the next morning.

Don't laugh, because John's not much better. He shows up at six-thirty with a bag full of sugar donuts and a cardboard box filled with assorted tools—two boxes of finishing nails, a set of pipe wrenches, four pairs of safety goggles, an electric drill, a hacksaw, and a brand-new roll of athletic tape. The items jingle and jangle together like Christmas ornaments as John sets them on the workbench. Dad's workbench—where he used to construct the mansions of the birdhouse world and notch out tenons and use freaking wood glue. Wood glue.

Boy, would he be happy to see me feeling my way through a box of tinker toys on the work bench he built with his own hands.

"Tell me," I say, "Did you pull a hammy on the walk over here? Because, what the hell are we going to do with athletic tape?" John shrugs and takes another tired bite of his donut. "This is a car we're fixing here. It's not a—man, I don't even know what you'd build with this mess. And what's with the safety goggles?"

"You can blame my mom for that."

"You told her?!"

I can feel the sweat begin to build under my pirate gear.

"No. Don't worry. I told her I'm working on a school assignment. Gravity-powered vehicles for physics."

That's John—the geeky lab rat in grease monkey's clothing.

"Alright, let's get serious," I say—which apparently entails spreading John's useless tools out in a line next to the car and staring, in silence, at the fender for twenty minutes straight. When that does nothing to improve the status of the vehicle, I kneel in front of the tire and wheel my nose to within centimeters of the pockmark.

"You don't know what to do, do you?" John asks after another full minute of silence.

"Not a clue. Best I can do is guess."

I had seen Dad do a little bodywork on the old Volvo. Not enough to really know what I was doing, but enough to send me in a direction.

I open a cabinet over the workbench and pull out a few strips of sandpaper. The words "coarse" and "16 point" are printed in small letters across the bottom.

"Observe," I say, and John shakes his head. I rake the grains of the paper across the scratches and watch a few flakes of red paint peel off and flutter to the ground. I stand back. There's a small patch of naked steel staring back and still a huge pockmark, but the scratches are almost gone.

"Looks better," I say.

"Depends who you're asking."

I give John a look, then step back up and continue sanding.

"This is gonna take a while."

"We'll take turns, save the shoulder. You know, for baseball season."

I stop sanding for a moment.

"Don't tell me you're thinking of trying out."

"Oh, hell no."

John laughs a little, and before we know it we're both hysterical. John playing baseball. Ha! Man, the thought of John playing anything without a video controller attached to his hand brings tears to my eyes.

"No," he says, "But, it's senior year. You need to start training. I mean, I think I can handle tossing a few balls to you."

"We'll see." I hand John the sandpaper and we trade places. No wonder Mr. Miyagi prescribed Daniel LaRusso a heavy dose of sanding.

This stuff is murder.

"Offer's always there," he says. "And the stakes are high, because there's no chance Marlie's going out with a guy who picks splinters out of his ass after every game."

"Not cool, man. And the answer's still 'we'll see.' You gotta understand. I'm afraid."

"There's nothing to be afraid of, Gabe. You've been playing this game—"

"I'm afraid you'll get hurt when I rip a screaming liner down your throat. I've seen you with a glove. It's freaking scary."

John runs his bare hand over the freshly-sanded spot on the fender.

"About as smooth as she'll ever be."

I nod and lift the lid on a metal trunk Dad used for all his detailing needs—shammies, waxes, touch-up paint, the works. I rummage around until I find a nail polish-sized bottle of touch-up. It says "Pontiac" on the label so I know it's for the Trans-Am.

"We can probably get away with leaving the dent," I say, "but let's get some fresh paint on her."

I hold up the bottle. John bursts out laughing.

"What the hell do you expect to do with that?"

"Paint the car," I say. "It's a small spot."

"Yeah, but it's not a finger nail!"

He laughs so hard the convulsions drop his entire body to the cement where he rolls around and laughs some more. When he rises, his shirt is peppered with chips of sanded-off paint.

"We'll make the best of it," I tell him.

But the best of it isn't very good. No, it's not very good at all.

In an effort to gain maximum paint coverage on a melon-sized gap of naked metal using only the contents of what amounted to a bottle of Wite-Out, things had gone horribly wrong. Blotches of deep red collide with the edges of the original paint and blend together in the same way you'd mix peanut butter and tuna fish.

In the middle of the disaster—front and freaking center—the pockmark looms larger than ever. Like an inverted volcano or a distant wormhole, all signs of light and color are sucked into its void. In a way it makes the car look like a giant juice box—maybe filled with Ecto Cooler—and someone has already jabbed a hole in its side with a stabby straw and sucked out all the fluid. Around this gaping nether eye is a patchwork of spidery brushstrokes that covers the virgin metal like a veil. Long, puffy streaks of raised red stretch down as arteries in places where the paint has pooled and collected. If you stand back, the whole thing looks like a giant, bloodshot eyeball. Without professional help, the car is basically ruined. And I can't afford professional help, so . . .

"Hey . . . . that's not too bad," John says. The kid's a gem. He really is. But he's also full of shit sometimes.

"Yeah," I say. "We should probably open a body shop together. Bag the whole school thing. Invest in a bunch of leather vests. Grow mullets. We're freaking naturals, man."

"Yeah . . . I guess it's pretty shitty," he admits.

"Pretty shitty?"

"Ok then . . . extremely shitty. Like if a cargo plane full of whale crap crash-landed on a mushroom farm."

"So you're saying that opening up a body shop is not a good idea?"

John doesn't laugh. He doesn't say anything. Just keeps staring. Then, all of a sudden, he's smiling, and I can tell he's thinking evil thoughts because he gets this look on his face where he's all pained and stoic like Abraham Lincoln, but also kind of devilish like, well . . . the devil.

"What?!" I ask before the kid's face explodes.

"Just thinking . . ." he says, casually. By now though, he's laughing like a Muppet. ". . . of you picking up Marlie for the prom in this thing. What a tool!"

I guess I can't really argue with him so I join him.

"She'd take one look at it and be like, 'Gary . . . I think I'll follow in my dad's Audi.'"

"Yeah. Or 'Gareth . . . it appears that your limo driver sideswiped the azaleas.'"

He says it in a real snooty voice, probably how people talked in *The Great Gatsby* or something, and it gets me laughing a little—but if a best friend can't put a stop to your corniness, who can?

"Gareth?" I ask. "Big time stretch."

"What? You didn't see what I was doing there?"

"Not your best. Besides, none of this matters. Marlie doesn't even know my name. I've never said more than two words to her. She wouldn't let me take her to a hospital if her hair was on fire. The prom? Please."

"Don't give up the dream, man."

"Whatever. Maybe I'll ask Sofia."

"Who?"

"Some girl I met at the veteran's hospital."

"What's she like?"

"I don't know. Kind of weird."

"How does she look?"

"She's pretty in her own way, but she likes to poke holes in herself."

"What?"

"Piercings. Tattoos. You know. The usual stuff."

"Usual?" He says it all weird, like if he were judging each letter in u-s-u-a-l as he said it. "Does she go to Schuylkill?"

"I don't know."

"That might be a nice detail to find out when—"

The latch on the door between the garage and the house moves and I freeze. I can see John out of the corner of my eye. He looks like a mannequin too. The door swings open and Nick staggers down the first step and steadies himself into the garage. John and I stand there like we're in a prison lineup. I resist the urge to shuffle to the front of the car to serve as a blockade between Nick and our mishap. That would be too obvious. Nick's pretty oblivious to most things. Maybe he won't notice. Then again, staring at him like we're a couple of prairie dogs is probably not going to throw him off the scent.

"Hey, Nick," I say, "can we help you find something?"

I walk as far away from the car as possible, flashing my palms and rubbing my fingers together like Nick's a stray cat and I want to lure him outside. "This place is pretty messy. Like a dungeon in here some—"

"What the hell happened to the car?" he asks. Wow! That was quick. Who knows? Maybe Nick isn't the slobbering baboon he appears to be. Maybe he's just playing a part—like a method actor or something.

"It's no big deal," I say. "Just a few scratches."

"It looks like you hired Picasso to do your bodywork." A Picasso reference? Damn, Nick. Maybe he's leaving his primate cousins behind after all. He has definitely been standing a little more upright of late.

"It's under control," I tell him.

But he's not listening anymore. He's lost somewhere.

In thought.

Nothing seems to be happening, but then he steps a bit closer to our handiwork and I see something. A glimmer. And he turns. Stares at me with enlightenment in his eyes. And I realize this monkey has suddenly become a man. He's climbed the evolutionary ladder and has discovered the human ability to perform mathematical equations—in this case the ability to put two and two together.

"You?" he asks, and his eyes flash like he's trying to brace himself for a punch.

I shake my head. "I rode my bike over to Perdomo's."

He glances over at John.

"John was home doing calculus homework," I tell him. "Mrs. Chen had the the place surrounded by federal agents."

Nick doesn't smile. Neither does John.

"But I heard the car," he says a moment later.

"You did."

"That means—"

I don't know why but I put my hand on his shoulder. It just feels like the right thing to do.

Nick looks at me and says, ". . . that means the worst."

10

BEN DAN OR 笨蛋

I usually sit in the back of Mastro's class like a sea sponge—silent and soaking up whatever nutrients happen to float by me before the tide changes on a forty-five-minute period. It's easier for me to concentrate that way. No chance of fumbling through words or saying something stupid. Dad once told me, "No one can know you're a moron if they never hear you speak." He was part joking and part trying to get me to shut the hell up while he was driving, but I guess I took his words to heart.

But today I can't help myself. I don't know what it is—I mean, we're still talking modern poetry like we have been for weeks—but something just pisses me off. Makes the rage rise a little between the vertebrae in my neck.

"It's obvious," I say without bothering to raise my hand. Everything in the classroom stops. Pencils rise from the scratchy surfaces of notebooks. Routine chatter in the back row is swallowed up on cue. Even the noisy second hand on the industrial school clock above the doorway seems suspended on its last tick. All eyes are on me. "He's talking about death, the dying of the light," I continue, "and the need to rebel against it. It's a poem about inevitability." The poem is Dylan Thomas's 'Do Not Go Gentle into that Good Night,' a classic I'd read probably a million times on my own before this class. I wasn't about to let my idiot classmates bastardize the thing.

"I agree, Gabe," Mastro says as if I've been a class participant all along. "And good word: *inevitability*. It's a part of human reality, isn't it?"

Mastro. You got love it when he gets all rhetorical on you. "The question Thomas poses here is: will you become a slave to it?" He pauses to write the word "slave" on the chalkboard as if any of us plan to copy it down. I swear, Mastro kills me sometimes. "Or, will you spend your entire life in an unsuccessful battle against it?"

Of course, some smartass named Dominic DiBruno has to chime in just to prove he's smarter than the teacher. He's one of these kids that looks like a rat or a weasel or something. And he's always annoyed by other people's opinions, as though he is the only person on Earth capable of thought. "Aren't both choices essentially the same?" he asks, and he's mad as hell—like Mastro's question had just ruined his life.

"That's a question I'll deflect right back at all of you. What do you think?" I see DiBruno's eyes roll and he exhales deeply, noticeably.

"I think we all know death is something we can't avoid," he says. "Is Thomas going to tell us all to rage against taxes next? I hear they're inevitable too."

There are a few muffled laughs in the back and I see Mastro's face tighten. He's smiling. He still appears amused, but I can tell he'd like to strangle DiBruno about as much as I do. Maybe more. So I jump into the ring and look to take my metal chair of literary knowledge to the misshapen gourd that is DiBruno's skull of ignorance.

"It's not that simple," I blurt out, and the laughter trails off like a record screeching to a stop. The silence startles me and, for a moment, everything I was about to say gets all jumbled up in my throat.

"Gabe?" Mastro asks when it seems I'm already out of material. "You were saying?"

"Yes. I, uh, said it's not that simple."

"Go on."

"Well, Thomas is not only talking about death. He's also commenting on sacrifice, determination, and regret—all feelings we can be aware of before the light goes out."

"Kind of how I regret not faking an illness this morning," DiBruno says in a loud whisper, which is the kind of crap guys like DiBruno do when they want everyone to hear them. Mastro frowns and takes a deep breath. He's about to unleash something on DiBruno, but I don't give him the chance.

"No. I think we're the ones who regret that decision," I say.

Everyone laughs, and suddenly I'm rolling—feeding off the healthy scoop of humiliation I just dished out to DiBruno. "When Thomas writes of the 'good men' and the 'wild men' and the 'grave men' who 'learned too late, they grieved it on its way,' he warns of those who didn't take full advantage of life's gifts."

"But one of life's gifts might be a couch and a television," DiBruno grunts. "If death is coming anyway, why not go out munching Doritos and watching *Tom & Jerry*?"

"Because that's selfish," I say. "To rage against the dying of the light has more to do with sacrifice than pleasure. Like a soldier, DiBruno. Or a firefighter. You've seen them before, right? Between cartoons, of course."

I get another round of laughter from my classmates and watch DiBruno slowly deflate in his seat. Mastro's lips curl up hard and his eyebrows inch toward his hairline. "And me," I continue. "Think about my situation. You really think I want to—"

But then the door swings open and Principal Geckhardt steps in. Everyone sits up a little straighter in their chairs. Even Mastro hops off his perch on the surface of his desk and starts walking around, as if moving around the room is proof he's working harder than anyone else.

The fluorescent, overhead lights reflect off Geckhardt's bald head. He fiddles with his pocket square as he speaks. "Mr. Mastrocola," he says, "we have a visitor who would like a word with one of your students." I look past Geckhardt out to the hallway, praying not to see a flabby, middle-aged man in a stained t-shirt. But it's not Uncle Nick. It's much, much worse.

"Can we borrow Gabe LoScuda for a moment?"

My legs go all numb and my heart starts to beat so hard I think it's going to burst. The man outside the door is in full uniform—a police officer's uniform. And police officers don't just roll into your class everyday with a hall pass so they can treat you to a slice of pizza.

I see Mastro's face tighten again, like he wants to protect me—like he wants to rage against the dying of the light—but he can't. He has a job and a wife, and the fate of some random Italian kid from Philly isn't worth losing all that. "Sure," he says. Then he glances at me with this nervous smile that tells me he's sorry.

I grab my books and stuff them in my backpack, but it doesn't feel like my own hands doing it. I can feel everyone's eyes on my back as Principal Geckhardt puts his arm around my shoulder and leads me out to the hallway. The door closes behind us and suddenly I feel like one of those guys in Thomas's poem who didn't make things count when they had the chance.

"This is Officer Patterson," the principal says in a soothing voice. "Nothing to be alarmed about. He'd simply like to ask you a few questions."

I nod because if I say anything they'll be able to tell I'm freaking out about now. "Good," he continues. "I'll leave you two alone. Please release Mr. LoScuda back to class when you're finished, Officer."

"Yes, sir," Officer Patterson says. His voice is low and monotone—like you'd expect from a veteran cop who probably drinks two or three pots of black coffee each day. He looks at me with eyes so dark you can barely see the pupils—reptile eyes that send a shiver from my head straight down to my feet. "Follow me," he says, and he's all business, like some mad scientist has removed all of his vital organs and replaced them with a central processing unit.

He leads me into a conference room that's mostly used by teachers for lounging around and having meetings. "Have a seat," he says. His gun makes little clinking noises against his belt as he takes a seat across from me. Then he opens up a manila folder and tosses three Polaroid photographs down on the tabletop.

"Recognize any of these?" he asks in a robotic voice.

I glance down at the pictures and recognize them immediately. One is a landscape shot of a red sports car—the Trans-Am. The other two are close-up shots of the handiwork John and I had performed a few days ago. My heart slows down from its steady rat-tat-tat and almost stops completely.

I'm screwed and it's inevitable. Thank God DiBruno's not around to see this. He'd never let me hear the end of it. Officer Patterson is staring at me, not saying a word. He knows his silence is the rope I'll use, like most criminals, to hang myself.

I start thinking about Grandpa being led away in handcuffs, rotting away in some squeaky gurney in a smelly prison hospital where they serve split pea soup four times a day and sponge-bathe the patients with paper towels. I think about Dad and letting him down, and about Mom—how she'd probably look at me with her doe eyes and make me feel all guilty for the rest of my life. And I think about Nick and me and how we'd never quite know if we could exist together on this planet. If he could be uncle and I could be nephew like in a normal family.

And I couldn't accept any of it. It's time to rage on, Mr. Thomas.

"Yes," I say. "I recognize it. That's my car."

"And it's currently parked outside of school?"

"Yes, sir."

Officer Patterson lifts one of the close-up shots from the table and holds it in front of me. "Can you tell me how this happened?" A few minutes ago this question would have blown me out of the water, but now I'm steely. Armed with the words of Dylan Thomas I know exactly what to say.

I let out a small chuckle, as if the whole interrogation is no big deal and happens to me on a daily basis.

"Oh, that? Funny story," I say, and I'm getting downright congenial. I'm suddenly feeling proud of myself. "I was trying to pull it into the garage the other night. It was dark and I judged it wrong. Scraped the fender across the doorframe and hit a couple of miscellaneous items in the garage. Kind of embarrassing."

Officer Patterson's expression does not change. If he's amused, he doesn't let on.

"And who did the repair work on the vehicle?"

"Oh, that would be my friend John and I. We basically sanded it down and repainted."

"Does Schuylkill offer an auto shop program?"

"Can't you tell?" I ask with a nod. Officer Patterson is unmoved, expressionless. I decide to change my answer. "No, sir," I say.

"Why didn't you bring it to a professional?"

"I'm not exactly rich," I tell him. "Thought I'd save a few bucks."

"And your mother and father? What did they say about it?"

"Nothing," I tell him. "Absolutely nothing at all."

"They had nothing at all to say about their son crashing into their garage?'

"My parents are dead," I say

Officer Patterson's eyebrows raise up about one millimeter—probably the most emotion this guy's ever expressed in his life. But something tells me he knew all along and just wanted to hear me say it. The bastard. I'm a little pissed so I fire back. "I'm sorry, but is there some kind of law I broke by being a horse's ass?"

He doesn't answer. Just keeps firing off questions.

"You live alone?"

"No, I live with my uncle and grandfather."

"Your grandfather?"

"Yes. We take care of him. He's sick."

"How so?"

"Alzheimer's."

"I'm sorry to hear that."

He says it like he's known for longer than just a second, and I don't respond.

After a moment or two of silence, Offcer Patterson then asks "So, can you tell me who fixed the damage to the garage?".

My heart bounces around a few times and it feels like I'm swallowing wool. Crap. I should have thought my story out a little better. But who shows up at school thinking they'll be under interrogation during second period? I try to stall.

"Again, is there something I've done wrong, Officer? I can't see how damaging my own—"

"I'm sure you've heard about the incident that took place on Montgomery Street last week involving a child."

"What incident?" I ask. I figure my best chance at playing it cool is to play it dumb.

"Come on," he says. "It's all over the news. The kid got hit a few blocks from your house." He shuffles through a few pages in his folder. "You're the Gabe LoScuda that lives at 2020 Maple Street?"

"Yeah."

"And you mean to tell me you know nothing of this incident that happened only blocks from your house?"

"Oh," I say. "Yeah. The kid with the broken arm, right?"

"Among other things. He's okay, but that's not the point."

Officer Patterson's demeanor stirs up faster than a squall at sea, and suddenly I can tell he's not screwing around with me. I guess since they sent him here without a partner he has to put on a one-man good cop/bad cop routine.

"We take this stuff pretty seriously, kid. And since you live in the neighborhood and your car fits the description given by witnesses, I need to do my job."

"But I didn't hit any kid," I squeeze out between my teeth. I'm suddenly aware that my jaw is sore and tight. That happens when I grind my molars—when I'm nervous as hell. "I swear, I don't—"

"Look, I believe you," Officer Patterson says, and he's back to being the good guy again. "The garage, right? Besides, you don't seem to fit the profile of the person we're looking for."

I don't know what to say so I force out a quick, "Thank you," as I hold back the impending sobs.

"Well, thank you for your time, Mr. LoScuda. You're free to go,"

Free to go? Did he really just say that? Suddenly, I can feel my legs again and I remember to breathe. I waste no time popping up from the conference table, gathering my things, and heading for the door. But I can feel Officer Patterson's cold stare on the back of my neck and, as I reach for the door, he says, "So, you never did tell me. Did you ever get the side of the garage repaired?"

"Oh, uh, yeah," I say. "Not a lot of damage. Just a few scrapes."

"Your uncle do it?"

"No, I took care of it. After my car, same process of sanding and painting, right?"

"That's right," he says. "Well, I appreciate your time Mr. LoScuda." He rises from his chair and strides over to me. "If you hear anything or remember anything else about this incident—anything at all—I want you to give me a call, OK?" He hands me a business card with his name and number and a big, official-looking policeman's badge printed on it. I slide it in one of my folders and escape to the safety of the hallway.

"Yes, Officer. I will. Definitely."

Phew. Freedom. And here I thought this whole situation would drag on forever. Like I'd become this crazy-bearded fugitive, constantly on the lam, hiding out in drainage ditches and seedy motels, and painting the Trans-Am a different color each week to stay one step ahead of the law. In reality, all I had to do was fire off a shitty paint job, a few barely credible alibis, and miss half a class period and I'm in the clear.

I turn the corner out of the administrative corridor and I'm back with the regular population—with all the prisoners, my classmates. I must have walked this particular hallway at this particular time of day at least a thousand times in my four years at Schuylkill. Only this time feels different. I can't put my finger on it at first, but the further I walk past opened backpacks and crowds of sophomores, and people jiggling locks on lockers, it becomes obvious. Instead of blending into the background like another speckle of beige paint on the vomit-colored walls—instead of floating by unnoticed like a ghost—all eyes are focused directly on me; the center of the freaking universe. And people are talking, in whispers but still loud enough to make out a stray remark here and there.

"That's him," one says.

"Gabe LoScuda?"

"Yep."

"Badass."

As I stroll past the guidance office and the school's mammoth trophy case, my feet feel lighter and my steps more assured. A group of freshman girls giggle up ahead. They stare in my direction and pretend to point at something else when I notice. They burst into giggles again, and I can tell right away that word has spread fast like it always does at Schuylkill High. It's like the second Officer Patterson crossed the threshold to Mastro's classroom and decided to throw me under the heat lamp, he somehow tripped the ignition on the rumor mill (which I hear is stored under the locker room toilets) and the gossip just flooded the hallways from there.

"I heard he spent the weekend in jail."

"He's cute."

A bunch more giggling. Wow. This is actually kind of awesome. Gabe "Freaking" LoScuda: celebrity. I'm almost to class feeling pretty good about my change in luck—about my dashing mastery over the ability to change a potentially horrible situation into a dream.

Then the best thing of all happens.

"Hey, Gabe."

It's a girl's voice and it's followed by a scented trail of baked vanilla cookies that makes me melt. I turn around.

It's her.

"Uh . . . oh, hi Marlie," I say. And that's it. I'm basically out of words. This celebrity crap is no easy business. Thankfully, Marlie saves me from stuttering all over her. I guess that's the kind of perk you get when everyone knows you.

"Heard about your little run-in with the law," she says. "Everything alright?"

"Oh, yeah. No problem. No problem at all," I say, and I stick whatever chest I have out as far as I can. I probably look like a deformed chicken hawk right now, but Marlie doesn't care because I'm a bona fide badass. So I decide now's the time to really lay it on thick. "Yeah, I just told that pig that before he comes sniffing around he'd better have his story straight. Had to let me go. I thought the dude was gonna cry."

She laughs. Marlie freaking laughs. I didn't know it was possible for me to do or say anything that would ever make a girl like Marlie smile, let alone laugh. But here she is cackling like an idiot in front of me—and all I had to do was lie to the police.

I tell John all about it over lunch.

"You should have seen me," I say. "Ladies drooling over me like I was made of chocolate or something. I'm a stud, John. A stud."

John rolls his eyes and does a quick pan of the lunchroom. Everyone is still staring and it's pretty clear that I'm the topic of conversation at most tables. About time. Only took four years, right?

"So you got your fifteen minutes," John says. "Who cares?"

"Me! I care! And you should too, John. Marlie knows my freaking name, man. She talked to me. Prom is back on in a big way."

"Right. If you're not in prison by then."

"What do you mean, in prison? I told you already. I'm off the hook. Patterson basically said so."

"For now, Gabe. But that doesn't mean he won't dig something up. You'd better . . . what's that phrase you always say to your Grandpa?"

"Keep your nose clean?"

"Yeah. Exactly. You'd better blow that big, freaking schnoz of yours very carefully until this is all over."

"Whatever," I tell him. "I'm just raging against the dying of the light."

John shakes his head. "Ben dan," he says under his breath, which in Mandarin roughly translates as "stupid egg," but really means nothing more than "dumbass."

Gabe LoScuda
English 4A – Personal Essay #4
Mr. Mastrocola
November 21

It Emits a Bronx Cheer

I've never been the popular kid, or the most athletic kid, or the smartest kid. Never held up a trophy after the big game. Never read a paper in front of the class or had a piece of artwork displayed in a hallway. Never even won a perfect attendance award.

I've always been the kid on the periphery; the kid with his toes hanging just over the boundary line waiting for Coach to send him into the action; the kid who blends in with the background.

Not famous.

Never famous.

So forgive me if my judgment falters in those rare moments when an opportunity for true recognition—or any recognition—stares me in the face. Forgive me if I lose myself in the pursuit. I'm surely not the first.

But do me a favor: remind me about Emily Dickinson. She wrote:

Fame is a fickle food
Upon a shifting plate
Whose table once a
Guest but not
The second time is set.

For I've learned that lesson too many times—but never in such a Dickinsonian a fashion as in Mrs. Lackey's class.

"I want this," I remember shouting from two aisles away.

I'd tossed the packs of *Garbage Pail Kids* back in their box and placed the bottle of invisible ink back on its peg-board rack. Then I bolted past an end-cap like I was rounding second base and pulled up in front of Mom and Dad.

"This is what I want," I repeated.

"Gabe, I told you. Nothing disgusting."

Mom remembered the last time we'd come to Edmund's Toy & Hobby with the promise of one toy for me. I picked a mad scientist's laboratory called *The Monster Lab*. The box contained a clear, plastic vat, a fake skeleton about the size of a pencil, and a bag filled with this rubbery concoction you'd form into organs and stick to the skeleton. Then you'd toss the whole thing in the vat with a little baking soda and some vinegar and watch your creation disintegrate faster than Arnold Schwarzenegger in *The Terminator*. Mom hated it, which literally doubled its awesomeness.

"Besides," she continued, "we're here to buy toys for the Christmas drive. This is not grab bag day for Gabe."

"But, Mom," I groaned, "I've wanted one of these forever."

I made sure to really drag out the 'r' in "forever" just to be extra whiney. Parents always fall for that crap. Even at age nine I knew that.

Mom grabbed the item from my hand and held it up to the light so she could read the comically small fine print through the windowpanes that were her eyeglasses. "It says right here 'Ages 10 & up.' So, no."

"For one lousy year? Come on, Mom. I'm not a baby. And it's not even that disgusting."

"It says right here on the tag: 'Emits a Bronx cheer.' That sounds pretty disgusting to me, Gabe."

Just then my father wheeled around a corner with about twenty board games stacked in his hands—from his waist all the way up to his nose. He sighed and then slid them mercifully into Mom's cart.

"Look at what your son picked out for himself." Mom dangled the object in front of Dad's face with two fingers like it was a soiled diaper.

"A Whoopee Cushion? No, Gabe. You're not sticking that thing under my ass every time I try to sit down. Pick something else."

"But I don't want anything else." I could feel the tears start to burn at the corners of my eyelids.

"Good," Dad said. "There's plenty of kids out there that do. So help your mother and I find a few more good, non-farting toys so we can get the hell out of here and catch the Monday night game."

Dad never did like shopping, and when he was forced into it there was really no way to communicate with the guy. He was like a rodeo bull, charging through stores without direction or purpose until he could toss the rider— usually Mom—and retreat to the comfort of his barn.

He handed me the Whoopee Cushion and I dragged my feet the entire way back around the end cap to replace it with the other novelty items. It was almost on the rack, too, when another idea crossed my mind. One that neither Mom nor Dad could ever hope to stop.

I moved a few items on the shelf in front of me so I could get a good view of Mom, Dad, and the shopkeeper from my toy store bunker. None of them were watching, all lost in their own simple tasks. I unbuttoned my jacket and slid the Whoopee Cushion down between my belt and my stomach. Then I buttoned back up and grabbed an R/C car off the shelf—probably the crappiest one they had. I carried it back over to Mom and Dad.

"Think the less fortunate children will like this?" I asked in the voice of a winged cherub. Mom and Dad smiled because apparently they'd done something incredibly right in raising this angel son of their's. The Whoopee Cushion shoved down my pants told a different story.

Like any nine-year-old boy would, I brought the thing to school the next day to show off to all my snot-nosed, little friends. Of course, John had first looksee, being my best friend and all.

"And when you sit on it," I told him, "It blows a fart louder than King Kong after a chili dinner."

"Right in front of everyone?"

"Yep! That's the best part," I told him. "Then everyone thinks you dealt one."

We started to laugh uncontrollably, the way little kids do when they think they've uncovered the world's entire supply of humor in a one-dollar piece of inflatable rubber. Mrs. Lackey jumped up from her desk and glared at us.

"Are you gentlemen finished with your work?" she asked.

"No, Mrs. Lackey," I said.

"Then get back to it. Only ten more minutes until reading group."

I folded the Whoopee Cushion up under my desk and slid it in my cigar box with the rest of my pencils and supplies. John was still smirking in the seat beside me.

"I dare you to set that thing off during reading group," he whispered when Mrs. Lackey rededicated herself to grading the stack of papers on her desk. I shook my head and went back to doing my work.

A few minutes later, Billy Wetzel tapped me on the shoulder and handed me a crinkled up piece of paper. I opened it.

Gabe is going to set off the whoopee during reading. – John

Freaking John. Even at nine years old he knew how to get what he wanted. Now that everyone was counting on me, I couldn't let them down.

At one o'clock, Mrs. Lackey rose from her desk and said, "Group One, please bring your textbooks over to the reading table. I'll meet you there in just a moment."

I grabbed my reader from under the desk with one hand and smuggled the folded up Whoopee Cushion inside the front cover with the other. Then I rushed over to the reading table and grabbed a seat between John and the head of the table—Mrs. Lackey's seat. Quickly and deftly I fumbled my pencil off the edge. It rolled under Mrs. Lackey's chair. Perfect.

"Oops," I said. "Let me get that." I dove under the table with the Whoopee Cushion in hand and had it blown up and set on the chair before anyone, even John, had noticed. It was all just a waiting game now.

"Now, Group One, please open up to page two-eighty-three in the textbook," Mrs. Lackey said as she stepped closer and closer to the table, closer and closer to her chair. "We'll be reading a selection from *Aesop's Fables* today," she said. Closer and closer. Bending. Crouching. "The story is called—"

FRRUUUMMMPH!!!

The Bronx cheer had been emitted, and it had been emitted loud and true. The echoes reverberated far past the ears of reading Group One, past the other members of the class startled from their seatwork, and out into the vacant halls to echo some more off the cinderblock walls.

Mrs. Lackey's face turned blotchy and pink, like an Easter egg gone horribly wrong. The members of reading Group One burst into hysterics for a brief moment until Mrs. Lackey shot them down with her teacher's stare. Then she popped off her seat like it'd suddenly caught fire and she stared down at the booby trap sitting there laughing back in her face.

"Which one of you did this?" she shrieked.

Nobody answered. We all just shrank a few inches in our chairs.

"Which one of you little monsters is responsible for this?"

Still silence. Nobody was willing to take the blame—especially me. My heart was beating so quickly I thought it was about to explode, but I remained silent.

A droplet of sweat rolled down the side of Mrs. Lackey's face and her ears burned red under her platinum curls. When it was clear there would be no confession, she reached down with an unwilling hand and hoisted the Whoopee Cushion up between her thumb and index finger—the way Mom had in the toy store—as if she were holding a dirty diaper. She looked at it closely, then spun it around and my heart dropped.

There'd be no confession that day because no confession was required. I had already seen to that myself earlier that morning when I'd scrawled my name in black magic marker across the back of the Whoopee Cushion. Hey, I didn't want to lose it after all I'd gone through to acquire it.

The letters G-A-B-E stared at me and I knew I was dead meat.

Mom waited for me on the porch when I got off the bus that day. The look on her face told me the school had already called. Thankfully, Dad was still at work.

The worst part was that Mom didn't have much to say. At least if she had shouted and screamed and told me what a rotten kid I was, I wouldn't have felt so bad. But her silence told me that she was beyond disappointment. Like, I'd have to do an awful lot going forward to make her see me as the angelic, little cherub she had in the toy store just the day before.

"You're going to write Mrs. Lackey an apology letter," she said—one of the only things she did say. "And you're going to explain to Mr. Edmund why you thought it was acceptable to steal from his shop."

I wrote the letter that evening and delivered it to Mrs. Lackey the next day. It went something like this:

Dear Mrs. Lackey,

I'm very sorry I for placing a Whoopee Cushion on your chair.

It made a really loud noise and people laughed.

That was not nice.

I will never play jokes like that in class ever, ever again.

Everyone makes these bathroom noises.

They are nothing to laugh about.

Please forgive me.

Your Friend,

Gabe

Mom brought me over to Edmund's Toy & Hobby the next day. She waited in the parking lot and made me go in and face Mr. Edmund by myself. He didn't want a Whoopee Cushion with "G-A-B-E" scribbled on the back, but he was interested in hearing my apology.

"I got this from your store yesterday," I told him.

"I don't remember your family purchasing that item," he said, his eyebrows raised and confusion stretched across his face.

"I didn't buy it," I said.

"I see."

"My parents didn't want me to have it because they thought it'd get me in trouble."

"But you wanted it anyway?"

I nodded.

"And it looks like your parents were correct about the trouble?"

I nodded again.

"Well, here's what I can do for you. The item costs a dollar and fifty cents. I'll start a tab for you, but I expect you to pay me back as soon as you're able."

I reached into my pocket and pulled out a dollar bill—my only dollar—that I'd fished from my piggy bank after breakfast. I handed it to Mr. Edmund.

"I can respect a man that comes prepared," he said. "Let's call it even. I appreciate your honesty, son. But if I ever catch you stealing from my store again I won't be so forgiving. Do you understand?"

I nodded for a final time and left the toyshop with the heavy burden of disgrace on my shoulders.

What a mess. About the only good thing that came out of my Whoopee Cushion incident was that Dad never found out. Mom sure knew how to keep a secret.

I wonder if she ever did tell him?

11

TATTOOS AND TRENCH WARFARE

It's been a few days since Officer Patterson grilled me, and I start to breathe a little easier. Maybe the worst to come out of Grandpa's mishap—apart from the kid's injuries and all—will be a nicked up fender. Not a bad trade for my newfound celebrity status and a chance with Marlie.

Grandpa's bruise is about twenty different shades of yellow, green, and purple—like an enchanted toad puked on his thigh. He hasn't complained about it but, with the fuzz falling off our trail a bit, Uncle Nick and I figure it's best if we let Doc have a look. So we head over to the veteran's hospital after dinner.

There's only one person in the waiting room when we arrive, and it's Sofia. Her face is about two inches away from the surface of a sketchpad and she's using a thick pencil to shade a section of spiked tail on what appears to be a dragon. Heavy guitar chords pump from her headphones, and I realize she's oblivious to everything around her. Thank God, because somehow Grandpa recognizes her. His eyes get all big and he shouts, "That's Gabe's sex!"

Danielle the receptionist, Nick, and I are struck dumb. We're frozen and staring at each other in round robin format. Sofia continues to sketch in her book as she mainlines her dose of punk rock adrenaline directly to the eardrums. Grandpa thinks we don't hear him, so he looks to Nick for reassurance. "She's for Gabe's sex, right?" Nick's mouth crinkles up and contorts—I can tell he's biting his lip. Danielle can't even go that far. She bursts out laughing and spits coffee all over her desk.

I run over to Grandpa. I don't want to startle him, but I need to get him out of here before Sofia notices us and Grandpa tries to proposition the poor girl right here in the waiting room. The last thing I want is for her to pull off her headphones in time for Gramps to say something ridiculous like, "How's two bits for a quickie in the broom closet with my grandson?"

Gramps's wrists seem bonier than ever, so my grip is gentle but firm enough to hook him off the stage like I'm that crazy clown on *Showtime at the Apollo*. He grunts a bit, but he allows me to guide him out of the waiting room and to a corridor that leads to the examination room.

"How long today, Danielle?"

"He'll be able to take you right back," she says from somewhere below the sliding glass window. "Why don't you take Ernie to room three while I clean up the rest of this mess?"

I start to lead Grandpa down the hallway, but I only move a step or two before Nick grabs me by the arm.

"You know what? I'll take him back again."

"Seriously? I mean, this is twice in a row," I say. "What's the catch, Nick? You trying to make up for something?"

"No. Not at all," he says, and he's smiling. Not just a happy smile. It's happy, yes, but there's something else in it. Then he whispers, "Besides, it's not for you. It's for your sex." The bastard. I should have known he was setting me up all along.

Still, I take Nick up on his offer. "I'll give you a holler if I need reinforcements," he tells me as he leads Grandpa to the front lines.

"I don't doubt it," I say as I retreat to the safety of the waiting room.

Sofia removes her headphones when she sees me walk in. Her sketchbook is closed on her lap and her pencils are tucked away in a cloth case.

"What planet did *you* just invade?" she asks as I unfold a chair and sit with a squeak.

"I don't know. Feels like a different one every day. Which one is this?"

She laughs. "Good question. If you hear anything let me know." There's a brief silence and Sofia's eyes catch mine staring at her closed sketchbook. She pretends to adjust herself on the seat and uses it as an opportunity to place the book and her pencils on the floor beneath her. "You know, I saw you guys come in," she says.

I feel my spine strain against the back of the chair. "You did?" I ask. "Why didn't you say anything?"

"I was busy."

"Did you, uh—"

"Hear anything?" I'm partially frozen but I manage a cautious nod. "Not really," she says. "I had Iggy Pop cranked up pretty loud." She pauses to pick at a ragged cuticle. "Well, nothing apart from the sex stuff. That was pretty damn hilarious."

"Oh, God." My forehead descends to the shelter of my palms.

"Don't worry about it. The old man doesn't know any better. Either that or he overestimates his grandson's game."

"I have plenty of game."

"Yeah, you're playing flag football while everyone else is looking to tackle."

I have no defense, and I can never fault a good sports analogy, so I simply say, "Nice."

"So, what's wrong with the old man this time?"

"It's just a bruise. Nothing major."

I must be boring her because she reaches down, pulls out her book, and goes into full sketch mode while I'm in mid-sentence.

"Don't you ever do any homework?" I ask. "You're always drawing stuff and listening to music. You never seem to have any real work to do?"

Sofia continues shading in the same area of the dragon as before. Then she erases, blows the spent bits of rubber off the page, and goes back to shading again. "*This* is my real work," she says.

"No, I mean school work."

"School?" Her hand continues to scratch across the page, but a smile rises on her lips as she shakes her head. "Nah, I haven't been to that dump in almost two years. Dropped out the day I turned eighteen, before I even graduated."

"You dropped out of school?" I don't know why, but I ask the question as if her decision to abandon her education was like deciding to chop off her own leg.

"Didn't really have a choice. Dad was long gone and Mom got cancer—that was her first bout with it. Shit needed to get done," she says, and for the first time I'm aware of some edge in her voice. Like she's getting pissed. "And, by the way, who are you to judge?"

Her question almost knocks me back off the folding chair, but I gather quickly. "I'm not judging. It's just surprising, you know?"

"Why? Because you stayed in school? At least you have your uncle."

"I don't think I'd use Uncle Nick as an argument in my favor."

"Well, he's better than no one."

And that shuts me up fast—because she's right. For as much of a pain in the ass as it is to have Nick squatting on my couch every morning, he's still present. He still absorbs some of the tension. He's still another soul who's in this thing with me—something Sofia has scarcely known in her life.

"So tell me about your work before I have to use your technique and spy on it over your shoulder."

"Not much to tell," she says, still a bit cold. "I'm an artist."

"I can see that. What kind?"

"Tattoo."

I'm a bit stunned. The girl is, by far, the most unique person I've ever met, but I just can't picture her—maybe anyone—jabbing inked-up needles into human flesh.

"You're kidding," I say.

"Take a look."

She spins the sketchbook around to reveal a traditionally designed dragon that is sprawled out across the page with back arched, ready to strike. "I'm sketching out the line work for a new piece. Some macho bodybuilder. He wants to drape it over his shoulder."

"Wait. You're serious?"

"Of course I'm serious." She rolls up the sleeve on her flannel shirt and her forearm is peppered with colors far brighter and more diverse than anything I saw in Grandpa's bruises. She points to a small floral design at the base of her wrist. "This one's a cactus flower. *La flor*. First one I ever did. Put the same one on Mom last time she went into remission. It was her idea. She says we're *dos chicas Mexicanas de culo duro*—two tough-ass Mexican chicks."

"I can see that, too," I say, and I'm serious as hell when I say it. This girl really does look like she eats kids like me for a protein boost between piercing sessions. I can only imagine the woman tough enough to give birth to her.

She points to a portrait in the center of her forearm—a woman draped in a gold and purple veil with white flowing robes. The face is smooth and serene, like a porcelain doll's. It's beautiful. "*Nuestra Señora de Guadalupe*," she says. "The patron saint of Mexico. I'm not big on religion, but she's Ma's hero. Or heroine. However you want to say it."

"You tattooed that on yourself?"

"I had to do it upside down so when I'm walking around on my feet she's not bouncing around on her pious, little head. Think about it."

It takes a few seconds, but I get a picture of Sofia with the tattoo machine in hand and her other hand outstretched in front of her. She's right. She would have had to sketch the portrait upside down if she wanted it to be right side up when she dropped her hand to her side—like for walking and stuff. Man, who knew artists had to think like freaking engineers half the time.

"That's amazing," I say. "Got any more?"

"Loads," she says. "I'm the best canvas I've got. I never complain when the artist's work looks like shit."

"Oh man, you have to show me the rejects."

"I prefer to think of them like Bob Ross would—happy accidents that I get to wear for the rest of eternity, or at least until this skin suit decomposes. Besides, we'd have to go on a whole lot more of these waiting room dates before you see any more of this." She takes her index finger and waves it up and down the length of her body the way Vanna White would display consonants or vowels.

"Dates?" I ask.

"Oh, don't get your geeky, little man parts all twisted up. I'm just having some fun with you."

"Oh, fun."

"You want to see something fun? Take a look. First tattoo I ever got—in the flat bed of an El Camino after a Ramones concert."

She turns her head and parts the black waves of her hair. Trailing down her neck is the outline of a battery with the words "Shock Therapy" woven inside in plumes of smoke. Yellow flashes of electricity crackle around the edges in a maniacal-looking border. I don't know if it's badass or just bad, but it's definitely unique. And it doesn't surprise me at all that it's a permanent fixture on Sofia's body. It fits.

"You're crazy," I say.

"Wasn't it Aristotle who said 'no great genius has ever existed without some touch of madness'? You should know. You're the one who gets dressed up in the schoolboy outfit every morning."

"All I know is it was Nigel Tufnel from *Spinal Tap* who said, 'There's a fine line between clever and stupid.' Dropping out of high school probably doesn't fall on the clever side of that line."

"Yeah, well, he never had a single mother fighting cancer. That fine line washes away pretty fast when the bills start to pile up. We needed money. And besides, why jump through the lion tamer's hoop when you already know how to attack and devour the lion tamer?"

"Makes sense," I say. "Guess it pays better than flipping pizzas at Perdomo's."

"That your new gig? I go there sometimes, especially when I'm looking for a discount." She winks at me and makes a big show of it so I know what she's suggesting.

"I don't work the register," I tell her. "I just do odd jobs, keep the place in order."

"You're a total rebel, Gabe. A real class-A daredevil, always living on the edge." She holds her tattooed arm in front of her and pretends to be mystified by my mama's boy charm. It kind of pisses me off a little, to tell you the truth—especially after the freaking parade of heroes that was thrown in my honor at school the other day. You know, after I handled Officer Patterson.

I don't know why I feel the urge, but it's strong. Like having a bunch of apostles at school all of the sudden isn't enough. I need everyone to see what Gabe "Freaking" LoScuda is all about. So, I pull my chair a little closer to Sofia and tell her in a low voice so Danielle doesn't overhear.

"You want to know about rebellion?" I whisper.

Sofia shrugs like she doesn't care, but then she moves in a little closer so she can pick up every last word. Tattoos or not, she's still a girl and she's still interested in this kind of crap.

I tell her everything. About how Grandpa hit the kid with my car. About how John and I tried to cover it up with some terrible bodywork. About getting pulled out of class and grilled by Officer Patterson, and the flimsy story I told him to keep Grandpa's nose clean. And about the new Gabe—or at least the old Gabe that now somehow matters at Schuylkill High.

I half-expected Sofia to jump out of her folding chair and offer a celebratory chest bump or pour a giant cooler of Gatorade over my head like I just won the Super Bowl. Instead, she says, "Are you freaking crazy? You lied to the police?"

"Jeez! Some rebel you are."

I smile at her because I think she's just screwing around with me again. But she's not. She's serious as all hell, and the look of motherly concern on her face tells me so.

"Do you have any clue what will happen if they find out you lied?" We're still whispering and she says it so quickly it comes out in one, long hiss like a snake.

"Relax," I tell her. "The police aren't even looking for my grandfather anymore. Remember? They let me walk."

"Boy, Gabe, you're the worst kind of rebel. One without a clue."

I can't believe I'm getting this crap from Sofia. John? Sure. The kid wets his pants if he finds a penny on the ground and he's not sure who it belongs to. He's the kid that dressed up as a brain surgeon on Career Day back in kindergarten and will one day actually become a brain surgeon. The kid sets his own lines in the sand and refuses to cross them. No matter what. But Sofia? The living, breathing version of a protest sign? And she treats me like I'm some dumb kid and she's my babysitter? No. That's just uncalled for.

"You need to call the police and turn in your grandfather," she says when I don't respond. "Before it's too late."

"What?! No way!" I say, and I realize I'm not whispering anymore. So does Danielle. She peers over the high counter of the front desk. "And . . ." I shoot a quick glance at Danielle and her eyes immediately descend onto the paperwork. Then I'm back to a whisper. " . . . you're not going to tell anyone about this either."

"Give me some credit, Gabe." Her eyes flash and her chin cocks back a bit. She's annoyed that I'd ever take her for a garden-variety snitch. Good. Now we're even. "But you need to listen to me. They'll—"

"Lock him away for whatever shitty moments he has left? Is that what you see as the best option? It's not happening."

"Gabe. You're making—"

"A mistake? If protecting my grandpa is a mistake, then—"

I want to tell her about Mom and Dad. About how much I miss them. How I'm just bouncing around from bumper to bumper like the last pinball on a man's final quarter. How the only way I can ever be with them again is through their wishes. But I can't—and not because I don't think she'll understand what I'm going through. It's because there's a loud crash followed by a deep voice that echoes down the corridor. As soon as it reaches the waiting room, I know—it's Nick.

Sofia looks at me and offers a resigned shrug of the shoulders. I guess saying goodbye under a hail of gunfire is, like, our thing now. I charge down the corridor with Danielle on my heels and hit the door to exam room three—and suddenly I'm in a recreation of the Battle of the Bulge. The exam table is pushed into the corner of the room, its roll of protective tissue paper strewn across the floor like a length of disemboweled intestines. Doc and Nick are pinned down behind it as Grandpa barrages them with tongue depressor missiles and cotton swab artillery fire. He mumbles a bunch of stuff under his breath about 'flushing out foxholes' and 'sweeping the flank.' Who knows what kind of war Grandpa was waging inside his own head.

I dive for cover behind the exam table with Doc and Nick. Their backs are up against it and their knees are huddled tight to their chests. Freaking shell-shocked. I have to take command, so I motion to Doc with my right hand and to Nick with my left. They nod their approval with the coolness of steel forming over their eyes. Then I grab a handful of stray tongue depressors off the floor and lead the counter attack.

"Men," I say, and I swear this is a true story, "we've got a soldier over the hill and he's moving like pond water."

"That's a big ten-four," Doc responds over the boom of the exam room mortars. "It may be time to ruck up and bring in the red team."

"Never!!"

Nick charges off the left flank and Grandpa peppers him with airborne cotton swabs and latex gloves. But then Doc covers him on the right, and I pop up from my foxhole and start winging tongue depressors in all directions—just to distract Gramps for a few seconds. Long enough for Nick to grab a hold of his right shoulder as Doc snags him around the waist. He struggles like a largemouth bass, but it's too late. Doc's examination is complete and he turns the prisoner over to his sentries.

Danielle and a few of her staff members surround the perimeter, as General Weston leads Private First Class Nick LoScuda and myself, Captain Gabriel LoScuda, to his bunker for another debriefing. I don't expect there to be any medal ceremonies in our future.

"I'll make this quick," Doc Weston says when we're all seated in his office. "His leg is fine. Just a bruise that'll heal up in a few weeks. You can give him Advil if he complains. But the real question is: how did it happen?"

Nick and I should have thought this through back at the house, maybe gotten our stories in order. Instead, we both blurt out our responses at the same time and it sounds all jumbled. Something like, "He fell down slipped the bathroom stairs."

Not our best moment.

"Wait a minute," Doc says. "Gabe says he slipped in the tub, and Nick, he fell down the stairs?" He pushes his glasses down on the bridge of his nose and stares at us. "Both are viable ways to get a bruise like the one Ernest has. But somehow I can't picture your bathroom being located in a stairwell."

"Well, Doc, what—"

"No need, Gabe. Look, I'm not here to play detective. I'm here to make sure you all stay healthy. And sometimes that includes more than just what you'd find in these anatomy books." He motions to the stacks of books on the shelves behind him. "Look, I think it's time you two at least give some thought to what we discussed on your last visit."

He slides a few brochures across the desk to Nick. I see the words "Assisted Living" at the top of one before Nick scoops them up.

This time we don't argue with the doctor—probably because we're still licking our wounds from battle. But the brochures never make it as far as the car. Nick chucks them in a wastebasket before we hit the parking lot.

12

INTERVENTION

It took almost four years, but I think I can see myself spending the next forty or so right here at Schuylkill High. It's amazing how the walls don't look so vomity and the teachers don't sound as nasally when you have an identity. And even if I happened to share that identity with guys like Al Capone and John Gotti, and other, even scarier dudes with nicknames like "Knuckles" or "the Nail," it didn't matter. Because it didn't stop girls like Mandy So-and-So from smiling at you when she passed your locker. And it didn't stop football team captains like Vince Barchetti from holding the locker room door for you, slapping you on the shoulder, and calling you "champ." I mean, I'm ready to ask the guy for his autograph and he's calling me "champ?" How freaking beautiful is that?

It's not as beautiful as the scene that unfolded in the parking lot after school—that much I can tell you. I'm getting in my car. John's not with me because I have a shift at Perdomo's. I swear, the kid's never around when the good stuff happens.

I open the door and a pair of hands reaches around from behind me and covers my eyes. I can't see a thing, but I can tell it's a girl because no guy with hands this silky would ever go up and let some other guy know about it.

"Guess who?" she says—and it appears we're gonna play this game, which I'm not too happy about because I don't exactly get accosted in parking lots by insistent female fans that often.

"No idea," I say. "I give up." It's my only real strategy, but it's effective. She releases her grip and I turn around. And it's her. Freaking Marlie!

I can feel my pulse race. I spend four years trying to get her to notice me and all it takes is a few days as a fugitive and she's tracking me down like Geronimo. She's gorgeous as ever, and the blue flame in her eyes is turned up extra hot. Even my newfound persona is no match for a girl like this.

"Oh, uh, hi," I say. Here we go again, Gabe, you sweet-talking devil.

"Everything back to normal?" she asks.

"Oh . . . yeah," I say. "Of course. You know me. Just doing my normal, everyday thing. Nothing out of the ordinary here."

"That's good to hear, Gabe." I start to wonder if she's talking to the right person. Like maybe all those Garys and Jerrys she thought I was a few weeks ago are the guys she's looking for today. But she keeps talking and I'm the only one here. "Nothing like a man who doesn't let the heat get to him," she says.

"Oh, definitely," I say mopping about a gallon of sweat off my forehead with the back of my hand. "I'm as cool as a cucumber. Nothing gets to me."

For a second I'm glad John is not here because he would have laughed in my face when I said that—and for another second I think Marlie might just fill in for John anyway. And who could blame her? Instead, she says something I thought was reserved for the jocks and the rich kids.

"Cool. I'll see you around?"

"Yeah," I somehow say without jumping out of my shoes. "Sure." Then I duck inside the Trans-Am before I can screw anything up.

And, boy, there's nothing like driving out of your dream and into the Perdomo's parking lot for an afternoon shift. But I guess working for Perdomo isn't so bad. He stays out of my way as long as I keep the counters and tables sparkling and the floor mopped fresh. Sometimes he lets me throw an order of fries in the hot oil and dump them in a basket when they're done. But he won't let me near the pizza. The dude is Philly born and bred, so pizza comes about half a notch below the Holy Grail on his list of important shit. Seriously. I think he keeps the freaking recipe under lock and key, buried seventy miles below the bedrock under the restaurant's basement—and you have to run a gauntlet through poison dart launchers and hidden trip wires just to reach it. I doubt even Indiana Jones could steal the Perdomo family secrets.

The place is pretty quiet this afternoon, so I take the opportunity to sweep the dining room and gather stray utensils from the tables. I swear, people are pigs. The five o'clock news broadcast plays on the old black and white television Mr. Perdomo mounted above the counter. It barely receives three channels, yet Perdomo has the nerve to advertise "Free TV" in blinking, neon letters in the front window.

Most of the time I tune out the news because it's filled with the most horrific crap you could ever hear. I can never understand why people want to listen to stories about murders and armed robberies while they're eating dinner. And since "the incident," I've been trying to avoid the tube like the plague. But the story has picked up steam—since the little kid who got hit is freaking adorable. Just my luck.

Every news station shows the same picture of the kid—at the height of his cuteness—with sandy, blond curls spilling out from under a toy store cowboy hat and each of his chubby, red cheeks kissed by perfectly round dimples. Like he pedaled his toddler-mobile straight off the label of a baby food jar or something. It's weird, but adults always eat that crap up. If you ask me, we're toast.

But I guess even my curiosity has its limits, and since I'm stuck between refilling napkin holders and emptying ashtrays, I decide to indulge in the latest from Channel Six:

"Still no suspect has been named in the Montgomery Street hit and run accident that rocked this community last week."

"Rocked this community?" Is she serious?

"Seven-year-old, Timothy Mullin, broke his tibia and two ribs when a vehicle clipped him as he rode his tricycle. Tonight, police are looking for any leads that will help determine who it was that sped down this quiet, neighborhood drive and almost took the life of a young boy."

I can't listen to much more, so I reach for the dial. But then I see Officer Patterson up on the screen and I freeze.

"At this point we do have a few witnesses and the department is using all of its resources to find the hit and run driver. But we must remember this is a community matter, and that means members of this community have an obligation to help us solve this crime and keep the streets safe for our children."

I flip the dial to another news broadcast. Same story. I turn the damn thing off.

"Hey!?" I hear Perdomo shout from the recesses of his pizza dungeon. "I was listening to that!"

Just as I turn the TV back on, I hear the bells jingle on the front door. Thank God. At least the customers will provide a distraction.

But when I turn around, I see that these aren't any old customers. It's John. And following closely behind is Sofia.

"What the hell?" I say before they can offer an explanation or even a greeting. John's eyes dart like he's just failed a polygraph test, and he dives for the nearest booth. Sofia doesn't look startled in the least. Her eyebrows rise a little and she quickens her pace behind John, but she appears unfazed—maybe even amused.

I'm not sure why, but I feel all the blood rush to my ears and then I'm burning up. The skin on my face radiates in waves of heat. I want to explode for absolutely no reason that I can explain. It frustrates the hell out of me, so I slam an empty napkin holder on the table, grab two menus, and walk over to the booth with a few beads of sweat trickling through my sideburns.

"So what in the hell is going on here, then?" I ask. My voice cracks a little and I think maybe Sofia is about to laugh me out of my own workplace, but she just hardens her glare on the surface of the table and cracks her gum. "Well?"

Sofia raises her eyes slowly from the table to meet John's, but they don't exchange a single word. Each one waits for the other to make a move, but nothing happens. Perdomo rips a pizza slicer through the crust of a piping hot pie on the counter behind me and John nearly springs out of the booth. But he still won't give me an answer.

"Look, I don't even know how you know each other, but are you two together or something? Is that what's going on here?"

Suddenly I'm aware of the menus collapsing between my hands like the many-folded vitals of an accordion. I toss them down on the table. John and Sofia exchange shocked glances and everything goes all quiet and awkward.

"Gabe?" John asks. "You feeling alright?"

Before I can unload on him, before I can tell him what a snake he is for showing up at my place of business with the only girl in the Delaware Valley that doesn't think I'm a charity case or an outright lost cause, before I can look Sofia in the eyes and tell her that maybe people are right when they see all the ink and think she's a felon. Before I can fire off any of those missiles, Sofia says, "Gabe thinks 'we're doing the nasty, John."

"No . . . Wait, what? The nasty?" John looks at me and his eyes tell me he'd rather be sitting at this table right now with Lily and Victor Chen, reliving their version of "the talk" where each and every part of the human anatomy has some awkward and super gross comparison to one of the plants in the Chen family garden. Chilling stuff.

"Go ahead and tell him, Gabe," Sofia says. "You know it's true."

And she says it in this flatline voice, like it's no big deal—like she'd just asked me to pass the dinner rolls instead of forced me to admit that

I believed in some insane conspiracy from outer space in which my best friend was trying to steal the girl that I might admit I kind of liked if I wasn't so afraid of her.

"That's what you think, isn't it?"

She stares at me. I can tell there's a smile hidden under her poker face but she keeps it concealed. And somewhere between the dark chocolate of her irises and the stone-cold brutality of her statement, I start to think maybe I'm being kind of ridiculous. Sofia and John? Come on. John and any other living creature on the planet seems kind of laughable. And, come to think of it, I was never worked-up about it in the first place. Not really. I mean, why would it bother me that two of my friends just happened to appear at my workplace?

"Gabe," John says, "Sofia showed up on my front porch twenty minutes ago. She mentioned your name and I took one look at her tattoos and knew she had to be the girl from the hospital. You know, the one you can't stop talking about."

"Shut up, John." I grunt it under my breath and Sofia pretends not to notice.

"I knocked on the front door," Sofia says, "and the tiniest, most adorable woman in the world came out to greet me. I swear."

"Your mom saw her?"

"That's the best part," John tells me. "Lily took one look at the black hair and the ripped up jeans and I thought her brain would explode into a million tiny fireworks right there on the front porch. It was awesome!"

I drift over to the counter, plop two slices of pizza on paper plates, and bring them back to the table. My treat. Just to keep them occupied. "How in the world did you break the front lines with the grim reaper of punk rock over here as your sidekick?"

"That's the second best part," John says. "Your friend here is such a badass that just the residual attitude problem emanating from her was enough to make Lily wilt. I wouldn't have believed it if I hadn't seen it with my own eyes. My mom was freaking powerless! I just grabbed my jacket and was like, 'later.'" I look at Sofia. She nibbles on the crust of her pizza and shrugs.

"But that still doesn't explain how or why you ended up at John's house," I say.

"Well..." Sofia says. "... even though I'm out of the prison population, I still have a few spies on the inside at the Schuylkill High State Pen. I asked around and got the scoop on your soul mate here." She drills John with a quick shin-kick under the table and he winces. "I heard that you two are inseparable. I'm kind of getting a Bert and Ernie vibe, but that's beside the point."

"This was all your doing?" I ask Sofia.

"Basically . . . Yeah, that sounds about right."

"And why, may I ask, are you here? Because I already gave you a free slice and I already told you Perdomo's discount policy: Gabe no work the register."

Sofia doesn't answer. She just stares down at the three or four pizza crumbs left on her plate, which is weird because normally she'd meet my wisecrack with six of her own.

"Sofia?" I say again. Her eyes rise slowly to meet mine.

"Yes?"

"My question. What are you two doing here?"

There's another moment of silence as John and Sofia exchange knowing looks

"We're worried about you," John says. He fires the words off at warp speed so that maybe I won't hear all the pity in his voice. But it's too late. I hear them loud and clear and it's pathetic when I think about how they rolled off the lips of someone who's supposed to be my best friend.

"So that's what this is? Some kind of intervention?"

I start to laugh. But John and Sofia are not laughing with me. They look scared. Ashamed. Their eyes dart back between the table and each other, avoiding mine completely.

"Not an intervention. I hate that word," Sofia says. Now she wants to get all humorous and I'm not sure I want to play along. "In-ter-ven-tion. Damn. It sounds dirty. Like what you think John and I did in the first twenty minutes of knowing each other."

"Yeah," John says. "It's not an intervention. Think of it as more of an enlightenment."

"An enlightenment?! You really expect me to fall for that kind of—"

"Yes, we do," Sofia adds, "and we're here to enlighten you to the fact that you're acting like an erratic ass."

"An erratic ass? Isn't that on the endangered species list?" And now I'm just spouting off crazy nonsense because if I don't keep things light right now Officer Patterson might need to add a few crimes to my record.

"Gabe. We're serious," John says, and the crackle in his voice tells me they are. "We don't want to see this whole thing blow up in your face. It's not too late. You can still make a deal and make things so much easier for your grandfather and yourself."

"You need to do the right thing," Sofia says. "Call the detective, Gabe. Turn your grandpa in."

I can't believe what I'm hearing. From my two so-called friends. Sure, Doc Weston—I expect this kind of crap from him. He's a professional. He has insurance people to keep happy, so he has to reason these things out like a damn Macintosh computer. But my friends? Damn. I thought at least I had the judgment to choose friends with a little bit of heart and a tiny shred of loyalty. I guess I was wrong.

"Turn him in?" You'd think Sofia just told me to light myself on fire. "Are you kidding me? Please tell me this is some kind of lame practical joke and that a cameraman's about to pop out from behind the counter."

I'm pissed, so I crane my neck all giraffe-like and make a big show of searching for the hidden camera jockey. Still trying to keep things light so I don't vaporize Perdomo's shop and turn it into a mushroom cloud on the horizon.

"This is no joke," John says, and he's getting this look on his face that I hate because it almost always precedes a freaking lecture from the good professor. I call him that sometimes, mostly when he annoys the crap out of me. His lips get all thin and his nose makes these tiny, flinching movements like a rabbit. Dude can't control them.

"Let me tell you a story," he says. That's how he always starts these little soapbox readings. "It's an analogy, really." Oh, boy, here he goes. He's starting to roll. "It's about this old man and a tiger. The tiger is chasing him and they reach a cliff. The old—"

"Oh, God," I hear Sofia grumble under her breath—thankfully.

John stops his tale midstream.

"What?"

"Does he always talk like this?" she asks to no one in particular.

"Yes," I say. "Yes he does."

Sofia shakes her head and scratches a dry patch of skin on her elbow just below the outstretched talons of an eagle tattoo.

"Does this kid think he's gonna live forever? I'll need to make funeral arrangements before the story ends."

I start to laugh at John's expense—I can never resist—but Sofia cuts me off and forces me to stifle it. "Not that I'd ever be seen at a funeral—dead or alive. They're phony as hell, but that's beside the point. Your situation is obvious, Gabe. Everything turns grey."

I'm not sure which one of these clowns is pissing me off more.

"What the hell are you talking about?" I ask, and there's nothing gentle about my tone—like I'm a New York City cab driver or something, and she's an obnoxious, drunken fare.

"Agent Orange," she says. "The band. It all turns grey no matter what you think or do or say. Or something like that. I don't know. I'm not the geeky poet here. But it's a line in one of their songs—a really simple way of saying you need to make a sacrifice, Gabe. And in about forty thousand less words than Faulkner over here."

I'm still pissed but I can't hold back on a second opportunity to ridicule my best friend. So I laugh. And John laughs too—I swear the kid was tragically born without an ego. And, suddenly, all three of us are cracking up at John's expense.

The laughter clears the fog for just a moment. Long enough to see the point my friends are trying to make—a point I wish they hadn't decided without me. Because it's not strong enough to make me turn my back on Dad's promise. Or on Grandpa. Nothing is that strong. I think even my Uncle Nick would agree, which is a pretty stunning development. I mean, it's not everyday I find my thoughts in alignment with Nick's. That alone should tell me to reason this thing through a little more, but every time I try I just think about Dad and I refuse to let him down.

"I'm not turning him in," I say matter-of-factly when the laughter dies and John and Sofia are back to munching on pizza. "You know, it really sucks having to worry about my grandfather every second of everyday. Even while I'm sleeping! I mean, I have nightmares where I'm trapped inside a Tetris board and all the falling shapes are Grandpa's pills raining down on me. And then I wake up from the nightmare and help the man take a bath. There's no escape. But if you think I would trade him away to avoid any of that stuff, then you don't know me at all."

"The only thing we want you to avoid is jail time," John says.

"And when the police find out the real truth," Sofia adds, "Things are gonna be a whole lot worse for you and Gramps." I just shake my head and reach for their empty paper plates.

"You two will never get it," I grunt as I carry the trash over to the counter. "This has never been about how I can improve my life. And it never will be."

Neither of them respond, they just go on sipping cola through their straws. I guess John and Sofia think they accomplished enough for one day. I don't tell them they're wrong, of course. It's more convenient to let them think they make a difference, even when they don't. So, I create a diversion and change the subject altogether.

"You know, Sofia is a tattoo artist," I say to John.

"I kind of figured that," he says as he motions up and down Sofia's arm with a shaky index finger. "You do all that yourself?"

"Every single line," she says. "And more. But Gabe knows the rules on seeing the rest of them." She winks at me—I swear, this girl has no fear of anything. I could probably unleash the tiger from John's lame fable on her and she'd send the poor thing back to me with a tattoo on its ass that says 'mommy.' I'm not much of a tough guy myself, so the blood rushes to my ears and I feel the red blotches form on my face.

"Yeah," I say. "Uh. You have to know her for a long time."

I'm nervous as hell all of a sudden and I don't know why. Sofia laughs. One big hearty HA! And it saves me.

"Lots of emergency room dates. That's what I call them," she tells John. As she says it, there's a quick flash of light like when the sun hits the face of someone's watch at just the right angle. My eyes move to the front window of the shop and I see him immediately. Officer Patterson. He's across the street and behind the wheel of a brown, unmarked sedan. He can tell I see him, so he rolls up the window and pretends to read the newspaper. What is it with this guy?

"Your buddy gets all middle school about the term," Sofia continues without noticing my wandering eyes. "Sometimes I think he might pee his pants." Now it's John's turn to laugh at my expense and he's not shy about it. He smacks his hand down on the table hard enough to rouse Mr. Perdomo from meditation above his afternoon espresso.

Boy, I'm so glad these two have met. Ugh. Nothing like being outnumbered. I think I'll keep the Officer Patterson sighting to myself.

13

TRANS-AMBUSH

It was only noon but Perdomo gave me the rest of the day off, which was pretty generous of him considering Saturdays are busy at the shop. "Don't worry about it," he told me as I finished wiping out the spill tray under the soda fountain. Thing's always sticky as hell. "You look stressed, Gabe. Enjoy the afternoon. Maybe take that vampire girlfriend of yours to a double feature."

"She's not my girlfriend," I had told him. What I really wanted to say was, "What the hell is a double feature, old man? It's the nineties for God's sake. Do you see any girls walking in here after school in poodle skirts and freaking bobby socks?" But I figured that might have jeopardized my afternoon off, so I thanked him and clocked out.

"Don't worry about me, Gabe," he said as I pushed through the front doors. "I been running this place forty years. I do it in my sleep." Trust me, there was no worry—at least not about Perdomo.

Officer Patterson is another story. It's been a few days and I still haven't told John or Sofia I'd seen secret agent man snooping around outside the shop. That would only lead to further lectures and even more detailed fablery from my best friend. I think jail might be a better option.

The story still leads the local news. Every time I see a report, there's little Timmy Mullins with a big cast on his arm and his gap-toothed, toddler grin. If the situation were different I might find him adorable like the rest of the saps in this town. Instead, every time I see him on screen, I get the urge to race around the block to his house, pick him up like a human-sized pigskin, and punt him into the cheap seats—on third down. But that's just me. Maybe I'm biased.

The police haven't named a suspect yet, which makes me feel a little queasy every time I think about it—because I'm pretty sure Officer Patterson wasn't lurking outside the Perdomo's parking lot so he could catch up on his reading. Somehow I know I haven't shared my last conversation with the guy, and each time I look at the macaroni collage

John and I constructed on the Trans-Am's fender, I'm reminded of it. And I'm powerless.

The only thing I can think to do is take another stab in the old LoScuda body shop. This time I'll keep it in the family. No John. I don't have patience for Tinker Toys today. I ask Nick.

He's in the bathroom, but the door's open a crack so I barge in without knocking. He's in front of the sink shaving—which is weird for Nick—and I see his eyes shoot to my reflection in the mirror. There's a glob of shaving cream encrusted with tiny flecks of spent beard hanging off one of his earlobes. A wet trail of the stuff dribbles down the side of his neck and piles itself on the stained collar of his tee shirt. He grabs a clean towel off the rack and wipes it away before I get the urge to do it myself.

"Any chance you want to help me repair the monstrosity in the garage?"

"The car again?"

"Yep."

"I'd do it, Gabe, but I'm all booked up today."

All booked up? The guy spends most mornings eating cereal from a Frisbee and trying to perfect the melody of the "Star Spangled Banner" in farts.

"What do you mean?" I ask.

"Got a job."

He glides the razor over a final patch of stubble and looks at my reflection again, this time with a self-satisfied grin on his face. I'm speechless. "Reconnected with an old buddy of mine. He's a supervisor over at McLeod's Trucking. Got me a gig in the warehouse. Nights, so we can split watch duty."

"You're serious?"

He nods and then splashes a handful of warm water over his face. For a second, the guy sort of looks human.

"You know today's Saturday, right?"

"Six days a week, Gabe. We need the money. Can you see if Perdomo will keep you off the schedule for Saturdays like he did today."

I'm stunned. It's almost like this bumbling, crazy-bearded, baboon invaded my house one day and all it took was a shave and he's suddenly a real human.

"That sounds great," I say, and I'm aware that I'm speaking in the voice of someone who'd just witnessed a UFO landing. "Gramps can hang with me today." I watch as Nick squirts aftershave from a green bottle on his hand and slaps it on his cheeks. Then he grabs a comb—a freaking comb—and runs it through his hair.

"I'm proud of you," I say, and now both of us are stunned. I don't know where they came from, these words. But there had been no chance of swallowing them up before they tumbled out of my mouth. There was no sucking them back now. They were out there.

But Nick doesn't make a big deal. He keeps the comb running through tangles and says, "Yeah, me too." Vintage Nick. The big ape.

I fetch Gramps from his room and tell him we're taking a trip to the beach. His eyes grow wide and they flash toward the closet—where he keeps all of his ancient swim trunks, ones with waistlines so high I'm afraid he might choke. I swing the closet door open and a ratty, leather bag filled with marbles—probably from a time when Gramps wore a freaking Angus Young-style schoolboy outfit—falls off the top shelf and smashes me in the face. Then all the little glass balls explode from the leather bag and shoot off across the wooden floor in no less than four thousand directions. Scattered, just like Grandpa's thoughts for the last few years. I gather as many of the marbles as I can and stuff them in the bag. If only it were this easy to collect Grandpa's thoughts and store them all in one place.

Before I have a chance to offer Grandpa one of my expert swimwear recommendations, he shouts "I want this one!" and nearly makes me jump through the freaking ceiling. He points at a green chest-hugger made out of some heavy material that would be better for covering the pool instead of swimming in it. I help him out of his robe—the thing smells like old milk so I toss it in a pile of dirty socks heaped near the door—and he climbs into the trunks. He must have lost a bit of weight because there's enough space between his gut and the waistband to fit a Chihuahua. Whatever. It's not like the beach we're going to will have any witnesses in the event of a total pants droppage. In fact, the beach we're going to won't have any other bathers. It won't have umbrellas or sand, or water, or even sunlight. Because it's the garage. Cape Freaking LoScuda.

I set Grandpa up in one of those beach chairs middle age mothers always sit in—the ones with legs that extend only about three inches off the ground so when you sit your knees are basically scraping your forehead and your ass leaves a crater in the sand. It's perfect for Gramps because there isn't far to fall.

I set up a multicolored beach towel in front of the chair with a bunch of smiling sea turtles printed on it. I even put my old plastic buckets and a dime store shovel on the blanket just to set the scene. Gramps plops himself down in the chair and sprawls out like he's catching some insane rays through the roof of the garage. It's another piece of trickery I'm not all that proud of, but at least he's happy.

I pop a CD into the stereo on Dad's workbench: Nirvana. The one with the naked, swimming baby on the cover. I figure I can use a little teen spirit right about now. I move a few of Dad's miscellaneous items off the surface of the bench: a torn carton full of penny nails, two rubber mallets, a socket set in an army green canvas bag, and his maroon and baby-blue Phillies hat. The fabric on the brim is all frayed so the plastic shows through the front, and there's a ring of salty whiteness around the bottom edge of the hat—probably a collection of Dad's sweat from a million humid Philadelphia summers spent grooming Mom's yard.

I think about slapping it on my head with my ears all tucked in like I used to do when I was three. But I know that'll just make the tears hang heavy on my eyelids, so I place it on one of the metal hooks Dad nailed over the workbench to keep his screwdrivers and pliers comfortable between birdhouse-making sessions. The old hat with its trademark Phillies 'P' in the center hangs like a tattered battle flag. Dad's flag. Seeing it holding sentry over all the other workings of the garage makes it feel like Dad's here with me. But the feeling only lasts a second before I look at the car and see the mess John and I had made of it. Man, if only Dad were here for real. He'd be pissed, but he'd know what to do.

An old piece of sandpaper lies limp and half-shredded on the cement floor—another casualty of the last repair attempt. This time I select a new strip with less grit. It says "fine" and "150 pt." in small letters across the bottom. With Gramps half asleep on his own private beach and Kurt Cobain belting out "In Bloom," I start applying some elbow grease to the fender.

With a few strokes, the raised, bubbly sections of paint are reduced to naked, metallic patches. By the time Kurt starts to sing "Lithium," all the crappy corrections we added to the fender are gone. I stand back and admire my handiwork. There's a bunch of powdery paint residue on the floor, but the fender already looks better. Gramps is still lounging away, sipping imaginary Mai Tais in his own imaginary paradise. Perfect.

There's a brown, paper bag on Dad's workbench. I grab it and empty the contents—a single spray can of red paint with the Pontiac symbol staring back at me. This time I did my homework. Stopped off at the auto store and had the guys match my paint up with whatever they had in stock. Asked for some pointers, too. The salesman—some dude with a ZZ Top beard and a pair of overalls—told me to cover up the parts of the car I didn't want slathered in paint and then spray away until my heart's content.

It's worth a try, so I grab a roll of butcher's paper Dad always kept in a tall cabinet beside the garage door. I cut off a few large pieces and lay them on the hood. Then I grab a roll of masking tape. I start to arrange the squares of paper over the untouchable areas of the car, but before I can tape anything down I hear footsteps.

They are brisk and they are close. I look out toward the driveway and see Officer Patterson, in his patent leather cop shoes, walking toward me. I pretend not to see him at first; shoot my eyes down at the pavement. But it's no use. I'm cornered. Like a rat. And what am I going to do? Run in the house? Yeah, that wouldn't be obvious. *Crap.*

"Mr. LoScuda," I hear him say as he enters the garage and stands near the tailpipes of the Trans-Am. "It's good to see you so hard at work on a Saturday."

"Yeah," I say. "Kind of tired of driving around in a demolition derby car. Girls think I'm a creep."

He chuckles a little, but I know it's fake because what I said was not funny, just desperate.

"I'm just stopping by to see if you've heard any new information about the case," he says. He glances over at Grandpa, pans his eyes from head to feet and back like he's studying an exhibit at the zoo. "You know, seeing as you live in the area and all."

"No. Nothing new, officer. Have you been questioning all the other people who live in this neighborhood or do you only have eyes for me?"

"I can't speak about an open investigation, son. Just be sure we are doing all we can—and I mean everything—to find the person who did this to poor, little Timothy Mullins." Man, am I ready to punt that little runt—second down is fine with me. "You mind if I ask a few questions?" he asks, and what am I supposed to say? No?

"Of course," I say. "I'll do anything I can to help."

Yeah, except tell you the truth.

"So you say you smashed the car here in the garage. Is that correct?"

"Yes, that's right."

Officer Patterson moves around the garage inspecting the walls, picking up stray tools, stepping over Grandpa in the process.

"And you say you did the repairs yourself?"

"Yes. That's correct."

Patterson looks over at Gramps again, doing that whole inspection thing he does. He reaches down on the beach blanket and snags the tube of Coppertone I had placed next to Gramps just to set the seaside mood — you know, since we're in a freaking garage and all. He pretends to read the label. What does he want to know? Whether the stuff is paba-free or something? He looks satisfied, as if he were about to slather himself up and catch some rays right there beside the old man. He tosses the tube back down on the blanket next to Gramps. I cringe because the last thing I need is for the ancient war hero to wake up and start ducking for cover like we're in the middle of a bombing raid. His eyes twitch behind his eyelids, but they don't open — thankfully.

"Mind if I see them?"

"Well—"

"It's your right fender," he says without waiting for my permission, "so that means you must have hit the garage somewhere around . . ."

He roots around on the right side wall, looks back at the fender and then slaps his hand against the spot he imagines to be marked with the "X."

"Here?"

He looks at me. I can tell he's waiting for a response now, but I have no idea how to talk my way out of this so I stay silent. "Would you agree, Mr. LoScuda?"

"Oh," I say. "Uh. It's hard to say exactly where the damage was. Definitely in that general area I'd say, but—"

"So, you must have done a phenomenal patch job here on the drywall." He looks back at the fender and smiles. Then he runs his palm over the drywall. "Wow. I'm impressed," he says. "I'll bet not even a seasoned contractor can make it look so seamless."

"Yeah," I say. "Guess I got lucky." He walks over, runs his palm over the fender, pulls his hand back, and inspects it like he'd just been cut by something sharp.

"Yes, it certainly appears as though luck may have been one of your tools."

He's no longer smiling. Now his eyes are narrow and his jaw is clenched. Bad cop's back in town. "So, I hear you play baseball," he says.

"Yep. Second base."

"Good hitter?"

"I'm alright, I guess."

"Have any problems seeing the ball?"

"Not at all. Just problems hitting it sometimes."

"I see."

He brings his thumb and index finger to his lips and stares up into the rafters for a second. There's nothing that catches his interest, so he moves along to the workbench. He picks Dad's Phils hat off the hook I'd placed it on—as if being a cop somehow gives him the right to paw at my personal stuff. It kind of pisses me off because I really hate rubberneckers. I want to tell him to get the hell out of my garage; to stay away from me and what's left of my family; to do anything at all—I mean, slap the freaking cuffs on me if he has to—besides steal the last few memories I have of my dad. But like I said, he's a cop, so I don't say a word. I just stand there with my fists clenched until he places the hat back on the hook.

"So, if a pitcher were to, say, throw a heater high and tight, you'd be able to jump out of the way?"

"Yeah, but I don't see what this has—"

"Reflexes, Gabe. You have them. The driver of the car that struck the Mullins boy did not. That's why I let you go the other day, because you don't add up to me as a suspect."

He turns and begins to pace the length of the garage floor. Up and back. In silence. Each time passing Grandpa in his slumber and eyeing him through narrow slits. In his beach chair, the old man looks like he could star in the movie *Weekend at Bernie's*. Like I'm about to pull a string and raise one of Grandpa's limp and wrinkled arms to a full salute. But the only string is a small line of saliva dribbling down his chin—and it's not really the best time for me to join the mop-up team. So I leave it there and hope the officer doesn't scoop it up and toss it in one of those clear baggies cops use to store evidence. And suddenly I notice my heart is bouncing all around in my chest, and not in a good way—like when Marlie sneaks up behind me in the school parking lot. It takes all of my energy to keep the damn thing from flying out of my mouth when I speak.

"That's good," I say.

"However, there's a pretty big elephant sitting in this garage right now."

He points to the car and I know I'm screwed.

"I took a few paint samples off your car the day I was at Schuylkill High. Had them tested in the lab. They match the scuff marks on the kid's bike."

Holy crap. Holy crap. Holy crap.

"Would you mind explaining how that could have happened?"

"I, uh . . ." *Holy crap. Holy crap. Holy crap.* "I—"

Just then, like a groaning zombie reanimating from its grave, Gramps pops up off his beach chair. He takes one look at Officer Patterson in his uniform and suddenly he's standing at attention—in full salute.

"Lt. Ernest LoScuda reporting for duty, Sir!" He says it crisply and clearly, like he'd somehow found a little voice left over from twenty-year-old Ernie. Officer Patterson's eyes bulge open and I pop up from my crouch in front of the fender in the hope I can wrestle him back into the house before he says anything stupid. But it's too late. Officer Patterson has already blocked my path, and there's a look of recognition in his eyes—like a devious plan has just been set in motion.

"At ease, soldier," he says, and Grandpa's shoulders drop a bit and his eyes focus on the officer.

"What are you—"

"See this vehicle, soldier?" Gramps looks at the Trans-Am and nods.

"Can you drive it, son?"

"Wait," I say. "You can't." I try to maneuver around Officer Patterson but he's big and he boxes me out and I've never been a particularly good rebounder, so he has me beat.

"Sir, yes Sir!" I hear Grandpa shout, and I don't like where this is headed.

"Did you drive it last week, soldier?"

"No," I say in the background. "No, of course he—"

"Sir, yes Sir!" Grandpa shouts over me.

Officer Patterson turns to me and he has this smug, little grin on his face. I swear if he wasn't a policeman and didn't outweigh and outmuscle me by at least thirty men, I'd smack that stupid look right off his ugly mug. Instead, I just stand there staring at him.

"Correction," he says, "It appears we have two very large elephants in the room. He points with his left index finger to the car and his right to Gramps, who's still standing at full attention.

"What are you suggesting?" I ask as if I don't already know.

"Witnesses at the scene couldn't give us an accurate description of the driver, but every one of them touched on one common point. Age. They all saw a driver much older than the boy who registered the car."

"I'm not a boy," I say. "And besides, that's impossible."

"How's that, Mr. LoScuda? I think it's pretty obvious that your—"

And then I do the only thing I can think to do. The only thing that can keep Grandpa safe and my promise to Dad intact. "Because it was me," I say. "I want to make a full confession."

"What? But—"

"I said I want to make a confession."

Officer Patterson is stunned, as if someone had actually slugged the smug grin off his face. He takes one final step toward Grandpa and says, "Dee-smissed!"

Grandpa slumps back in his beach chair and begins to nod off again.

Patterson shakes his head and leads me out of the garage.

"You're making a big mistake, son, but that's where my jurisdiction ends."

He nudges me forward and I feel my feet shuffle a few steps across the pavement. The handcuffs click against each other as Officer Patterson pulls them off his belt. I feel the cuffs tighten first around one wrist, and then the other.

"You can't take me anywhere," I say and I hear my teeth chatter against each other like hollow Chiclets. "What about my grandfather? I can't just leave him here."

"But he didn't do anything wrong," Patterson says. "You said so yourself. Now, if you'd like to amend your story—"

"I'm not changing my story."

"Then your grandfather is a law-abiding adult. And he looks like he's comfortable." I don't say anything and Patterson takes the silence as an opportunity to tighten the steel on my wrists. "Gabriel LoScuda. I am placing you under arrest You have the right to remain silent. Anything you say can and will be used against you in a court of law. You have the right to speak to an attorney . . ."

And that's all I hear before I tune the rest out.

Gabe LoScuda
English 4A – Personal Essay #5
Mr. Mastrocola
December 19

Pie in the Skye

Charlotte Bronte, perhaps one of the most influential feminist writers of her time, has something in common with my Uncle Nick. Trust me, I'm as surprised as you. Probably more, because all it takes is one shared meal with the guy and it becomes obvious you better keep your valuables, any stray body parts, and maybe even your soul far away from his mouth. Dude's like a human vacuum cleaner at the dinner table—a sight that would have surely made a refined, sophisticated lady like Ms. Bronte shrivel up and disappear right there in her seat.

But her poetry remains and, from that standpoint, it becomes hard NOT to notice the connection. At least for me. See, I have the benefit of history. You take, for instance, Bronte's poem "Regret." In it, she writes, "Long ago I wished to leave / The house where I was born; / Long ago I used to grieve, / My home seemed so forlorn."

Like Nick, Charlotte Bronte saw the grass on the other side of the street and thought, "By God! It looks greener!" Like Nick, she left the place she'd called home and realized, much too late, "how utterly is flown / Every ray of light." Like Nick, she made a snap decision and it rewarded her with nothing but the weight of her regret.

But, unlike Charlotte, it never had to turn out that way for Nick.

"Hold on tight," he had said one morning as he wrapped his thick fingers around my waist and pulled me back against his body. "I'm gonna send you to the moon, Gabey!" Uncle Nick grunted and heaved me forward. The soapy scent of lavender from Mom's bushes rode the spring breeze and tickled my nostrils as the tire swing catapulted me toward the treetops. I squealed like a little idiot and relished in the ride as the tire swung lower and lower on its pendulum. Then Nick grabbed the ropes again and the swing lurched to a stop. I rested there on my stomach, panting, my tiny, five-year-old heart still humming at a thousand miles per hour.

"Again," I said to Nick, and the big bear churned his shoulder muscles and blasted me off into the stratosphere.

"You're gonna be the next Buzz Aldrin, Gabey-Boy!" he shouted from below.

When the swing slowed to a stop I asked, "Who's Buzz Aspirin?" Uncle Nick laughed.

"Buzz Aldrin. He was an astronaut. One of the first humans to walk on the moon. Nobody's done it since."

"Think I'll walk on the moon some day?"

"If I toss you any higher that day may be today," he said, and then he grabbed my nose between two of his fingers and squeezed. Not hard enough to hurt, but just enough to be annoying. I snorted. "You gotta start learning how to live without oxygen," he said. "Figured I'd help you out a little."

Even back then—minus twenty pounds of back fat, the perpetual odor of whiskey, and a whole lot of ear hair—Uncle Nick still knew how to piss me off. So I took my tiny, five-year-old fist and socked him in the arm. I was serious, too. But Nick played along. He turned it into a game, and before long we were chasing each other around the yard, howling like morons, and attempting to recreate wrestling moves that were best left to guys like the Junkyard Dog and Jake "the Snake" Roberts.

Just as Uncle Nick hoisted me into pile driver formation and pretended to talk a bunch of fake wrestling smack to an imaginary audience, I heard a car roll up and park along the curb. Dad's car. I always knew when Dad was home because I'd memorized the muffled p-p-p-p-p-p of the Volvo's engine and the quick, rickety thwack of Dad's traditional yank on the parking brake.

Uncle Nick's voice dried up mid-speech and he replaced me, upright, on the ground. He watched as Dad stalked up the driveway without acknowledging Nick. Dad vanished into the shadows of his garage, but the sounds of a slammed cabinet door and some under-the-breath cursing told us he hadn't ventured inside.

"Go play on your swing," Uncle Nick said. "I need to talk to your father."

I listened because that's what five-year-olds do when confronted with directives from people who could probably eat you for breakfast. But I wish I would have gone with him, because then he and Dad wouldn't have had the argument, and then I wouldn't have had to hear all the stuff I heard. And then maybe, just maybe, my Uncle Nick wouldn't have disappeared for all those years.

"How can you be so goddamned irresponsible?" I heard Dad say from my perch on the swing. He didn't sound happy, like he was trying to use his words in the same way my G.I. Joe figurines fired missiles.

"I studied, Sal. I really did. I just didn't pass."

"Bullshit!"

There was silence for a few seconds and then Dad's hammer clanged off the side of his vice grip. He was building a birdhouse again. That's what he did when something was on his mind. Never hung them in the yard. Just built them.

"It's the stress," Nick said when the hammering died down. "It was killing me. I need a break, Sal."

"A break? Your whole life has been a break!"

"I just need to get away for awhile. Clear my head."

"Yeah, well you already cleared out Dad's bank account. You might as well work on your head next."

The hammering started up with greater intensity, and for a moment I thought the conversation would end and the two brothers would cool off. But then Dad stopped pounding on the birdhouse and said, "How can you be so inconsiderate? What the hell is Dad supposed to do now?"

"Look, I won't be gone long. I'll come back, and I'll be prepared, and I'll pass the thing this time. Ernie's investment won't be wasted."

"Investment!" My father spit out the word like it was a bad taste in his mouth. Then he continued his hammering. When he stopped, it was Nick who looked to further the argument.

"Look . . . his money won't be wasted . . . I promise. It's just . . ."

"Here we go again," Dad muttered.

". . . that me and Skye. We're . . . It's Jerry Garcia, Sal. I just need a few months."

"Months?!" Dad said, and his voice rose two octaves like he'd suddenly transformed into Frankie Valli.

"Get your teaching license, then you can have months—it's called the summer. Until then, just grow the hell up."

"But Skye and I, we're—"

"And to hell with this Skye girl. She's not for you, Nick."

"But I love her."

"So what? Get out of love with her and do it quick—before she talks you into tattooing Buddha on your ass or strangles you with her love beads."

There was no more hammering. No more talking. Only the reverberations of a slammed door echoing off the garage walls.

Nick trudged out onto the driveway a minute or two later with a canvas backpack slung over his shoulders. He kneeled down in front of the tire swing and looked me in the eyes. His were red, puffy—the way mine looked after a tantrum over bedtime.

"Hey, Gabe! I'll be on the road for awhile," he said as he ruffled the hair on my head. "Won't be gone long. But I need you to train hard while I'm away. Get that swing as high as you can—and don't let your daddy convince you it can't touch the clouds. You understand?"

"Where are you going?"

"Oh, here and there. But don't worry about me. I'll be back to get you before you know it."

"Get me for what, Uncle Nick?"

"For our trip to the moon," he said, smiling. "That's what all the training's for. Weren't you listening?"

I nodded but, even then, something told me Uncle Nick's idea of "before you know it" was a lot different than my own. If only I'd known about Charlotte Bronte back then. At least then I would have felt comfort in her words. At least then I would have grown up with the knowledge that regret— the evil but necessary demon that perches on each of our shoulders—would eventually bring Nick back home.

14

BARS

It's hot, and I stare at the ceiling from my squeaky cot. The mattress is about as thick as the bars that hold me from the outside world. I lie there quietly, listening to a distant prisoner sing an old country song that could be Hank Williams, but might well be made up on the spot. I can't tell. He sings about his old truck and how it's still in better shape than his woman, but he misses them both equally. And it has this Christmasy feeling to it, like something he might sing if he were out caroling with a pack of bearded Tennessee farmers.

But maybe it's just my imagination.

Maybe it's what I want to hear. Because, this time last year, I was busy helping Dad string lights on the boxwoods and eating baskets full of Mom's pizzelles. I could never eat enough of those things, and I don't even like the taste of black licorice. But, damn, something magical used to happen when Mom would ladle a few tablespoons of batter on the old iron and scoop off one of her thin, waffle-shaped delicacies a few moments later. She'd stack them all in cellophane bags and send them off to the neighbors and her coworkers, and then she'd spend all of January retrieving thank-you letters from the mailbox and whitewashing the refrigerator door with them. It always made it feel like the holidays.

I doubt I'll see anything resembling a pizzelle behind these bars. I mean, Officer Patterson might have the license to carry a firearm, but a pizzelle iron? Those were best left to the professionals. Like Mom. Makes me want to cry to even think about it.

So I think about Emily Dickinson instead, and her obsession with death. And I think about the many thousands of lines of poetry she managed to crank out in her lifetime—all of them great, but all boiling down to one short set of lines that will cling to me always, but never more stubbornly than at this moment.

In this short life
That only lasts an hour

How much — how little — is
Within our power?"

Apparently not much. I mean, all I did was ride my bike a few blocks and eat a slice of pizza. Now I'm in jail. How's that for a short life with little to no power, Emily? Good enough for you?

I stare at the cinderblock walls, absent of everything including color, and I think about all I'll miss while I'm stuck in here rotting away like freaking Doctor Manette, until I'm some old man cobbling shoes in an abandoned attic. Baseball. Marlie. Graduation. College. Kids. Everything. But at least my promise to Dad is intact. I hope that's enough to keep me company behind these lonely bars.

I roll over and trace the line of Dickinson's poem on the blank wall with my naked finger. I do it over and over and over again, like if I do it enough they'll actually show up. Then I'm rudely interrupted.

"How are the accommodations?" Officer Patterson asks through the bars. I don't answer, just keep tracing. *How much — how little — how much — how little.* He continues. "I pulled a few strings, got you a private suite. Didn't want you in with real criminals."

"Thanks a lot," I say. I don't mean it and I don't even try to make it sound polite. What does it matter?

"I have a lot of respect for you, Gabe," he says. "Not too many boys your age would find themselves in a predicament like this."

"I'm not a boy."

"And mostly," he says, "it's because they don't have the spines to do what you're doing."

"Trust me," I say. "Laying around in here all day isn't much of a challenge."

"I think you know what I mean. And I think, maybe right about this moment, you're thinking 'I'm ready to get out of this dungeon. I'm ready to tell the nice officer who was really driving that car.'"

He goes silent and I can feel his eyes, like freaking laser beams, scorching the back of my neck. I hear the hinges squeak on a cell door somewhere on my block. Then the metal clangs on metal, and the tinny reverberations bounce from one hollow wall of the cavern to another. It makes me jump a little, but I'll never admit to being scared. Even Patterson doesn't scare me, though he could probably slice me through the prison bars like a hard boiled egg if he wanted. And so I go back to tracing. *How much — how little — how much — how little.*

When I hear him turn and start to walk away I say, "I'm ready to tell."

He stops, shuffles back to front and center.

"Go on," he says. "I'm listening,"

"I did it."

I turn and look him square in the eyes, no blinking. He shakes his head—the same way he did when he slapped the cuffs on me.

"Someone's here to see you," he says.

He turns and disappears around the corner of the cell next to mine. A moment or two later I hear another set of footsteps. Slow ones. Lumbering ones. I sit up in my cot, hoping this looming beast is not my new cellmate. Please don't let him be my new cellmate.

The steps grow heavier, closer. They're rounding the cell next door and closing in. A droplet of sweat oozes from my back and rolls down into my underwear. I'm about to scream and make this whole prison experience a heck of a lot worse for myself when:

"Gabey-boy!"

It's Nick. Freaking Nick. Oh, thank God it's just Nick. He knew I was here, of course. He was my "one call." I phoned him at work on his first day to tell him I was locked up and his father was passed out on a beach chair in the garage. Somehow, Nick got his friend to cover for him so he could supervise Grandpa, but we agreed that he'd keep Gramps away from the police station at all costs. And speaking of cost, neither of us had two pennies to rub together, let alone the five grand it would take to make bail—so coming by for a visit was kind of pointless. Besides, it's not like I need anyone to protect me in here—not like I'm scared or anything.

"Nick, what the—"

"Before you say anything, Grandpa is at home. He's fine. John and his mother are looking after him until we get home."

"We?"

"Yeah, I posted bail. You're free to go."

The officer who escorted Nick to my cell pulls a key ring off his belt with no less than forty-six thousand keys on it. He pulls one out of the mix and unlocks the cell door on the first try. Lucky bastard.

Or maybe that's me. I don't know. And I sure as hell don't know where Nick pulled five grand from. I mean, the dude never wears hats and rarely wears sleeves—it's not like he's a freaking magician or a wizard or anything. So, what the hell? I decide to wait until we're in the car to ask him about it.

"Cab's waiting outside for us," he says as we pick up my belongings at the front of the precinct and head for the door.

"Cab? Why didn't you take my car? There's an extra set—"

"The Trans-Am's been impounded, Gabe. It's evidence now."

Crap. *How much—how little—how much—how little.*

You keep one promise to Dad and another one somehow ends up in an impound lot.

"Let's just go home," I say. And we exit the precinct and head out to the street where our chariot awaits.

The interior reeked of old lady perfume mixed with anchovies, and the driver had this hideous wart on the back of his neck that I thought would sing to me at any moment.

I slide the Plexiglas shield to its closed position—for a little privacy—and say, "How did you manage this, Nick? You holding out on me? Are you a rich oil baron or something?"

"Archie. My buddy down at work."

"Yeah?"

"We negotiated a payroll loan. I'll work it off in a few months."

I shake my head and watch the meter on the cab increase with each quarter-mile. What have I done? Here I am complaining about Nick every day, telling John and anyone who'd listen how horrible the guy is, and I put him in this position—starting day two of a job already in the hole for more than I've ever made in my life. What the hell is wrong with me?

"Uncle Nick," I say. "I'm so sorry. I—" and I have to pause because my throat's getting all tight and I have to strain to get the words out.

"Hey, Gabe. It's not your fault, man."

He pats my leg like he used to do when I was about three years old. "And you're not alone. He's my father, not yours. What happened is a tragedy—for all involved, including what's-his-name?"

"Timmy." The adorable bastard. I can feel my punting foot start to twitch.

"Yeah, Timmy. And all of us. We're gonna make the best of this and we're gonna get through it."

I appreciate all the optimism from my Uncle Nick, but come on. Does he listen to himself speak? We have no money. Scratch that. We have less than no money. Significantly less. We have no one to take care of Gramps on a consistent basis. I'll probably spend the rest of my life in prison and the Trans-Am is being stripped for parts as we speak. And Nick says 'we'll get through this?' How exactly will we get through this? Things are looking pretty bleak.

"I can't afford a lawyer," I say, "They'll probably appoint me with one of those guys who studied law at the Collegiate University of the Grand Bahamas or something."

"You do have a lawyer," Nick says calmly.

"I do?"

"Yeah. It's me!"

Suddenly I'm thinking about settling for the Grand Bahamian. I laugh—actually just start cracking up because the idea of my oafish uncle strapping on a monkey suit and organ-grinding his way around a courtroom is the most ridiculous thing I've ever heard in my life.

"You?" I ask, incredulous. "Did you say *you*?"

"Yes. Me, Gabe. I did go to law school. You were pretty young, so I doubt you remember but—"

"Wait. What? Law school? *You*?"

"I never passed the Bar," he says. "I ran off with some girl. Your dad warned me."

"Skye," I whisper, and I'm not even trying to say it out loud. But I can't help it—that day on the tire swing. The argument. The memories keep flashing before me. Only this time they make sense.

"What's that?" Nick asks.

"Oh, nothing," I say. "Never mind."

The cab pulls up in front of our house and Nick fumbles through his wallet. He gathers his final few bills and folds them over in his hand. Studies them. "Sometimes your life can take a detour without you seeing it."

"I know," I say. "And I'm proud to have you defend me."

Nick smiles and hands the money to the driver.

"Thanks for believing in me," he says. Then he reaches inside his jacket and pulls out a thin, waffle-shaped disk. The smell of anise overpowers the stench of the cab for a moment. "I tried to keep your mother's tradition alive," he says. "It's the only one that didn't crumble into a million pieces. Merry Christmas."

He offers the pizzelle to me and I take it in my hands.

"Doesn't look too freaking bad," I say. Then I take a bite. It's rock hard and tastes like a burnt Twizzler. I cough a few crumbs out on the back of the driver's seat.

"Merry Christmas, Nick," I say. And then I choke down the rest of that disgusting pizzelle right in front of him. I figure it's the least I can do for my new attorney.

15

BREAKING FREE

We're pinned down behind enemy lines. A commando unit of starstruck, freshman girls holds the front along corridor A, brandishing giggle rifles and firing them off with reckless abandon. A bunch of nosy bastards—the world's supply of future journalists—form a rag-tag group of mercenaries that have corridor B sealed off with muckraking mortar fire. And the doorway to the outside world is blockaded by the most evil and destructive force known to man—the local media.

John and I swing our packs over our shoulders and strap them on tight. Our steely eyes meet and lock in a hollow glaze. It's "the 1000-yard stare" a soldier gets after being under siege too long.

A slight nod is all John needs to set our strategy in motion. We're lifelong platoon mates, the two of us. We share the same brain, so we both know there's only one way to negotiate the field of battle.

We take brisk strides, pretend nothing is different even as enemy hands clutch at our packs and breathe on the backs of our necks. When we reach the concourse leading to corridor A, John takes a quick left and I bounce off to the right so we can flank the enemy on both sides. All attention diverts from John, and the rebel fighters mount their efforts on me alone. Perfect. Our plan is in action. Between heads and passing shoulders, I catch a glimpse of John moving undetected toward our rendezvous.

I push forward through the swarm. Questions and phrases drone together in a constant buzz so only a stray word or syllable here or there can find a clear path to my eardrums. My pace quickens, and the cinderblock walls swell around me. The bite of the cold linoleum collides with the soles of my sneakers. First the left. Then the right. Then the left again—each individual step a power plant full of friction that slows me down, keeps me from our checkpoint. And the words and phrases zing past me like stray artillery fire:

"Wanted for . . ."

". . . serious?"

"Gabe is so . . ."

". . . to the police."

". . . his life."

"such an outlaw . . ."

I can't avoid them all. A catch phrase or two pelt my skin like tiny polysyllabic bullets. Up ahead I see John reach the end of the hallway and cut down a dark set of stairs beside the entrance to the theater—our rendezvous. I know it's now or never.

I hook the straps of my pack with my thumbs, fake like I'm about to turn around and head the opposite direction. Then I burst through an opening and sprint half way down the hallway. But I'm not much of a stolen base threat, so the swarm gains on me. The tips of John's fingers swing wildly on his arms down below the stairs. I'm almost to the safe zone. I'm picking up ground.

But then something crashes against the side of my foot. A stray book. And I'm teetering. Rumbling. I'm stumbling and fighting with every last ounce of strength to keep my balance. A hand clutches the canvas of my backpack as my palm squeals against the waxy linoleum. And that's all I need. Momentum.

Suddenly, I'm back upright and gaining speed. I hit the top of the stairs and watch John's eyes expand to the size of grapefruits. He sees the horde closing in on me from behind. He spins and punches a tiny code into the Sentry lock on the door handle—one that every senior knows by the end of four years at Schuylkill. I take two steps at a time and watch as a sliver of sunlight seeps through the open door. John swings it open and we're smothered in light. I hit the bottom stair and dive through the opening. John slams the door shut behind us and we hear the horde on the other side crashing and banging against it. But it's too late. We made it to the student parking lot, therefore, we are free. Or so we think.

"What are you two doing?" I hear as I push myself up off the asphalt and brush off my pants. It's Coach Foley. He looks puzzled, but something's missing—the red face and the bulging veins, I suppose. For once, the guy doesn't look totally pissed.

"It's a mad house in there," I say. "We had to make a grand escape." Foley looks at me. He stares down at my shoes and works his way up to my face. He's sizing me up. Seeing if I'm full of shit. This is usually about the time he reminds me how bad I am at baseball and makes me wonder if maybe I should take up bowling instead. But he doesn't say anything. Just keeps looking at me, and there's something weird. Something soft in his eyes like, I don't know, maybe the guy feels sorry for me.

"Sir?" John asks when the whole situation starts to get a little creepy.

"Oh," Foley says. "I, uh, was just thinking." He pauses when a few more of the horde pound loudly on the other side of the door. "Just thinking, LoScuda. Are you coming out for the team this year?" I start to say something but he cuts me off. "You know, assuming everything works out."

"Yes, sir," I tell him. "I'm planning on it. Second base."

"Well, I'll see you out there," he says. Then he walks past us, punches in the same code John used on the door just moments prior, and bursts through to cover us—and sacrifice himself to the horde on our behalf.

"What the hell was that?" I ask John. He starts to shrug, but there's no time to continue his thoughts because, suddenly, we're right back in the line of fire. I look over my shoulder and see a battalion of reporters with legal notepads tucked under tweed jackets and cameramen wielding cameras on their shoulders like bazookas. We've been spotted and the enemy is in hot pursuit.

John and I take off at a full sprint into the open canyon of the Schuylkill parking lot. With the Trans-Am in the impound lot, our escape vehicle is Lily Chen's Honda Prism—not exactly a road warrior, but better than boots on the ground. Mrs. Chen, in a moment that should be recorded in the annals of history, felt sorry for me—and maybe for herself at the thought of having to transport her driver's-licenseless son all over town each day. She entrusted the car to me. I'm serious.

"For school purposes only," she said sternly as she handed me the keys. "No joy riding or craziness. Drive slow, Gabriel."

Something told me "driving slow" was not something she'd expect me to abide by when a legion of hell raisers was hot on our tails. With reporters firing off questions, John and I race for the Prism. I pull out the keys as we hit the doors and immediately start fumbling them around in my hands. Typical, Gabe. So much for second base. The battalion of reporters is nearly upon us when I find the right match and slide it in the keyhole. John swings himself inside the car like he's in an episode of *Dukes of Hazard*. He slams the door and punches the lock down. I'm about to follow suit when I hear my name.

"Gabe?"

I look up and see Marlie approaching from the next row of cars. Her hair shines in little ripples. I'm glued to the spot. The reporters are now within firing range.

"Mr. LoScuda!" I hear one yell. "Are you the one responsible—"

I look at Marlie. She's smiling and her blue eyes twinkle at me, like they're saying, "Come here Gabe. Come here and see what I need from you. Gabe—"

"Gabe!" It's John and his voice jars me from my trance. I still can't move.

"Just a couple of questions, Mr. LoScuda!"

"Mr. LoScuda, please—" then I feel a tight grip on my backpack, as if freaking Hulk Hogan himself is yanking me like a yo-yo, and I'm in the car. John snatches the keys out of my hand and cranks the ignition.

"Mr. LoScuda!"

But it's too late. The car is in gear and we're off. I take a speed bump at about twenty miles per hour and feel the shocks wince under us. But John's not even phased. He keeps shouting, "Go! Go! Go!" over and over again like he's stuck in a loop. The reporters and Marlie and the rest of the cars in the Schuylkill High lot shrink in the rearview and we both ease back in our seats. We're safe. For now.

Even though I promised Mrs. Chen that her car would be used for school purposes only, there's one more thing to do before I take John home.

"Where the hell are you going?" John asks when we pass the turn for his street and head toward downtown.

"One quick stop," I tell him.

"But my mom said—"

"My mom said blah. My mom said wah." I say it like we're in kindergarten and John had just stolen my modeling clay or something.

"Look," I tell him. "It'll only take a minute. I promised Sofia."

"Oh, I see," he says.

"You see what?"

"Nothing."

I keep driving, not interested in where this conversation is headed.

"Just that it's getting pretty obvious."

"What's getting obvious? What the hell are you talking about, John?"

"You like her."

"Who?"

"Oh come on, Gabe. Sofia. Are you gonna sit there and — "

"Yes, John. I am. She's a friend. We're both going through some shit right now in case you haven't noticed."

John doesn't say anything. I look at him out of the corner of my eye. He shrugs. "Besides," I continue, "did you see Marlie today?"

"Yeah, I saw her. She almost got us ambushed."

I shake my head.

"She's the one, John. She's the one."

"Yeah. Whatever."

I pull the Prism into a parallel spot next to Liberty Park, which is nothing more than a glorified traffic circle with a bench and a couple of potted plants. I guess that's the extent of city beautification projects these days. The park is right outside the main entrance of the veteran's hospital, so we meet Sofia there between visitation hours.

She's sitting on the bench when we step out of the car. She seems oblivious to everything around her, headphones blaring as usual a few decibels above the passing traffic and her eyes focused down on the surface of a steaming cup of coffee. She pulls on the filter of a cigarette and blows the smoke out through her nostrils in a single, industrial puff. She brushes a stray ash off her black skirt and then runs a black fingernail the length of her black fishnets down to the laces of her black, Converse All-Stars. She fiddles with the laces as we sit down. She's not startled. Big surprise.

"Hey," she says as she rests her headphones down around her neck. "How was school, kiddos?"

"Like being hunted down by cannibals," I say.

"I figured," she says. "Your ugly mug was on the news all day in there." She waves her cigarette in the direction of the hospital.

"How's she doing?" I ask.

"Not one of her best days," she says. "But she's tough. I've seen her get through worse." Her voice trails off and, for the first time since I met her, she seems scared. Vulnerable.

"Yeah," I say as Sofia grabs a small sketchpad off the bench and buries her face in it. "If she's anything like you, cancer better run and hide." That perks her up a little.

"How about you?" she asks.

"Don't let him tell you differently," John chimes in from his perch behind the bench. "He's enjoying every minute of this crap."

"What?" Who the hell is this kid? Ten minutes ago he was my platoon brother. Now he's making me look like a dipshit—not that I care or anything. But he keeps it up. Just won't let it go.

"You should see yourself, Gabe. Pretty soon I think you might set up a table at lunch and charge for autographs. It kind of makes me want to puke."

"Puke? Are you serious? Didn't you see me running from that place with you today? Was I imagining that?"

"Maybe for my sake. Once Marlie was in the picture I thought you were gonna negotiate me to the enemy."

I'm about to lay into the kid like never before when the whole damn argument gets interrupted. By laughter. Sofia's laughter. Her sketchbook is gripped tight against her chest and she's about two loud chuckles away from rolling off the bench and into the street.

"What's so funny?" I ask and I'm feeling pretty crummy right now— the way you feel when everyone's laughing and you don't know why.

"You," she says between breaths. "I just imagined you and this Barbie girl together."

"Marlie," I say.

"Whatever. Is there a difference?"

"Not really," John says, and now they're both laughing in my face. I swear I can't win with these people. Laugh at me because I'm a nobody and then laugh twice as hard when I actually become a somebody.

"Yeah, yeah, yeah. Keep on laughing," I say. "We'll see if that's still the case when I take Marlie to the prom. We'll have to double date, of course, with John and his hand. Maybe we'll drop by the hospital afterwards and see what kind of imprint the folding chair leaves on your ass, Sofia."

I stop, realizing I have stepped a little beyond the realms of friendly sparring. John looks shocked—like he just swallowed a blowfish and it's all caught up somewhere near his Adam's apple. Sofia is stone-faced, but she dives back into the rescue of her sketchpad. I feel kind of guilty, so I try to soften the blow.

"Whatever," I say, "I want all of this to end. I want to go back to my quiet, little nothing life and just move on."

"Then confess."

The words come out of her mouth like jagged icicles and she doesn't bother to lift her gaze from the drawing.

"I did confess," I say. "That's why—"

"No, Gabe." John's voice is forceful, steady. He means business. "She means the truth. Confess the truth."

And here we are again. Back to sitting with the two imposters who pretend they're my friends; spineless cowards who know nothing of the power of a man's word; who know nothing of the bond shared between father and son, and the promises one makes to his own blood—living or dead.

"No way!" I say flatly. "Out of the question."

Then I'm up off the bench and I'm gone. I mean, I just escaped a raving horde of lunatics at Schuylkill High; I'm not about to sit here and get devoured by my so-called friends. I leave John and Sofia sitting on the bench together and walk home alone. They deserve each other. The bastards.

Oh, and I hope John has fun driving home on the merits of his Schuylkill High School student ID. Something tells me the yearbook committee doesn't hold the same jurisdiction as the Department of Motor Vehicles. Whatever. He'll figure it out.

Promise

Dad often claimed the best way to watch a baseball game was not to watch it at all. And yet he never missed a single game of Fightin' Phils action in my life. His trick consisted of three objects: a cooler full of Yuengling, a beach chair, and a handheld radio that was so old it looked like he mined it out of the archives of the Smithsonian.

I once came across a few lines of poetry by a Serbian-American poet named Dejan Stojanovic fittingly titled "Simplicity." In just four lines, Dejan captured my dad's pre-game Phillies routine better than I could have done with a video camera and a doubleheader on tap. He wrote, "The most complicated skill / Is to be simple. / To say more while saying less / Is the secret of being simple." Taking that as a universal truth, my father might have been one of the simplest creatures on the planet.

On hot, July days Dad would carry his simple items about twenty feet from the back of the garage to the driveway. He'd set them up like he was in the parking lot at Veteran's Stadium before a game, tailgating with the rest of the Philadelphia wildlife. He'd crack the cap on a Yuengy and tune his radio to 1210 AM. "Screw TV," he'd say. Then he'd fiddle with the extendable rabbit ears with only a few of the softer vulgarities under his breath. Sooner or later the static would give way to the hush of the stadium and the bass-drenched voice of one Harry Kalas—Dad's play-by-play man. Maybe the greatest of all time.

"Why would I want to miss this, Gabey?" he'd say. "Sitting in a hot ballpark? No Harry? That's not baseball." It was stone cold, middle-aged logic at its best.

Of course, Dad would never make the connection between his choice of profession and our annual, Cal Ripken-like streak of rarely seeing the inside of an actual ballpark. At least not out loud. But it always kind of bothered me. See, Dad being a teacher gave him all sorts of time in the summer to go on any number of adventures with his family. Problem was, the salary—you know, only getting paid ten months out of the year—didn't help us accomplish much of anything. By my calculations, we missed exactly eighty opportunities to watch a live Phillies game every season. At least that left us with one home game. Dad's promise—his once a year departure from the simplicity he thrived upon. I guess promises trump the simple life in the same way an ace beats a deuce. In fact, I'd guess a promise trumps most anything.

He'd say, "If I have to leave my beach chair for a game, we might as well do it right." And that's what we'd do. Once a year. One game. Great seats. All-you-can-eat. Just me, Dad, Gramps, the sounds of the game, and about two pounds of ballpark franks. It was glorious.

A few weeks after my eighth birthday, Dad hoisted me up on his shoulders. He walked us out through the garage—past his beach chair leaning up against the wall, and his radio lying silent on the workbench. There was no cooler in sight.

On the driveway, he popped the Volvo's passenger door and slid me in the car. "I promised you a game," he said as he slid his weather-beaten Phillies hat out of his back pocket and slapped it down over his neatly combed hair. "We got the Astros today. What do you think?"

"Ten nothing, Phillies," I said. To be honest, I didn't care about the result. All I could think about were pink puffs of cotton candy and rivers of chocolate ice cream melting down the side of a cone.

"Ten nothing? With Nolan Ryan on the mound?" He chuckled a bit under his breath, then said to no one in particular, "My son must be crazy." Then he hopped in the driver's seat, and flicked on the radio while the car was still in reverse.

The game was in the top of the first already. We were late. As usual. Sometimes I think Dad made it that way on purpose—almost like a compromise. It allowed him to keep his one-game promise to me and still catch a few minutes of playful banter between Harry the "K" and his on-air sidekick, Hall-of-Famer Richie Ashburn. It was a cool tradition, I guess. I'd pop a whole pack of Doublemint—all five sticks—in my mouth and pretend I had a full lip of chew stored in there. Dad would swing by Grandpa's house on the way, and we'd head east on the expressway, following the winding glaze of the Schuylkill River as it slogged casual canoe paddlers and UPenn crew teams alike between the columns of ancient oak trees and brick-faced boathouses. We'd snake past the art museum on the way and I'd make Dad swear to me that the mountainous pile of steps in front were the same ones scaled by Rocky Balboa. Every time. And then we'd pull off into South Philly, park a few blocks off of Broad Street, and be inside the stadium by the bottom of the second.

Veteran's Stadium stood there on Broad, waiting for us like a 70s-era fortress. Dad grabbed my hand and turned our tickets over to the usher, who ripped them at the perforations and handed them back. Then we stepped through the turnstile into once-a-year glory.

"Section 326," Dad said to Gramps as he glanced down at the ticket stubs. "Right behind the plate."

"As always," Gramps said. He tipped the brim of his Philadelphia A's cap to his son—Grandpa always had to be a throwback—and Dad nodded in reply. Sometimes it was easier to steal a sign from the visitors' third base coach than it was to figure out the simplest communication between these guys.

We walked around the interior concourse of the 300 level—a hollow cavern with sticky floors, fans in their red and white pinstripes zigzagging in all directions, and the perpetual stench of stale beer rising up in plumes like mustard gas. Dad gripped my hand and led us past a set of old bleachers, down a ramp, and out into the open air. My eyes darted to the green of the artificial turf; to the thick, white lines that cut precise incisions from each corner of home plate to the imposing, yellow foul poles that loomed overhead; to the pennants—all perfect, little slices of pie—that waved at me from the top of the stadium; to the tops of the dugouts—one painted in the triumphant, script lettering of the home team, the other simply printed 'visitors.'

It was like a supersonic slideshow of boyhood wonder. A kaleidoscope of our nation's pastime. And it was like that, for me, every time Dad fulfilled his promise and brought me there. To the Vet. Philadelphia's own Roman Coliseum. The only place where three generations of LoScudas could sit side-by-side, spit sunflower seeds on the ground, and shout obscenities at perfect strangers—all while solving every flaw in the basic structure of the entire franchise, while second-guessing every single call made by the manager (and probably the umpires), and forecasting the complete statistical output of every Phillies player from now until 2055. That usually started around the fourth inning—the Phils' second time through the order.

"This kid's got promise," Grandpa said to Dad. I cracked a seed between my teeth and watched Von Hayes stride up to the plate. He was all arms and legs; a tall left-handed giraffe with a mullet hanging out the back of his helmet. Dad shook his head.

"Yeah, but will he live up to it?"

"He knocked in eighty-two runs with the Indians," Grandpa said. "I think that shows promise." There was a loud crack and a wave of people poured out of their seats in the next section. A second later a foul ball—just a tiny speck from this distance—shot back past them like a bullet. Strike one.

"Well, he'd better show something," Dad said as Hayes reset himself in the box. "We gave up the farm for him." There was a smattering of boos on a low outside pitch. Hayes shook his head at the umpire. Strike two.

"Trillo and Vukovich are washed up," Grandpa argued.

"Forget Trillo and Vuke. What about Franco?"

"Julio Franco? He's a prospect. They never pan out." Hayes took a mighty swing-and-a-miss and the catcher fired the ball down to third like a missile. I watched it bounce from infielder to infielder like a pinball machine. Around the horn. I love that stuff.

"We'll see," Dad said. And Gramps decided to drop his side of the argument.

By the end of the sixth inning, with the Phils unable to get anything going against Nolan Ryan and the defense unable to catch anything not in virus form, the score was barely memorable. Eight to one or seven to two. I can't remember. But I can say I'd filled myself, by the mid innings, with everything from popcorn to peanuts to Cracker Jacks. I might have actually been the kid they sang about in the song. But I wasn't satisfied. No cotton candy. And you haven't actually been to a ball game unless you've had yourself a cotton candy. Maybe that's just my rule, but it's a good one. I wasn't leaving the Vet without at least one huge, puffy mouthful of the stuff.

"Dad, when can I have cotton candy?" I asked.

"As soon as you see a vendor."

Problem was, I hadn't seen a cotton candy vendor trucking his usual eight pack of pink, fluffy globes all night. I knew, once we hit the seventh inning stretch, all would be lost because that's when the vendors seemed to up and vanish. It was like there was a dastardly mastermind hidden somewhere under the concourse level—in the Cave of Concessions. He'd push a button midway through the seventh and all his little vending minions would dematerialize on the spot and converge before his throne. And they'd spend the next three innings bashing all the whiny brats they were forced to serve that evening. Kind of like a form of concessional therapy that went something like:

"See that snotty bastard in Section 326?"

"The one crying for his cotton candy?"

"That's the one. Well, I've got his cotton candy right here." And then he stuffs the whole damn lot—tray and all—in the toilet, and there's a loud flush.

I noticed these kinds of things at the ballpark. They stood out to me a lot more than the depth and positioning of the second baseman with one out and runners at the corners—much to Dad's displeasure. But hey—a kid's gotta get his sugar.

"I don't see any vendors," I told Dad when it became impossible to stifle my anxiety for even one more pitch.

"Be patient, Gabe. They'll be around."

"It's almost the end of the seventh inning," I whined.

"We can get one out in the parking lot."

"I don't want parking lot cotton candy!" My whining reached a new level of annoying—by design, of course. Dad hated that kind of crap, especially during a baseball game.

"Look, Gabe—"

"But I want ballpark cotton—"

"Alright, alright," he said and he looked over at Gramps who shook his head solemnly. I knew this would work. "I'll take you when the inning is over."

This was unacceptable. An outrage. I would never let it stand. "I can go myself," I said.

"Oh, sure. It really seems like you're grown up enough to handle yourself here—in a crowded ballpark."

"I know where it is, Dad. I—"

"Sal." The voice of reason as always, Gramps was golden. "Let the kid be a man today. We're at the Vet. He's not a baby anymore."

Dad was silent. Brooding. He looked at Gramps with a blankness in his eyes. Then he glanced over his shoulder to the tunnel along the concourse. I looked, too. It was empty, but for a single usher in his white Phillies polo shirt and a pair of khakis. Very official. No danger there.

"Make me a promise," Dad said. "Go directly to the cotton candy stand, buy what you need, and come directly back." He pulled a ten-dollar bill out of his wallet and held it before me. "Will you do that?"

"Yes," I said. "I promise."

"I want change." He handed me the bill and watched as I climbed the mountain of stairs up to the tunnel and passed through into the darkness.

Once inside, I realized the concourse at Veteran's Stadium was not built with the intention of ever having someone less than six feet tall walk on it.

It was like being trapped in a stampede. I took two steps and was nearly beheaded by a stroller the size of a tank. I sidestepped my way around a group of staggering Phillies fans as they shouted epithets of the "You suck!" "Go home!" variety to an elderly couple that happened to be wearing Astros hats. I clung to the wall and inched my way along it like a little kid trying to skate his way around an ice rink for the first time. The cotton candy stand was in sight. Only thirty or forty more paces.

And then I realized, man, I really needed to use the bathroom. I looked up and, as luck would have it, a sign with a two-legged stick figure—not wearing a little triangle for a dress—hung above me. I knew I'd promised Dad just to the candy stand and back, but I figured he'd be pretty annoyed if I sat back down and then asked him to take me to the bathroom two seconds later. So I pushed through the doorway—it was door less, really more of a gaping crack in the concourse wall with a putrid odor emanating from it. Old men, young men, little kids with their fathers standing behind them, all pushed forward at once like a school of salmon swimming upstream. Only the stream we were all pushing towards was like no stream I'd ever seen. It flowed directly through the room along a flatiron trough that'd been dug into the floor for just this purpose. Men and boys stood elbow-to-elbow, pieces in hands, and relieved themselves all over the wall, the floor, most likely on each other. I wanted no part of this, so I spun around and swam back downstream, through the wreaking chasm, and out into the concourse. I could hold it.

I resumed my path along the wall, pushing past old men in maroon and baby blue Phils gear with the name "Schmidt" stitched on the back. I stepped on half of a mushy hot dog bun and squashed it off the bottom of my shoe, leaving it gooey and sticky with each new step.

I finally reached the stand and got in line. There had to be twenty people— like Pope John Paul was making change behind the counter or something. I stood there with my hand in my pocket holding back the flow, sacrificing my own dignity for a chance to eat a bunch of sugar spun around in a giant hairdryer. It was starting to seem kind of ridiculous, even to me, after ten minutes of standing in the same spot. Then something caught my attention. A loud thud. The kind of noise you might hear if, say, a gymnast mistimed a jump and landed belly-first on a wrestling mat. It intrigued me. Then I heard a few cheers—and they weren't coming from the field.

I spun around in line and craned my neck as high as it would reach. And then I saw it. Probably the coolest thing I'd ever seen in my young life. Just across the stream of people on the concourse was a mass of black netting that hung from the ceiling in a distinct square—like a cage. Planted inside was a giant, yellow cushion with a cartoony-looking catcher printed on the front. The words 'Speed Pitch' were scripted out above him, and there was a tiny instrument with flashing, red numbers planted beside the whole set up. A radar gun. I watched as a kid in his late teens reared back and pounded the mitt. The gun flashed a few digits and the kid shook his head in disgust. He handed the attendant a ten-dollar bill and grabbed three more balls from the bucket below him.

I looked down at the crinkled bill in my hand. Then I stepped a bit to one side and noted how the candy line was still longer than one of those dragons you see during Chinese New Year. The decision was made. I popped out of line and froggered my way across the mass of pedestrians on the concourse. I walked right up to the Speed Pitch attendant and held out my money. He looked at me for a minute. Then he smiled.

"You big enough to reach, son?" he asked.

"Of course I can reach," I said. "Just give me the ball." He handed me a ball and I took my spot on the portable rubber. The full windup, just like Dad had shown me. I reared back and fired the biscuit with all the juice I could muster. The laces flipped and spun through the air and the ball collided with the backstop. A little outside, but plenty of distance. My eyes shot to the radar gun. The digits blinked and rolled a few times, and then a bold, red number registered on its face: 36.

Thirty-six? That's not even fast enough to get a speeding ticket in my neighborhood. Thirty-six. Ugh. The attendant looked at me from atop his snooty nose. "Want to take another stab?" he asked, holding back a laugh.

"No, thanks," I said rubbing a fake sore spot on my shoulder. "Think I need to stretch it out."

"I see," he said. He handed me this cheesy certificate that documented my results, and then he was on to the next concourse-level pitcher. I was once again cast aside into the sea of pedestrians. Only this time I wasn't thinking about getting flattened by fat guys with funnel cakes, or about holding a pink wad of cotton candy between my cheeks. This time I was thinking about one thing—the number thirty-six. Mark of the wuss. Printed in big, black numerals on this crappy, cardboard certificate I'd already folded in half before anyone could see it.

Of course, with all the focus on my lack of pitching prowess I kind of forgot about the actual game and about Dad and Grandpa and the big-time promise I'd made them. I had forgotten how simple my original task had been and about how much more complicated I had suddenly made it. By the time it all dawned on me and I spun myself around for a venture back to Section 326, it was too late. Nothing looked familiar. Or maybe everything looked familiar because the whole place was a repeating line of the same stands over and over again like some kind of grease-riddled equation.

I was lost. No matter how many times I turned around or ventured up a new tunnel, there was nothing that made me feel like I was getting any closer to Section 326. Suddenly, the concourse felt like the pits of Hell, like the temperature had risen to at least 75,000 degrees and the sweat rolled down from under my cap in tiny, repeating marbles. I started to panic and could feel my eyes start to well up. *Should I tell someone? Would it be okay to trust a stranger in this case? Should I talk to one of the ancient mariners they employed as ushers?* I was too scared and too embarrassed to do any of those things. So I continued to wander the stadium, up long hallways and through the spherical arteries of the old fortress.

Finally, when it felt like all my breaths were somehow stalled inside my lungs, I decided to walk back out through one of the tunnels and see the light of day. When I did, I was in for a big surprise. Section 326 was completely on the other side of the stadium, across an entire baseball field, behind a reinforced mesh screen, and at least one hundred feet closer to sea level. I was in the freaking cheap seats. The upper deck. All the way up near the Jumbotron—which also greeted me with a surprise message. My face, on a picture I recognized from inside Dad's wallet. It was plastered up there on the screen under the words "Have you seen this child?" in a place normally reserved for the stats and bio of the current batter—in this case, Mike Schmidt.

I looked down to the plate. Even Schmidty was staring up at my ugly mug on the Jumbotron and shaking his head. *Great.* It wasn't bad enough that I was lost in a stadium that was so infamous they had to build holding cells under it, or that the Phils were losing, or that I never got my cotton candy, or that my fastest pitch couldn't break a pane of glass. I also had to see my freaking hero laugh right in my face—a face that was standing behind me at least three stories tall for all of Philadelphia to see. I guess that's what happens when you break a promise. I guess that's what happens when you fail to keep things simple.

I sat down in an abandoned seat, in an abandoned row, in the most abandoned section of the ballpark and lowered the brim of my cap over my eyes. I could feel the warmth of my tears between my fingers, and then I felt a touch. A hand on my shoulder. The smell of Aqua Velva.

I don't know how he found me or what he thought I was doing way up in the rafters where they hang the division pennants and where no one has officially bought a ticket since the early 70s. I never bothered to ask and he never questioned me. When he saw me sitting alone among an empty row of seats, Gramps just laughed a little under his breath and shook his head. "Come on, Champ," he said. And that was it. Sweet relief.

Maybe too much relief, because the last thing I remember from that dreadful trip to the ballpark was something I'd forgotten to do earlier on my concourse-level expedition. Take a leak. And, well, it's a darn good thing I'd never promised Dad I'd keep his car seat dry on the ride home.

16

GABE PLEA(SE)

I had a whole week to let the betrayal sink in. To hear Sofia say "confess" and John whisper "ben dan" over and over again like echoes through time. In the shower; at my desk as Mastro droned on about Elizabeth Browning or Mary Shelley or one of the Bronte sisters; even in that half-second between awake and sleep—where my eyes flip open and search the room for someone, anyone. But they're only whispers. Not real. Just reminders of a drastic split in the path. I'm on one side—the one with hanging limbs and bramble and thick brush. John and Sofia are on the other—the one with a yellow brick road. But they don't know those bricks are forged in pyrite—fool's gold. I do. And I've already made up my mind. Long ago. Like Robert Frost, I'm taking the road less traveled. I hope, at least for Grandpa, it will make all the difference.

I haven't seen or heard from Sofia since our meeting at Liberty Park. When I stormed off, I wasn't trying to be dramatic. I wasn't looking for her to chase me down the street like in one of those romantic comedies where, somehow, in mid-chase, the love interest is able to hire out the services of a traveling harpist who'd plant herself at just the right spot—the crescendo of the chase—and strum a melodious tune that I will meditate on and then realize, in a flash, "They're right!"

I wasn't looking for the grand gesture, because nobody in real life is really looking for that kind of crap. No. I simply wanted to get away—from the people I knew could never understand the decision I've made.

So I avoided Sofia and the hospital completely. I still had to ride to school and back each day with John. Somehow, the car—Lily's car—appeared mysteriously on my driveway the morning after the argument, even after I left it behind and walked home from Liberty Park.

We drove together both ways in total silence, me flicking through stations and pretending to know the lyrics to songs, and John with his eyes burning holes through the pages of his chemistry textbook. At school, we were strangers. We split in the parking lot in the mornings, avoided each other's paths all day, and then reconnected for the same, silent ride home. About the only time I'd see John during the school day was at lunch. He'd sit in a remote corner of the cafeteria, never raising his eyes from the same chemistry book.

But it wasn't my concern. I was at Marlie's table. I had better things to do. Like captivate my fans, starting with Marlie and Mandy So-and-So. I was more than happy to reply "Yes, I did really start a prison riot," when Marlie asked about the many assorted perils of my single night in a holding cell; and I may have jumped a little at the opportunity to say, "Oh, of course Officer Patterson's scared of me. Do you see him anywhere?" when Mandy asked me about my run-ins with the good detective. In fact, not having John around is kind of great. I've been carrying the kid around like a bottle of girl repellent for years.

I had Mr. Perdomo jack-up my hours so I could keep busy and focus on tasks that only comprised my present and not my imminent future. The rest of my time was spent preparing with the lawyer—which was great because I live with the guy. Uncle Nick's really been surprising me. He might actually know what he's doing when it comes to this legal stuff.

In fact, he saved my butt a few times this week already. Like yesterday. The phone was ringing off the hook. I knew it was a reporter from one of the local papers because they'd been relentless ever since news came out that a date had been set for my preliminary hearing. I only found out about the hearing when this creepy guy in a hoodie with slicked-back hair knocked on the front door a few days ago. I answered it and he handed me a yellow envelope and made me sign my name on a clipboard. The top line of the return address read, "Bucks County Courthouse", so I felt a little dizzy as I tore into it.

But before I could rip the letter out, a voice on the television report caught my attention and ruined my surprise. The reporter said, "All eyes in this suburban community will be on Gabe LoScuda next week as he takes the stand to enter his plea in the hit and run accident that injured little Timmy Mullins . . ." That's when Uncle Nick burst out of the kitchen with a roast beef sandwich in hand. He flicked off the television mid-report. Then he swiped the letter out of my hand before I could read a single line.

"Let your lawyer handle this garbage," he told me. "Anyone asks you a question from now on, the only acceptable answer is 'no comment'. You got it?" I nodded. So, when I answered the phone yesterday and a reporter from the Bucks Dispatch asked, "What plea do you plan to enter in the—"

I cut him right off with Nick's response of choice: "No comment!" Then I hung up, just like I'd done for the ten or twenty identical calls I answered in the past few days alone. Only, each time I slammed the phone down on the hook it made me worry a little more about what I'd say when I was up in front of the judge and jury.

"So, what's this hearing thing about," I finally ask Nick as if I'm not petrified by the thought of it.

"The whole thing is procedural," he tells me. "If we do it right, it shouldn't take long. All you have to do is say 'guilty' when the judge asks for your plea."

"Then what?"

"He'll hand down his sentence. No need for a trial if you already admitted to the crime."

"It's a good thing we prepped for this, Nick."

"Yeah, well, I was getting my legs under me." I feel my eyeballs start to roll back in the sockets a bit, but I steady them because I know he's just trying to help.

"What do you expect out of the sentence?"

He's silent for a moment, which scares me.

"Hard to say, Gabe. A crime like this could get you five years in Pennsylvania."

"Five years?!"

"But there's nothing on your record and you're admitting to the wrong doing. Judges love that crap, Gabey. I think I can talk you out of the jail time and bargain for a stack of lesser penalties."

Nick jots a few notes on his legal pad and pushes the pen back behind his ear. I have to say, the dude really looks the part. I never thought I'd say this, but I actually have confidence in the guy.

"What kinds of lesser charges?" I ask.

"Loss of license, probation, fines, community service. Stuff like that." The options don't sound great, but picking up trash and sucking down gas fumes on the side of some highway beats having a cellmate any day. Maybe this decision to shield Grandpa and live up to Dad's promise will be the easiest one I ever make in my life. Maybe Uncle Nick will come to the rescue after all and this whole thing will blow over without detonating every aspect of my life. "Of course," Nick continues after jotting a few more notes, "you never can tell with cases like this one. Lots of people following it. You might get a hard-ass judge." Maybe I better prepare myself for the worst. Maybe the bailiffs are cooking my last meal as we speak, and the warden is already inking up the rubber on the stamp that'll punch my way straight to the electric chair.

"I guess we'll just have to wait and see," I say.

"Yep. That's all we can do."

On the morning of the hearing I'm up before the sun. Only slept a few hours, but I'm energized—charged up with a surging, nervous electricity that fires me from task to morning task without letting me feel a thing. I don't know what it is. Most likely fear.

I take my shower and get Gramps dressed and medicated for his trip to the courtroom with us today. We need him on his best behavior. But something odd happens as I tie the laces on his brown hush puppies. He looks at me. Right in the eyes. And I can tell he recognizes me. Like he can't quite wake himself from the trance, but that he's somehow aware of my good deeds. I guess that might not seem odd to most people. Most sane people, anyway. But most people like me—the ones who get to see their loved ones transform from adults into infants in a matter of a few years—are we really sane? I'm just glad to see that Gramps is still in there. Somewhere.

I make Gramps a few pieces of toast with some butter and jelly, and stuff a handful of Cocoa Puffs in my mouth as the old man eats. His jaws compress on the bread at roughly the speed of a trash compactor. I start to think I might be here a while. Then Nick walks in and pours himself a juice. He's in a clean undershirt and he's wearing a pair of grey dress pants I never knew he owned. His hair is slicked back and there's a few tissue remnants stuck to his face in places he cut while shaving. I swear, I barely recognize the guy these days.

"You ready?" he asks over the top of his legal pad.

"Just a few minutes," I say. "Can you keep an eye?"

Nick nods and jots a few more notes as I head outside to put Mom's garden hose into hibernation before the frigid temperatures turn it into a dry-rotted corpse. She'd be proud. Her only son is possibly headed to the clink, but he still makes sure there will be a way to keep her Dahlias from sagging once summer rolls in. What a thoughtful freaking kid I am—like I'm starring in an after school special or something.

I twist the nozzle off the faucet and start to unravel Mom's ancient, perpetually kinked garden hose. But that's as far as I get because I happen to glance down to the bottom of the driveway and notice the little, red arm on the mailbox is up like a hitchhiker's. I don't remember mailing any letters in the last twenty-four hours and, up until a few days ago, I wasn't sure Nick could use a writing utensil to form letters let alone maneuver the insurmountable obstacle of affixing a stamp to an envelope. And it couldn't have been Gramps. I doubt he even sees the mailbox as a mailbox anymore — probably thinks it's a weapons cache or a field marker or something.

I drop the hose and take a cautious stroll down to the mailbox — one of those walks where it feels like people are watching you, like Ed McMahon is about to jump out of the bushes with a check the size of a mattress and crown me the king of Publisher's Clearinghouse.

But there's nobody watching. No giant checks. No white-haired talk show hosts. The street is empty. So, I open the mailbox and peer inside. There's no letter. No bills. Not even a wrinkled-up, old supermarket circular. Just a cassette player connected to a bunch of tangled wires. Sofia's bright yellow Walkman and headphones. I'd recognize them anywhere.

I pull the contraption out of the mailbox. There's one of those comically tiny Post-it notes stuck to one side. It says "Play Me." I pop open the deck and pull out the cassette. There's a bunch of sloppy writing on it in blue magic marker that reads: "Pixies – Where is My Mind?"

Freaking Sofia. And John. I can tell they were in on this together because I'd never given Sofia my address, and the only thing John knows about Pixies is that he can rip open the top of a paper straw and guzzle down about four hundred grams of sugar in one gulp.

I'm pissed they won't just shut the hell up, respect my decision, maybe even support me a little. But I pop on the headphones anyway and press "Play" because that's what you do when you wake up one morning and there's a mysterious device in your mailbox. That's what you do when you realize someone's entrusted you with her most-prized possession.

It's a catchy little song with an actual melody — a major departure from the adrenaline-inducing, hard-driving stuff that usually spills from Sofia's headphones. I've never heard the song before. Never heard of the band either, but it doesn't take long to uncover the message my ex-friends were trying to tell me. It comes in a flash when I hear the opening lines — which amount to nothing more than a sneaky soapbox lecture straight off the lips of John and Sofia. Some garbage about planting your head on the ground instead of your feet. I guess that's supposed to be some kind of statement on my decisions of late. You'll have to listen to the song yourself because I got so pissed I tapped the "Stop" button about ten seconds in. And it's much better than what I wanted to do, which was smash the Walkman against a tree and watch the shards of plastic rain down on Mom's dormant rose bushes.

I mean, this is all pretty insulting stuff if you come to believe Sofia's intent was to make fun of an old man whose mind is no longer his. But it's almost unforgivable when you realize the lyrics are intended for me, the almighty *ben dan*—the boy who puts a stupid value, a damn promise, ahead of his fate. A total moron who must be completely insane because his word and his duty mean something.

At least that's how John and Sofia see it. I know that without question now, and without question I am filled with more resolve than ever. For a second, I feel all the heat in my body rise to the tips of my ears, and the blood quickens through the chambers of my heart. I feel it again—the urge to smash the Walkman, the headphones, and the cassette all over the driveway until there's nothing left but those tiny bits of reflective plastic you see in the street after car accidents.

But again I stop myself, because why should I stoop to their level? Why should I attempt to destroy something another person holds dear? That's not what friends do. Maybe that's a note I should leave in Sofia's or John's mailbox. But why bother?

I place the Walkman on the kitchen table and watch Nick stack all his legal pads, pencils, and loose notes in a pile.

"You ready?" he asks. I nod. I can't say anything back because my throat suddenly feels like it's filled with rubber cement.

This thing just became real. Much too real.

17

Guilty

Three generations of LoScuda are piled in the backseat of a cab on the way to the courtroom. Sounds like the hook of some legendary, barroom comedy routine, but it's not. It's my actual life, with Nick and I flanking the window seats and taking turns slapping Grandpa's hand away before he yanks on the driver's earlobe like it's a pull cord on a Teddy Ruxpin bear. Add a couple of eye gouges, a bowl-cut hairdo, and film the whole thing in black-and-white and you could probably slip us in on a Saturday morning between episodes of *The Three Stooges* and no one would know the difference.

The whole slapstick routine is as routine as routine can get by now — it's like freaking breathing to me. I slap at a withered hand and straighten a threadbare tie and lose myself in thought all at once.

I think about my future. Not, like, years and years ahead. Like, my future in the next few hours. When I step out of this cab and into the next phase of my life — the one where I'm a convicted felon. *No future for you!*

I imagine myself gliding out of the cab and onto a red carpet that floats weightlessly an inch off the four hundred ninety-nine cement steps that rise all the way up to the federal courtroom nestled snugly on the hilltop above. I see myself behind a pair of dark sunglasses — maybe Ray-Bans with a hazy, black finish to the lenses — and I am a study in stoicism, like a wrongly-accused defendant or a small fry fighting the big company on one of those episodes of *Law & Order* that fed Mom's addiction. I don't even crack an expression, face as barren as a slab of granite, as flashbulbs sparkle like in a Dick Tracy comic and reporters shower down questions like rancid confetti. Me, Gramps, and Uncle Nick just glide up that mountain of steps and through the heavy, courtroom doors as if transported on a chariot made of clouds. Nothing can touch us.

But reality is often the most worthy opponent to imagination.

For starters, when the cab sputters around a turn and closes in on our destination, I notice the courtroom is not atop a hill. It's set back within an enormous parking lot where I imagine you could pack the combined vehicular inventory of all five branches of the armed forces—planes, ships, tanks, freaking aircraft carriers, they'd all fit here no problem. The courtroom forms the large "L" of a building that also houses an ice cream shop, a dry cleaners, *two* coffee shops, and a Hair Cuttery. Pretty low budget crap for a governmental institution, if you ask me.

The Texas-sized parking lot is empty except for a few random sedans, a police car, and a couple of news vans from Channel 3. Great. They'd been riding my ass all week, calling the house bugging me for quotes, sound bytes—anything into which they could sink their pointed, yellowed, journalistic teeth. Freaking jackals, I tell you. I said 'no comment' so many times this week it became a sort of mantra. I wonder if Gandhi used the same one to endure his hunger strike. Doubtful.

As the cab approaches, more reporters stir from their metal hives. The door swings open on the police car and an officer, in full uniform, steps out. It's Patterson. The bastard. Here to watch me fry, I guess. All of my imaginary stoicism dissipates in a single rush of heat and sweat. I feel it melt like an oozing, drippy glob of ice cream on a scorching-hot day in mid July. It forms a little puddle in the hollow just above my shoulder where my neck runs into my collarbone.

And then I realize it's not melted stoicism or ice cream at all. It's saliva. From Gramps. Somehow, amid the hand slapping, and the Three Stooges routine, and the media circus, and the somber sound of taps playing on a lone and distant trumpet (that perhaps exists solely for my ears), he was able to pass out with his face all twisted and scrunched up on my shoulder. Great timing, old man. I glance over at Nick. There's a glimmer of recognition in his eyes like he knows what I'm thinking—that half-carrying, half-wrestling a helpless old man out of a cab and into a courtroom wouldn't make me look all that endearing if it happened to play on the evening news as people sat down to eat their dinners. Because one thing will always ring true in this society, and Sofia, the traitor, would agree—elder abuse and meatloaf just don't mix.

But my "high-powered" lawyer is not about to let me walk the plank. At least not yet. "Pull around to the pavilion entrance," Nick tells the driver, who nods. The tires wobble a little and a loose belt squeals under the hood as the cab bypasses the crowd of gawkers in front of our patriotic strip mall courtroom and heads for a deserted corner of the shopping center lot.

"I'm thinking we could cut behind the row of shops on foot and slip in the side entrance," Nick says to me.

"Wake up Gramps."

I jerk my shoulder a few times and watch Grandpa's head bob up and down like a buoy on high waters, but he's still snoring and drooling like a madman. The cab stops along the curb and already I see something disheartening reflected in the side view mirror. The news vans, once again armed to the hilt with their assorted drones, their killer bees with legal pads, back out of their spots in front of the courthouse as Patterson speaks furiously into his walkie.

"Gramps!" I shout, and I ruffle my hand through his white mane once or twice. Nothing. Nick slips a twenty into the driver's hand. I can feel the low rumble of the twin news vans as they complete a rotation around the parking lot and lumber toward us. "Keep the change," Nick says, and then we both shake Grandpa and tug at his sleeves and the front of his shirt—not the ideal awakening for someone with dementia. But it works. His eyelids flutter. Then he coughs, and suddenly the power's back on. Gramps looks around. I can see the confusion in his eyes—likes he's an alien and he just crash-landed on our planet with no understanding of the laws or the land or the customs of its people. I can see the panic rise, the pupils dilate, the whites nearly disappear as if the irises are splotches of ink bleeding through the fibers of a page. I have to reel him in before it's too late, before he's off the cliff and down the embankment—and before those damn news vans get any closer.

"We're almost to the ballpark, Grandpa," I say in a voice that's maybe me at age eight, all squeaky and pre-pubescent. His eyebrows perk and he looks around. "Ryan's on the mound tonight," I say. "Think our boy can take him?" A smile washes over Grandpa's face and the creases in his forehead soften. I look over at Nick. He's stunned, but he nods his approval to continue the ruse. "Hayes might be the man for the job," I say.

"Hayes," Grandpa grunts as we lead him down a cobblestone walkway and behind the Hair Cuttery to the abandoned strip of employee parking spots businesses provide to their employees—the ones next to the smelly, grimy loading docks and trash receptacles. "Hayes is a gamer," Gramps says under his breath.

"He sure is," I say, still like I'm singing a song to a two-year-old. "I think he'll take Ryan deep at least once today."

And we're making good progress, already nearing a short breezeway that connects the main thoroughfare of the strip mall to the crumbling backbone behind it. We hang a quick right and guide Gramps up the narrow alleyway and, for a brief moment, it feels to me like we could be at Veteran's Stadium. Then the spell is broken by the clatter of voices—questions fired off from long range—and the swoosh-swoosh of vinyl jackets as they brush against canvas messenger bags. The media. And Gramps's eyes are bulging out of his head. And so are Nick's. I can't see mine, but my head feels hot and my stomach churns like I had better find a bathroom five minutes ago.

"Come on, Grandpa. It's almost the third inning already!" I yell and somehow I have him captured again. Nick notices and snatches Grandpa's wrists and we run and trip and pull and scuffle our way down the alley with the flood gaining on us.

We slip out the other side of the alley into daylight, and I can tell Gramps is gassed. He's hunched over and there are little whistling noises coming from his nose and mouth. "Is Hayes on deck?" he asks. He pushes the words through exhausted lungs.

"He's on deck all right," I tell him and he perks up. Takes a few steps toward the courthouse. Then a few more, and by the time the journalistic hoard squeezes its way through the bottleneck in the breezeway, we're back to a light jog, or at least a compromised sort of half-stagger, half-leg drag. Whatever it is, it's not fast enough. I feel the questions ping off my back first. They rain down like artillery fire:

"Do you plan to take full responsibility?"

"Are you sorry for—"

"Why didn't you turn yourself in before—"

"Care to comment on—"

"NO COMMENT!" I shout for the final time, and now Nick and I pull at Grandpa without remorse. But he won't budge. He's like a statue—a very heavy and very immovable statue. The hoard approaches. More questions, then the patter of footsteps. Closer. Closer. Nick shoots me a deer-in-headlights look and then he reacts. He bends down and attempts to hoist Gramps over his shoulder, but the old man resists. He turns himself into a limp noodle and wriggles out of Nick's grasp. The hoard surrounds us. Six or seven microphones and several cameras are thrust into the pile like hot pokers:

"Do you have anything to say to little—"

"Why didn't you hire professional representation?"

"Are you prepared to do time?"

And then, suddenly, the buzzing ceases and the swarm erodes. All at once, Gramps stands fully erect (and under his own power) and the hot poker microphones are off point. I look over my shoulder and see our savior. The freaking almighty Messiah himself. Officer Patterson.

"Any further questions can be directed to the commanding officer on the case," he says with deadpan authority. There's a smatter of disapproval among the hoard, then a loudmouth decides to speak up.

"But we have a right to report this story. He's not even inside the courthouse yet. He's not officially off-limits."

Officer Patterson snaps on his words as deftly and businesslike as if he were snapping the guy's neck. "Code two-dash-four two-dot-seven of the commonwealth penal code states 'the grounds of the courthouse can be extended up to one hundred yards beyond the interior structure to provide imminent safety to all officers of the court, its principles, and any member of the jury as deemed necessary by a ranking official.'"

"And where might we find this official?" one of the reporters asks.

"You're talking to him," Patterson says, and for a second I think he might be Dirty freaking Harry. But that passes quickly. "You're late for the proceedings, Mr. LoScuda," he says without looking at me. "I suggest you escort your two counsels inside." Two counsels. The bastard. But, at least, he's the best kind of bastard you can be—the kind who can Dirty Harry the hell out of a bunch of local reporters.

We get Gramps situated in a chair outside the court chamber and I pull a paper bathroom cup out of my jacket pocket (I always carry one with me since I adopted Gramps). I hand it to Nick and he fills it with water from the fountain so Grandpa can take his pills before the show gets started.

"Hayes is due up soon," I say as I plop two pills in his water and tell him to drink until the whole cup is empty. I know you don't believe me, but it works for some reason.

Nick checks us in with the clerk and fills out a couple of forms. I hear the clerk, a mousy-looking lady with a sour expression, say, "You're lucky you got here when you did. Your case is next on the docket and Judge Waner simply does NOT accept lateness." Nick accelerates the pace of his pen across the surface of the last form in the stack. "Courtroom Two," Mouse Lady says. "Sit in the back and wait to be called."

"Come on," I say to Gramps, "we're heading to our seats."

"Three twenty-six?" he asks.

"Always," I tell him as we tiptoe into the back of a wood-paneled chamber with proceedings already in full session. A few heads pop up to gawk at the old man as he bumbles and stumbles his way to a pew at the back of the chamber between Nick and me. We push our thighs up close to his like the slices of bread on a sandwich. To the innocent bystander, Nick and I probably resemble either hyper-vigilant bodyguards or extremely reserved body snatchers. Take your pick, because I can never tell either and it's my own freaking life.

Gramps nods off again, this time on Nick's shoulder as Judge Waner issues this long-winded lecture to a thirteen-year-old kid accused of stealing his neighbor's bicycle.

"We all make decisions in our lives," he says, "and we all need to learn how to live with them. My late grandfather, the Honorable William J. Waner, Esquire, once told me 'there is a day time, and a night time, and a tea time, and a mean time . . . . but there is no right time for dishonesty." The judge lowers his Ben Franklin spectacles (he probably bought them directly from old Ben) and scans the silent courtroom like he's aching to find a stray syllable, or even a poorly-timed cough vibrating at the edge of anyone's mouth. There is only one such vibration—from the young defendant himself.

"But Javon left his bike in our garage," he says. I can barely make out a whitish outline, stained by a long, salty tear, that streaks down the right side of his face. His words sputter in his throat a little, and he has to wipe his nose before he can continue. "I never made any decision, sir. I didn't even know the bike was there until the next—"

Judge Waner holds up one withered hand like he intends to stop the entire courtroom at a cross walk. The gesture serves its purpose. Complete silence, which the old judge enjoys for a moment by staring at the mahogany surface of his bench and providing the court with a magnificent view of the seven or eight grey threads clinging to his liver-spotted scalp. Then he raises his eyes and bores them deep into the defendant.

It's kind of bone chilling—even from back here in the nosebleeds. I mean, it's not bad enough the guy has absolute power over your future, or that he's a virtual doppelganger of the Crypt Keeper from that show *Tales from the Crypt*—but those beady, black eyes. Ferret eyes. They are cold and vacant and full of hate. They can see well beyond the cotton knit drab of the defendant's freshly-pressed dress shirt, past his puffy lips and boyish dimples, right through to the boy's brain matter and into all the tiny neurons pumping fear hormones every which way, maybe even into his soul. Because, what looked to me like a normal, everyday, pretty nice kid—kind of a mama's boy if you ask me—Judge Waner saw as the devil incarnate.

"You did not notify the authorities, Mr. Reynolds!"

"But—"

"And you did not contact the owner of the bicycle, Mr. Reynolds!"

"But—"

"And you retained the bicycle under lock and key for multiple days, Mr. Reynolds!"

"But—"

"Enough of this! My sentence is for one hundred hours of community service and two years probation." The defendant is motionless except for the slow deflation of his shoulders. "You're lucky to be a minor," Judge Waner continues. "Don't let me see you in my courtroom again, Mr. Reynolds, unless you desire lodgings in the local jailhouse."

Damn. All the kid did was keep his friend's bike dry in his garage for a couple of nights and Waner's got him going to sleep with visions of the chain gang in mind. I give Nick a look that says, "Can you freaking believe this guy?" He receives the message and returns a nod that attempts to say "don't worry, I have everything under control," but which actually comes across as "looks like we are freaking screwed."

Typical LoScuda luck. All the judges in the world and I get to the one that unearthed himself from the grave in time to host a popular horror show on cable and send a good Samaritan from Scout Troop 117 to the chair. I'm picturing the whole thing unfold—the defendant in his long, brown socks, khaki shorts, and goofy shirt with all the patches on it getting strapped down and read his final rites—when Waner slams his gavel on the bench and calls for a recess. The crack of wood on wood reverberates through the court chambers.

Gramps springs to attention and his giant skull nearly smashes Nick's eye socket to smithereens. "Gah!" Grandpa shouts and twenty heads spin around at once to gawk at the psychotic old dude. Man, I hate rubberneckers. But I hate embarrassment more, so I think quickly. "Just a foul ball, Grandpa," I say with my arm around his shoulders. "Strike two."

His eyes scan the rows of pews and all the people in brown, tweed jackets and dress pants moving around the "concourse." I feel his back relax against the seat. "Hayes?" he asks.

"He's up soon," I say. "Couple more batters and Hayes will have his revenge." He nods and stares straight ahead, then tapers off into catatonia again. Nick rubs his eye, which is already swollen and red with a noticeable lump rising along the socket-line. He reaches over and pats my knee.

"You're a good kid," he says. "A good freaking kid, you hear me?"

I nod and we sit in silence and watch the courtroom fill back up with the tide of clerks, legal teams, and onlookers for the next session.

"All please rise," a stocky bailiff trumpets the moment everyone is seated, "for the Honorable Milton J. Waner." The Crypt Keeper emerges from his dark chambers in his sod-encrusted robes and snails his way across the courtroom floor awash in a storm of creaky joints and sagging skin. He ascends the heights of the court bench, his vantage point above the crypt. My crypt.

The bailiff continues his song. "Now hearing case number one double zero eight two, dash jay: The State of Pennsylvania versus Gabriel LoScuda."

When I hear my name, it's like one of those times when you're half asleep in class, or busy thinking about girls like Marlie, and the teacher calls on you just because she notices how you're tracing weird geometric shapes on the desk and your book's under the chair. My feet get all hot and sweaty and my legs go numb, and I can't tell if the courtroom has gone deathly quiet or if it's just me—like a giant hand keeps forcing my head under water and my eardrums are submerged in silence.

It takes a few seconds before I remember I'm the one operating the body that houses the riddled mind of this LoScuda fellow they keep mentioning. A few heads bob up and down in the pews in front of us, and a couple of people stand up. They turn around and gawk. Ugh. I guess they wondered if I'd bothered to show at all. One of them is Officer Patterson. He makes eye contact with me—expressionless, of course. He offers a nod, and suddenly my head's above water again and the symphony of disaster is about to begin.

"Gabe that's us," Nick says in a low, growling whisper. He reaches across Grandpa's lap and tugs a button off my sleeve. "Gabe!!"

There's a scattered burst of voices, like the clumsy caws of buzzards over a rotting carcass. More sleeve tugging. My legs start to tingle. Maybe functional. Can't be sure.

"Mr. LoScuda?" I hear over the noise. It's the Crypt Keeper. I lift my head and levitate drunkenly from my seat. The Keeper's empty glare meets mine with a twisted grimace I can only imagine is his best attempt at a smile. "Glad to see you've joined us. Will you and your counsel please take your positions so we can proceed?"

I'm dazed, so my "counsel" takes over.

"Yes sir, your honor," Nick says. "Nicholas G. LoScuda, defendant's unc, er, counsel." There's a goofy grin plastered across his face that in no way matches the force with which he wraps a single bear hook around Gramps and me at the same time and drags us up the center aisle.

"Gah!" Gramps is all stiff and his hackles are up like an old bloodhound.

"We're going to see Von Hayes," I whisper, but the courtroom is so quiet and so focused on us that shouting it through a bullhorn would have had the same effect. I get a few puzzled looks from members of the peanut gallery, but at least Gramps is back under control.

Nick plops the briefcase he bought at Goodwill down on the table reserved for the defense team (boy, what a team!). I wonder, for a moment, if the thing is just a prop—either totally empty or filled with a stack of peanut butter and jelly sandwiches or something. Not that it would matter either way because there's always the inevitable: I'm just moments away from complete and utter personal destruction.

I get Gramps situated in a chair behind the heavy, oak table and I sit down beside him. The Crypt Keeper glares down on me from the height of Mt. Justice and taps his wretched fingernails on the bench. "May we proceed, Mr. LoScuda?" he asks.

I shudder and start to respond, but then realize he's talking to the other Mr. LoScuda—freaking Nick.

"Mr. LoScuda?" he repeats over the silence. I slap Nick in the back of the head. Nothing hard or overly noticeable. Just a little something that says, "On guard, you big ape." He looks at me, surprised, and mouths a question: "Me?" I nod.

"Yes, uh, yes sir, your honor, sir," Nick finally says, and he finishes in a flourish of grotesque throat clearings and a wheezing cough that doesn't help my case in any way—though, sadly, it doesn't hurt it either.

The Crypt Keeper exhales. "Clerk, read the charges."

"The defendant is accused of one count of each of the following: hit and run without intent to do bodily harm, leaving the scene of an accident, and reckless driving."

Hearing it all laid out like that makes me sound like a real badass—

like I'm one pinprick away from owning a new teardrop-shaped tattoo on my face. Traitor Sofia would be proud. Or not. Whatever. None of it matters anymore. John doesn't matter. School. Baseball. My stupid job at Perdomo's. Marlie. None of it.

The Crypt Keeper's over-poached Adam's apple is already moving, vibrating, pulsating. And he's about to ask me that one question to which I have one possible answer. And that answer will not be the right answer no matter who you get to judge it or grade it or push it or pull it.

"Mr. LoScuda, please rise." The Crypt Keeper's voice echoes down from above and the walls of the crypt tighten around me. I rise from my chair, wobble a bit, then steady myself. "Mr. LoScuda, in lieu of the signed confession this court has in its possession, how do you plead?"

I know exactly what I have to say, but the word is trapped somewhere behind my uvula—you know, that weird, hangy flap of skin at the back of the throat. I'm parched and sweaty and shivering and sick to the stomach all at once. My biggest fear at the moment—besides the prospect of rotting away in a prison cell for the rest of eternity—is that I'll spontaneously combust and release half my breakfast in a sour, milky blob on the defense table.

"Mr. LoScuda? Your plea?"

I feel a large paw scrape against my back and I look over and meet Nick's eyes. He winks at me and tips his head forward as if to say, "You've come this far, Gabey. You've got this." And I do. I've had it all under control, to some extent, from the beginning.

I think about Dad. What would he do if he were standing here in front of all these people getting ready to trade in his life for the lives of those he loves? He'd make the trade without a shred of regret or a moment of delay. That's when my own decision solidifies; when I know that my next word is not destined to be the wrong answer after all.

"Guilty," I say, and the word comes out all hollow-sounding and heavy like the thud a splintered branch makes when it tumbles from a tree after a storm and hits the ground.

There are a few seconds of hubbub that trails its way through the peanut gallery before the Crypt Keeper continues. "Thank you, Mr. LoScuda. If there's nothing else to add I'll be happy to issue a sentence before we move down the docket."

Nick and I stare forward. We've nothing to say. Gramps neither, though for a different reason altogether.

The Crypt Keeper interprets our silence to mean "proceed" and so he lifts his gavel in one wrinkled hand and glares down on me with those beady, black ferret eyes.

"You injured a young boy, Mr. LoScuda. Could have killed him. And you didn't have the decency or the maturity to stop and check on the damage you'd done. You have a lot of growing up to do before the state will grant you the privilege of another driver's license. In addition," he says as he lifts his gavel a few more inches above the surface of the bench and sends my heart into painful spasms, "I am sentencing you to two years in a fed—"

"Wait!" Just then the doors to the courtroom burst open and John is standing there looking kind of disheveled, panting and confused. He locks eyes with me for a second before his dart to the floor. Something is weird, or rather, even weirder than my ex best friend bursting into court in the middle of my proceedings.

The door opens again and Sofia leads Mr. Perdomo into the chamber. They stand next to John and absorb the stares of an entire gallery of peanuts. What the hell were they doing here?

"Please, your honor," John continues with a waver in his voice. "We'd like to present more evidence on behalf of the defendant."

"John!" I shout, because it's not his freaking place to present anything on my behalf. I can only hope the Crypt Keeper agrees.

"Mr. LoScuda, who are these people who so rudely intrude upon my courtroom?" The old judge looks a little pissed and I'm not about to piss him off any more while he's right in the middle of handing down my sentence. I open my mouth to explain—to tell the whole court that I'd never seen any of these psychos before in my life—when Sofia cuts me off. "We are friends of the defendant, witnesses to his character, and first-hand observers."

"First hand observers?" The Crypt Keeper suddenly seems intrigued. Great. Way to drag this moment out for me, friends. "I didn't think we had any of those in this case. I don't believe there is a legal precedent in this situation, but I'm inclined to hear your evidence, if only out of curiosity."

What is going on here? I said the magic word already. Open and shut, just like Nick told me. Let's not wade through any more garbage. I confessed already! I glance over at Officer Patterson, sitting two rows behind the prosecution team. He raises one of his eyebrows. The bastard. He's been on to me from the start.

"What is the new evidence you plan to present?" the Crypt Keeper asks. "And how is it relevant?"

"We'd like to call Mr. Joseph Perdomo to the stand," Sofia says, and I have to say she sounds more like a real lawyer than my real lawyer. Maybe I should have hired her, if she wasn't such a damn traitor. "We intend to show that Gabriel LoScuda could not have been driving the vehicle that struck Timothy Mullins."

What!? What the hell did she just say?

"Sofia! What are you doing?" I squeeze out the words in a harsh whisper, as if all the people packed into rows of pews can't hear me.

"We're saving you from yourself," she says without even looking at me.

"Call your witness," the Crypt Keeper says, and he actually looks kind of amused—like watching this tattooed nightmare of a girl make me squirm in the seat gives him some kind of vampiric power. The bloodsucker.

Mr. Perdomo walks up to the witness stand and swears to tell the truth with one of his tiny hands held firmly on the bible. He sits and faces the gallery, and Sofia begins her interrogation.

"Mr. Perdomo," she says, "How long have you known Gabriel LoScuda?"

"I'd say eight or nine years.."

"And how would you describe him?"

"He's a delightful young man. Always polite. Never in trouble. A model student. A great athlete with a high level of maturity. He's a hard-working kid."

"Is that why you decided to hire him?"

"Absolutely."

"And when did you hire him?"

"Back in September, close to the start of the school year."

"September, you say?"

"Yes."

"The hit and run accident also occurred in September, did it not?"

"Yes, I believe it did."

"It occurred on the morning of September 23 to be exact."

"If you say so."

"Not only me, Mr. Perdomo. It's tattooed," she pauses to look in my direction for a moment when she says this. Typical Sofia, can't even be serious in a serious-as-shit situation. "across every page of the police report and in all the local newspapers."

"Then it must be correct."

"Yes. And could you tell me the exact date of Mr. LoScuda's hire?"

Perdomo pulls a stack of check stubs out of the chest pocket of his red, flannel shirt. He fans through them a few times, then he looks the Crypt Keeper in his beady eyes. "September 23," he says flatly. "A Saturday. The date is stamped here on all of Mr. LoScuda's check stubs."

"Do you remember interviewing and hiring the defendant on that date?"

"Absolutely. As clear as day. He came in around noon. We talked and I offered him the job. Then he pedaled away on his bike."

"His bike?"

"Yes."

"Not a red, 1981 Pontiac Trans-Am with silver accents and a tee-top?"

Again, Sofia looks over her shoulder and directs a stone-faced expression my way.

"No. I distinctly remember him riding a bike because it was leaning up against the front window of the shop during our interview."

"Mr. Perdomo, did Timothy Mullins get run over by a really fast bicycle?"

There are a few muted cackles from the peanut gallery before Perdomo responds.

"Definitely not," he says, and then he looks down at me from the witness box and repeats, "Most definitely not."

"Thank you, Mr. Perdomo. We have no further questions."

"Prosecutors, do you wish to cross examine?" Both the man and the woman in their custom suits look confused and decline the Crypt Keeper's invitation.

"Good," Sofia says. "That gives us time to call Gabe LoScuda to the stand."

I'm floored. How can these bastards just storm into the courtroom, into my life, and dismantle all the plans I had for me, for Gramps, for Uncle Nick and the future of the LoScuda family? How can they expect to roast me and then make me stand up in front of all these people and admit my shame? They are not friends. They've never been friends. They are parasites. Parasites that suck every last ounce of dignity from me and my family, and from Gramps and even my parents.

"Mr. LoScuda, I am inclined to hear this out," the Crypt Keeper says. "Approach the stand."

I don't even remember walking from my chair to the witness box, but suddenly I'm standing up there with my hand on a book swearing I'll finally tell the damn truth. And then John takes the baton from Sofia and pounces on me before my ass is even touching wood. His litigation style proves to be much less measured than Sofia's.

"You didn't hit that kid, did you?!" he shouts as if he was starring in the movie *A Few Good Men*. I don't respond. I'm completely startled. John seems like he's not going to give me a chance to say a word. "You never drove the car that day, did you!?! You're not the one responsible, are you!?! You're just covering, Gabe. You stupid, freaking idiot! You're covering."

There are streams of tears running down his cheeks and, for some reason, I feel the same sting encroach at the corners of my eyelids. My throat feels like it's coated in molasses and wallpapered with cotton balls. I don't know what to say. I don't know what to do. There's no one to rescue me from this moment, so I just stare down at Gramps and think about how much I love him and Dad and Mom and even Nick. And I think about how I'd do anything—literally anything—to protect them. And then the strangest thing happens.

Gramps opens his eyes wide and he looks at me. I mean, he really looks at me the way he used to at baseball games and when I'd fall off my bike and skin my knees and he'd wipe them down with a cool cloth and slather a bunch of Neosporin on the wounds.

He looks at me with all the recognition in the world and he says, "Keep your nose clean, kid. Please. Keep it clean." And there's nothing more I can do for him. I know it now. He knows it. Nick knows it. And now an entire courtroom full of strangers knows it.

"I'm not guilty," I say to the tabletop. "Someone else was driving the car."

Gramps sits at the table—still looking at me with the eyes he had ten years ago—with that gentle smile that makes me feel, at least for a moment, like a little kid again.

18

OVERTURE

The Crypt Keeper cracks his gavel against the surface of the bench. It's like mortar fire exploding in my head. I can almost feel a hail of imaginary shrapnel knife through my skin, and my head gets all woozy like I've just been concussed. The whole world goes mute, with all the members of the peanut gallery and the court reporters and officials moving about the chamber in a silent ballet—chaotic but still with some semblance of order and precision. These muted dancers rise up around me. They wash in on a high tide of clunky pirouettes and curious aggression, and they overpower my compromised senses with their blinding flashbulbs and the evil, blinking eyes on their video cameras. Their lips move and their gums smack in time with the vacant symphony, but it all feels more like a silent film to me—one of those grainy black-and-whites, but without the trademark and necessary title cards.

I sit in the chair behind the witness stand and watch it all unravel: watch the Crypt Keeper fold up his paperwork, slip it in a pocket within his robes and retire to high ground in the safety of his chamber; watch Uncle Nick fend off an entire hunting party of reporters with the rat-tat-tat of his "no comment" machine gun; watch Grandpa's face twist and contort in fear, the pupils dilating again, as two bailiffs approach him with handcuffs swinging; watch John and Sofia sit in the gallery, the horror broadcast across their stupid faces.

Then I'm up out of the chair and bounding across the courtroom floor like an assassin or a special forces militant. A bailiff already has my grandfather up and out of his seat. He spins Gramps around and snaps one end of the cuffs around a bony wrist. I'm about to pounce, to rescue Gramps one last time, but the other bailiff—a large man with the shoulders of a linebacker—gets me in a choke hold and drags me in the opposite direction. I try to scream out to Grandpa. Try to tell them all they're a bunch of bastards. That they need to unhand my grandfather before there's trouble. That cuffing the old man could inflict irreversible trauma to his already damaged mind. But I either can't push the words past my lips or they're lost on the current of chaos rushing through the courtroom. And there's nothing Nick can do as the smaller bailiff drags Grandpa off into the bowels of the courthouse, to a place where a set of steel bars are a man's only company.

The monster bailiff releases his grip on my neck, but still has me wrapped up in a bear hug. He drags me past the gallery, past a quietly weeping John and a Sofia with her brown eyes all soft and sympathetic in a way I've never seen from her before. And all I want to do is walk past them forever and never talk to either one of them again for setting this whole scene in motion; for decimating the structure of my family so we're like the tiny, jagged shards of a broken wine glass; for their ultimate and untimely betrayal.

I turn my head and give in to the strength of the bailiff as he forces me back behind the Crypt Keeper's bench and pushes me through a small door that leads into an even smaller chamber. Uncle Nick, Doc Weston, and the Crypt Keeper are all seated in leather chairs beside a bulky desk. The monster bailiff escorts me to an empty folding chair. The big goon exits the chamber and, with the click of the door handle, all sound rushes back to my ears.

"Thank you for being here," the Crypt Keeper says, "to all three of you. This is a unique situation. One that can only be solved by a village and not an individual."

"Glad I can help," Doc Weston pitches in. The bastard. When the hell did he arrive? From the looks of his wrinkled suit jacket and the loose knot on his purple and gold striped tie, he may have slept here last night. Man, it sure would be nice if somebody, anybody—my employer, my best friends, our family doctor (you know, the people you're supposed to be able to trust)—were on my side. But I guess that's not my fate. See, I'm a LoScuda—which apparently is Italian for "punching bag."

The Crypt Keeper shuffles a few loose pages on his desk and lifts his ancient, beady eyes to the rest of the chamber. "Mr. LoScuda," he says, and both Nick and I cock our heads to the sound. The Crypt Keeper notices and raises a single, bushy eyebrow. "Young, Mr. LoScuda," he says with a roll of the eyes. Boy, Nick really has some work to do in the lawyering department before he makes any appearances on freaking *LA Law*.

"Son," the Crypt Keeper continues, "I don't recall a time in my career when my sense of justice has risen to the highest heights and then collapsed into despair in the course of such a short period of time." His whole career? What are we talking? Centuries? "What you did was both noble and completely irresponsible; both heroic and highly illegal."

"Illegal?" I repeat.

"You perjured yourself, Mr. LoScuda—an offense that could result in stiff penalties or even jail time if you find the wrong judge on the wrong day." I look at Nick for a second. His eyes are wide with the panic he's trying to hide. Or maybe it's fear. Fear that he's about to lose *two* of his family members in the course of a single morning. "But don't worry, Mr. LoScuda. This particular court, though quite strict, plans to exhibit considerable leniency on your behalf."

"Doctor Weston," the Crypt Keeper continues, "the court would appreciate your recommendations in this matter."

"Of course," he says sitting up a little taller in his chair. He fixes a pair of black, wire frames on the bridge of his nose and averts his eyes from my glare. "Your honor, I've been treating Ernest LoScuda for the past two years."

"And young Mr. LoScuda has been the guardian you've dealt with during that time?"

"For a portion of it. Gabe's parents originated the patient at my office, but the young man has taken over since."

"And where are the boy's parents at this—"

"Dead," I say in a hollow, lifeless voice that stops the Crypt Keeper mid sentence and attracts Uncle Nick's hand to my shoulder. "They're both dead," I say again. "Car accident."

There's a subtle change in the Crypt Keeper's demeanor. His shoulders stiffen a bit and the beady eyes somehow appear softer and less rodent-like. "I'm sorry," he says. "How long has it been?"

"It will be a year this summer," Uncle Nick says as he pretends to consult a handwritten note on his legal pad. Boy, Perry Mason better watch his back before he's out of a job.

"I see," the Crypt Keeper says with a contemplative thumb tucked under his baggy chin.

"This is an amazing young man," Doc Weston says out of nowhere. "He's taken on the role of caretaker in one of those tragic and unexpected twists life often throws us. And he's succeeded even while continuing his roles as nephew and student, friend and employee." Doc smiles at me. Maybe the guy's not such a total bastard for showing up here. "But his grandfather . . . Ernest . . . his condition is, frankly, far beyond what can be managed by non-medical personnel." *Bastard!*

"How would you describe the patient's condition?"

"Ernest LoScuda is in the latter stages of Pick's disease, your honor. All patients respond differently to the disease and to the pharmaceuticals used to treat it. This particular patient has lost most of his ability to communicate. His memory is compromised. He often becomes disoriented, and his fears—as I have witnessed first hand in my own exam rooms— are sometimes carried out in violent bursts or are acted out as flashbacks. There is little doubt that the incident involving Gabriel's car and the hit-and-run accident itself were products of Ernest's disease."

"I see," the old judge says again. "And how would you recommend I proceed?"

"With Ernest LoScuda? I'd say he needs professional assistance. He cannot care for himself, and I fear there's not a man in this room—myself included—capable of taking care of him without such assistance."

He looks at me. The traitorous bastard. I can feel all the blood and rage boiling in the tips of my ears. I kind of want to slug the guy for saying I can't take care of my own grandfather; for making Gramps out like he's a worthless lump of mud; for coming between me and my father's wishes; for painting me as a helpless, little kid. But I'm resigned to my failure. I don't even have the will to take a swing.

"As for the young man . . ." Doc continues, but then he's suddenly cut off.

"I'll take this, your honor," Nick says. "My nephew is the only man . . . and I say 'man' in the truest sense of the word . . . he is the only man I've ever met who is basically flawless. He's pretty much perfect. Strong-willed, thick-skinned, hard working, and persistent. He has all the traits a parent could ever wish for in a son. And his only true flaw is one that all of us—every damn one of us in this room—should aspire to achieve. He cares too much. Plain and simple, the kid cares too much. About his family. About his friends. About anyone or anything in need. You see, he does all this caring and working and worrying about all these other people, and if there's a few seconds left at the end of the day, he might think about his own needs. But that rarely happens. He's a good kid, your honor. He's a good, freaking kid. But he's an even better young man. Please, your honor, don't punish my nephew for that."

Nick ends his sentence and there's a layer of pristine silence, like silken fabric, that blankets the chamber. Freaking Nick. In spite of everything— the slovenliness, the drinking, the bad manners, and the fly-by-night attitude—I love the guy and I always will.

The Crypt Keeper jots a few notes on a pad and then his eyes meet mine.

"You're a lucky man to have an uncle like this one," he says. "You're free to go, Mr. LoScuda. Congratulations. You are an impressive and puzzling enigma, and I wish you well. You may regain ownership of your vehicle from the impound lot behind the courthouse.

"And what about Grandpa?" I ask. "Where can we get him?"

I'm afraid to hear the answer.

"Your grandfather will spend the night in custody at the veteran's hospital. Doctor Weston has volunteered to keep a watchful eye. He will be assigned a temporary caseworker that will make observations over the next twenty-four hours, and then offer an official recommendation. The likely outcome? He will be assigned to an assisted living facility."

"No. That's out of the question," I say, as if I have any jurisdiction. "My grandfather can not—"

"Mr. LoScuda, the only other alternative for your grandfather is jail time. That's the reality, son."

The words strike my face like a heavyweight's fist and, for a second, I think maybe they've knocked my teeth down my throat because my mouth feels all dry and the gums are all sore and swollen. There's nothing I can say. I nod and rise to shake hands with all the gentleman in the chamber. "We'll make arrangements for your grandfather and contact you with the information within the next forty eight hours," the Crypt Keeper says. I thank him—though I'm not all that thankful about the results—and leave his chambers.

Only there's a part of me I feel I've left in that room forever. Locked up where I can never get to it again. It's the part of me that knows I've failed my mission. I've let my father down. I've proven that if a bullet is headed in your direction it's best not to expect me to stand in front of it. It's the part of me that can't accept—will never accept—my grandfather as a beaten-down old man in a hospital gown. It's the part that will lie awake in bed each night and wonder if Gramps got into the hospital commissary and swiped a six pack of pudding snacks, or if he treated the nurses to a one-man game of trench warfare in the recreation room, or if he also lies awake in his bed, miles away, and thinks of the grandson who took care of him all of those nights. Or if he can still remember that grandson at all. It's like I'm saying goodbye forever to a man who hasn't truly disappeared. And yet somehow he has.

I squeeze Nick's arm a little tighter and he leads me to the clerk's desk to pay the fine. We don't talk. Nick slides a short stack of fifty-dollar bills under the window. The clerk takes it and then slides my keys out in return. She points down a long hallway that culminates in a door. A thin beam of sunlight filters through a slim, rectangular window cut directly through the center of it. Nick and I continue our silent trek through the courthouse. We push through the door at the end of the hallway and into the outside world—an asphalt nightmare entombed behind random lengths of chain-linked fence and barbed wire, and covered in jalopies from here to the horizon.

The Trans-Am is parked right in the front, but there's something screwed up about it. Something is attached to the rear bumper that really pisses me off. It's John and Sofia. They're out here freaking waiting for me. The no good, traitorous, bastards. They sold Gramps and me down the river and now . . . what? They think I want to grab a slice of pizza with them or something? I walk right past them and slide the key in the lock.

"Gabe," John says, "what else were we supposed to do?"

I try to ignore him. I try to get in the car without even acknowledging that either one of these traitors exist. But I can't resist the urge.

"How about anything other than what you both did in there?" John and Sofia both stare back at me, dumbfounded. It's amazing. Suddenly they have nothing to say. All of Sofia's sneaky, little insults and John's sermons from the freaking mount. Where are they now?

"You know what I thought you were *supposed* to do?" I ask them. I get nothing—not even the blink of an eye or the twitch of a lip. Nothing but absolute shock. So I answer the question myself. "You were *supposed* to be my friends."

I hop in the Trans-Am and slam the door before John or Sofia can build up the courage to respond.

"Don't worry," Nick says. His voice is all muffled through the locked-down tee-top, and I can't hear if John or Sofia say anything back to him. "He'll come around," Nick adds before he closes the passenger door. But I don't think he's right. I think Uncle Nick's calculations are vastly off base.

And, just to prove a point, I crank the ignition and put the Trans-Am in reverse. I watch in the rear-view as John and Sofia scramble out of the way—just like a couple of backstabbing rats.

Gabe LoScuda
English 4A – Personal Essay #7
Mr. Mastrocola
January 28

My Crummy Kingdom

For passion tempts and troubles me
A wayward will misleads.
And selfishness its shadow casts
On all my words and deeds.
— Robert Louis Stevenson, *My Kingdom (5-8)*

I always hate when writers plug in a few lines of poetry or an overused quote at the top of an essay and hope beyond hope that someone with an IQ score that gets dwarfed by a half-dollar is the first person to read it. That way, the idiot might mistake the sage words of an established, professional writer for the ones vomited onto the page by a hack. It's an awful ruse to pull on someone. What's worse is it strikes me as selfish. I mean, Robert Louis Stevenson probably wasn't planning to have Gilbert J. Pitsniffer from Mrs. Swanson's third period class in Wichita, Kansas stealing his ideas a hundred years after he wrote the poem "My Kingdom," but that's how it is. We all like to lift each other's glory, cup it in our hands, and then pawn it back off as our own. We can't resist it. Stevenson knew that in the year 1913, and countless hack essayists have no doubt ridden the same wave ever since.

Of course, I probably shouldn't sit here and pretend I'm immune to this basic human weakness. I'm not. I'm just as guilty, maybe more, since my glory pilfering—my hairy streak of selfishness—victimized one of my dear friends instead of some faceless author who died half a century before I was even a sparkle in my father's eyes.

I doubt the victim I speak of would ever refer to me as a friend anymore, and I wouldn't blame him in the least. His name is Carter Willis. He, John, and I spent most of our elementary years and part of middle school tooling around the local ball fields, riding bikes through the neighborhood, and visiting the municipal pool on lazy, July days. We were inseparable.

John was the brains of the group, and Carter and I were the "athletes." We were ballplayers with everything in common. We both played second base, had sloth-like moves to our backhand, hit for power like church mice, and worshipped Ryne Sandberg (why did the Phillies freaking trade him?).

John was our resident statistician. Out on the sandlot, he'd keep a running tally of all our swings-and-misses, all of our booted ground balls, and every one of our arguments about who was better than whom. Carter and I were none too appreciative, because John's patented status reports only served as daily reminders of how unlikely it was that either of us would stand an ice cube's chance in hell of making the middle school team.

So, when John would accost us on the other side of the chalk line with quips like, "Gabe, that's your fourth strikeout of the day," or "Carter, you only managed to field three out of ten ground balls cleanly," he'd be met with all sorts of groans and grunts and shut-the-hell-ups. But our displeasure never stopped John from reporting. He was much too dedicated to statistics to blow a chance at making out with his precious numbers.

By the time we'd climbed the educational ladder to the lofty heights of seventh grade, Carter and I figured we'd left some of our best baseball out there on the sandlot where stats and wins and gold glove plays were meaningless. It was time to lend our debatable talents to the team that bore our middle school crest on its jerseys. Plus, both Carter's dad and my dad were shaking us down on a daily basis because they couldn't bear to live in a world where their only sons had no connection to a sanctioned and organized ball club. Dad would remind me of this each time I loaded up my bag after school for another fruitless (according to him) trip to the sandlot.

"It's time to shit or get off the pot," he'd tell me, which still kind of puzzles me because I can never see how dropping a deuce and playing baseball have any real connection—unless you happen to be a Mets fans (and for that I am sorry).

Carter and I finally buckled and signed our names on the sheet Coach would post on the bulletin board outside the cafeteria. It read: TRYOUTS – NEXT WEEK! "That doesn't give us much time to prepare," Carter told me as he dotted the i's in his last name.

"We're as ready as we're gonna be," I said. "It's time to shit or get off the pot."

"Disgusting," he said.

"Yeah, well tell that to my dad."

We spent most of the weekend fielding ground balls off the fungo bat of John Chen (when he could actually make contact), and doing a drill we called "soft toss" where John would flip a ball at us from the side and we'd slug it into a section of chain linked fencing around the field. By Sunday afternoon,

Carter and I felt as ready as ever. By Sunday night, I was ready to take Dad's advice and get the hell off the pot.

I was terrified. So I called Carter.

"I don't think I'm gonna show up tomorrow," I said.

"What? Are you wussing out on me, LoScuda?"

"It's a waste of time. I'm useless compared to the eighth graders."

"So am I," Carter said. "But I'm showing up. And you should too."

"What's the point?"

"To show Coach you have what it takes . . . or at least to let him know you exist. Come on," he said, "We can suck together."

"We'll be the crappiest second base tandem in the Delaware Valley. Even worse than Steve Geltz and Juan Samuel."

"Well, probably not that bad."

We laughed a bit more and made fun of each other's rag-armed throwing styles for a while and then we hung up. Carter always knew the type of treatment I needed to wipe away the fear and get motivated. What Carter didn't know was the meaning of the word 'selfishness.' Because for him, the monster had never "cast its shadow on all his words and deeds" like it had for Stevenson, and as it would for me at the conclusion of tryouts.

We toiled on the diamond all week long, running sprints from foul pole to foul pole, taking over a hundred swings a day off the tee, and fielding ground balls until our forearms and chests were covered in baseball-sized bruises. Carter would go out and get the best of me one day, and then I'd outperform him the next. We passed cuts on Tuesday and Wednesday, and had only one more to go on Thursday before that sweet blue and gold pinstriped uniform was folded up in our sports lockers.

Each day, John would sit on the bleachers and compile statistics for everyone trying out. It was annoying, don't get me wrong, but his maniacal scribbling did serve to make one thing clear: the real competition for a spot on the roster was shaping up between me and Carter, since the rest of the players—mostly older guys—were performing at a level that left our statistics looking pretty pathetic.

On Friday morning, Carter and I raced to the cafeteria with John biting at our ankles like a neglected terrier. There was already a crowd of *real* ballplayers surrounding the list—eighth graders with stocky shoulders and peach-fuzz mustaches and five to six inches on either of us. They congratulated each other in front of the bulletin board—the final cut list, where Carter and I would probably find a lot of white space in the spots where our names could have been if we didn't suck.

We waited for the smoke to clear and then slowly, cautiously—like terrified wolf pups leaving the den for the first time—we boxed out positions in front of the list. Carter reached one of his dark hands up and ran his finger from the top of it to the bottom. Then again. Then once more. His shoulders dropped. His eyelids lowered. Then he spun away and trudged down the hallway. He didn't wait for John or me. I guess he wanted to give us a few minutes to adjust, because the very last line of the final roster—way down at the bottom where the edges were frayed and repaired by bubbled-up squares of Scotch tape—was the following entry: LoScuda, G. – 2B.

There was barely a millimeter of space beneath it—not nearly enough to fit: Willis, C. – 2B. And so, without me even knowing it, the end of my friendship with Carter Willis had begun.

It was kind of subtle at first. The sandlot games and the horsing around after school took a back seat to my baseball practices and my late evening homework sessions. John's statistical reports were born out of the team's sanctioned practices and made no comparisons between the playing styles of Carter and me. Instead, they focused on how far I alone lagged behind the nine regular starters. The phone calls ended. So did our travels together between class periods. We didn't even meet up on weekends to enjoy marathons of *RBI Baseball* or *Mike Tyson's Punch Out* on John's Nintendo game system.

About the only time I'd see Carter once the season began was in the locker room where we changed into our gym uniforms for PE. The locker room—long a true bastion of bullies everywhere—was a dungeon where geeks and nerds received cruel and unusual punishment that harkened back to the Dark Ages. Being the last person cut from a horrendous team (we finished 5-15 that year) somehow placed Carter squarely into both categories. If his life after baseball were illustrated in a Venn diagram with one circle representing "NERD" and the other "GEEK," poor Carter would find himself directly in the middle of that annoying inner circle where most things never fit. And that couldn't have been more true for Carter, who didn't belong anywhere once he deemed himself unfit for friendship with anyone wearing pinstripes—even if one of those guys had been his friend since the days they stored clay in the same cubby hole.

One particular day in the PE locker room, about midway through the baseball season, Carter approached me. And I was pretty darn happy because I kind of missed the guy.

"How's the batting average?" he asked as he punched the combination into his lock.

"Is it possible to bat .001?"

"Not unless you had a thousand at-bats," he replied and he actually had a smile on his face for once.

"Did John figure that out for you?"

But he never got to answer, because a whole gang of my teammates—the real players—filed into our row of lockers with their voices cranked up to full volume. As they entered, a few of them slapped me across the back or shoulders in a playful, teammatey sort of way. None of them acknowledged Carter . . . except for our shortstop, a tall, lanky beast with a shock of bright blond hair named Clint McWilliams. Kid was good at two things: baseball and being a douchebag to anyone not wearing the uniform.

"What's up, LoScuda?" he said.

It kind of startled me, to tell you the truth, because McWilliams was one of those goons who rarely noticed the little guys. I mean, we were already eight, nine games into the season and this was the first time he'd thrown a single word my way.

"Hey," I said trying to sound all casual and unfazed. Carter turned around and pretended to root around in his locker.

"Good play yesterday at practice," he said, and suddenly I found it a lot harder to hide my excitement. I mean, the captain of the team had taken notice. This was a big step. Sure, I'd made a sweet, diving grab on a line in the hole between first and second—probably the best damn grab of my life—but I was a third-string nobody and, worse than that, a seventh grade nobody. But now it was starting to look like Gabe "Freaking" LoScuda was about to rise to the top like so much cream.

"Thanks," I said all nonchalantly, still doing my best to maintain composure.

"Keep making plays like that and old Sparky will be picking splinters by season's end."

Old Sparky was our starter at second, Stevie Sparkleson. Pretty obvious—and very fortunate for him—why his nickname was what it was.

"Of course," McWilliams continued, "you keep hanging around with losers and darkies." He paused to nod in Carter's direction, and he made a big show of it, winking with both of his eyes in tandem and holding out the pause long enough to attract a few chuckles from my teammates. "You're only as good as the people you surround yourself with, LoScuda. And Nelson Mandela over here ain't doing you any favors."

I stared at McWilliams and his stupid, pie-eating grin for a second. Then I stole a glance at Carter, whose lips were quivering a little. He looked like he wanted to cry but he didn't want to give McWilliams the satisfaction. He also looked scared, like he wanted to stand his ground but had to use every last bit of strength to will himself to the spot. I could tell he wanted to run.

It was obvious what I needed to do. And I wish I can say that I grabbed McWilliams by his collar and jacked him up against the bay of lockers, and that I punched and punched and punched until I could feel the blood streaming against my knuckles. But I can't say that. Because, as I stood there between my lifelong friend—who'd just been wronged and dejected and mentally abused—and a collection of my teammates—a crew to which I desperately sought acceptance—the clear and obvious choice of how to proceed somehow wasn't so clear and obvious.

"You still hang around with this turd?" McWilliams finally asked with a sneer on his face that told me I better choose carefully.

And then the words—words that I continue to regret to this very day—slipped out past my tongue before my brain could reel them back in.

"Me?" I said. "You think . . . you think . . ."

For passion tempts and troubles me

A wayward will misleads.

". . . you think I'd be seen with this scrub?"

And selfishness its shadow casts

On all my words and deeds.

I'd said it. And I'd said it like I meant it. Like I was mountains and clouds above my friend who'd trained by my side for the better part of ten years; who gave me (I now know) a position on the team simply by being born with a different color of skin. And worst of all, I said it as if being a third-string second baseman on a last place middle school team gave me that right.

They were the last words that ever existed between Carter and I.

I'm ashamed they'd been "cast behind the shadow of my selfishness."

What a crummy kingdom I had built.

19

TATER TOTS AND KIDNEY SHOTS

I take a bite of my cafeteria pizza with my free hand and squeeze Marlie's hand under the round table. She squeezes back. It startles me for a second. Not because I don't expect her to respond, but because there'd been a point in my life when I never thought I'd gather the courage to talk to the girl. Now, here I am her, uh, boyfriend—though I wouldn't dare say that word in front of her. Don't want her to think I'm all into defining stuff like that.

Of course, I'm a badass now. Signed and certified. I'm the kid who spent half his childhood locked away at Alcatraz and then, against all odds, sprang the joint. I sacheted my way past the gunfire of prison guards on fifty-foot garrets, and swam the shark-infested waters of San Francisco Bay to safety. Probably paddled right past Al Capone taking a dip in the frigid drink; maybe even used his fat gut as a freaking flotation device to guide me to shore.

At least, that's what you'd think if you believed any of the rumors circulating through the halls of Schuylkill High. And I tend to believe them—because the formula seemed to be: convert to badass-ism, get with Marlie. It wasn't brain surgery.

Without John or Sofia acting as freaking shackles to drag me back into the dungeons of my high school invisibility, I'd spent nine lunch periods eating crappy food, listening to crappy conversation from the likes of Mandy-So-and-So and her troop of bleach-blond idiots, and enduring some craptacular looks from the guys at Schuylkill who'd rather be sitting in my chair—which was basically all of them. It was glorious.

I take another bite of the French bread frozen junk. I don't know why they serve this crap like twenty times a month. Perdomo would never forgive me if he found out I was cheating on him with such a cheap, floozy piece of pizza, but only dweebs pack their lunch. Marlie made a point to tell me that little nugget of wisdom on our very first lunch "date" early last week. Even though the pizza tastes like dishwater and oregano, I'm still thankful for it because it fills my mouth and excuses me from the predictable conversations of the day.

"Did you hear about Susan Cafferty?" Mandy asks Marlie at warp speed.

"Oh, I couldn't care less about that drama queen," Marlie says with a trademark eye roll. I swear she rolls those baby blues more than she freaking blinks. But whatever. I'm not complaining because she's got my hand locked in the softest and smoothest vice grip in human history.

"What about her?" she says after taking a tiny mouse sip of chocolate milk.

"She's all 'Gabe LoScuda this' and 'Gabe LoScuda that.' I think she has eyes for your man, Marlie."

I feel my face go all flush when Mandy calls me "Marlie's Man." Am I her man or am I just some goober sitting next to her who's trying his hardest not to spit little pieces of mozzarella on her when he talks? I really don't know the answer to that because I'm kind of drawing the map as I explore.

Marlie makes a little coughing noise in the back of her throat and says, "Pleeeease, Mandy. You think I'd ever lose aneeeeething to Sue Cafferty? I mean, aneeeeeeeeething?" Marlie loves to drag out those long 'e' sounds when she wants to be really descriptive in her arguments. It's like the girl never heard of adjectives. "I mean, did you seeeee what she was wearing yesterday?"

"Those shoes?" Mandy asks, as if Sue's shoes had been molded from raw sewage. "Ugh."

"I know," Marlie says, and I can feel the conversation turning a corner like a race car leaving the pit and speeding out into an open lane at two hundred miles per hour—and, I have to say, it's entirely possible that race car has no chance of catching up with the rapidity of these girls when they spoke. I knew my quasi-involvement in this particular race was about to take a back seat. For real. "Oh my Gawd," she says, "and-those-tights-she-wears-under-that-plaid-skirt-OHMYGAWD-I-can't-believe-aneeeeone-would-wear-blah-blah-blah—"

"I know! I-can't-stand-how-she-thinks-she-can-blah-blah-blah—"

"And-she-thinks-she-can-take-my-man-and-blah-blah-blah—"

"Don't-worry-there's-no-way-blah-blah-blah—"

That's about the point where the conversation, the actual words, fall to the background like the incessant buzzing of engines at Talledega Motor Speedway, or if your head happened to be trapped inside a beehive like Yogi freaking bear.

I scan the cafeteria as Marlie and Mandy continue their clucking, and I make eye contact with John. He has his dorky lunch bag in hand and he smooths out a dollar bill for use in the soda machine beside the round table—the Land of Babes, as some of my male classmates liked to call it. Kind of lame, I know, which is why I never repeat it in front of Marlie or her friends.

John sees me, it's clear. How the hell could he not? I mean, I fit in at this table like a toddler at a saloon in the Old West. But he avoids acknowledging me and instead pretends to gaze at a spot well beyond me, presumably over at the janitor's closet at the back end of the cafeteria. Whatever. Kid's a freaking traitor anyway. If not for him and that other do-gooder, Sofia—man, and I really thought that girl was a rebel—Gramps would still be at home instead of locked away in some facility across town where they only allow visitors on weekends and holidays.

John passes the table at a near cantor and I tune my ears back into Marlie and Mandy's high-speed word race. I think they're approaching lap five hundred and I'm half-expecting Mandy to whip a giant, checkered flag out of her purse and start waving it across the cafeteria.

"No, I saw him at Miller's party last week," Marlie is saying. "He looked pretty drunk."

"He was," Mandy says. "Tried to kiss me out on the driveway."

"No way! Oh . . . my . . . Gawd!"

"I know. Normally I wouldn't mind, but he smelled like a brewery and kept slobbering all over me."

I see John swivel his head over his shoulder. His eyebrows slant downward like darts.

"What a pig."

"I know, right? Like I'd ever be seen kissing some drunken idiot on a random driveway."

I take another bite of the rock hard French bread and keep my eyes trained on John. He slides the wrinkled currency in the bill receptacle and it promptly spits it back out. He grabs it, smooths the bill, and then slides it back in the receptacle again. The machine hurls the bill out again and John snatches it with hatred in his eyes. He tries to smooth it out by stretching it around the square corner of the machine. Marlie and Mandy keep ranting about slobbery kisses and all sorts of assorted crap—the kind of conversation to which I could never hope (or even desire) to contribute.

"Oh my Gawd, I hate that," Marlie says about something—don't ask me what.

"Me too," Mandy says. "It's the worst."

And then John coils up like a cobra and, man, he looks pissed—like the soda machine and Mandy-So-and-So had taken his entire family hostage and he was the Rambo-like force destined to set them free.

"No it's not," John says out of the blue, "YOU are the worst!"

I'm stunned. I didn't think the kid could hear us through the insane rufflings of his dollar bill, and here he is more involved in Marlie's conversation than me.

"Do you honestly think you're so far above everyone here that you have the right to complain about every little thing they do?"

His eyes are wide with anger when he says it and there are little beads of sweat forming on his upper lip.

"And you—" He points a shaky finger at Marlie. "Can you even hear yourself? I mean, I've met parrots with more original things to say!"

Marlie's face turns about a million shades of red and pink, and she may have actually looked like a parrot (a very good-looking one) if someone flicked a few stripes of green or yellow paint on her at that precise moment.

But John doesn't relent. "Are you a parrot, Marlie? Is that what you are?" The wrinkled dollar bill extends from his hand like one of those pointer sticks teachers use to, well, point at stuff. Each time he extends it, I see Marlie shudder and rock back in her chair a little. She's speechless, probably because no one has ever had the guts to talk to her this way. She keeps looking to me with these swirling, little eyes that say, "HELP!" But John doesn't notice. He keeps firing shots.

"That's the problem with girls like you! Everything's on the outside. How about, I don't know, you choose one day—just one freaking day—where you don't act like an immature, judgment-dispensing robot? Just one day, Marlie. Then at least—"

"Hey! Leave her alone," I say, and it sounds like the words come trumpeting out of some hollow speaker behind me instead of through my own lips.

John stops his speech mid rant and the entire cafeteria falls into a hush over the course of a second.

"What?" John exclaims. And he sounds like he means business. Like he's a tough guy or something instead of being this frail, Asian kid who's allergic to athletics and grass and a million other things.

"You heard me. I said leave her the hell alone, you chump!"

John's eyes flash. I can tell he can't believe his best friend—his ex-best friend—would call him out like this in front of the whole school. He's angry and hurt and insulted all at once.

"What did you say to me?"

I'm up out of my chair before I'm aware of what I'm doing, and I walk slowly, casually—but also menacingly—over toward him. My nose is about two inches away from his and I stare at him with eyes like freaking Clint Eastwood's.

"I said you're a freakin' chump, Chen. Are you deaf or something?"

Then I push him—not enough to move him off his spot, but enough to let him know, "Hey, I'm right here, pal."

John returns the favor with a slightly harder push that forces me to take one tiny step back. But then I'm right back in his face and I realize I have a handful of John's shirt balled up in each of my extracted claws. He tries to pull some kind of crazy self-defense move on me—probably some crap he saw in a safety pamphlet for the elderly— where he slides his forearms inside mine and attempts to snap them free. It doesn't come close to working, so he grabs my arms in desperation and, suddenly, we're hanging all over each other like a couple of dog-tired heavyweights in an undercard prize fight. It's kind of awkward, to tell you the truth. If either John or I were even a tad bit more graceful, everyone in the cafeteria might think we're engaged in some bizarre form of the waltz.

We struggle for a few seconds before I get super pissed and go into total badass mode. Like blind fury or something. I twist and push and pull and gouge like a deranged bull in a red room. I'm not sure how it happens, but before I know it we're on the floor and I'm kneeling over John looking at his stupid, inconsiderate, insulting face. I want one good shot. Just one. For Gramps and for Marlie, but most of all for me.

The muscles in my shoulders tense. My hand lifts off John's chest and pulls back behind my head like a pinball plunger. I pick my target—his stupid, freaking nose—and I'm just about to strike when a hand, strong and rough, tightens around my wrist. Then I'm yanked off the ground by the same arm and a loud and sudden buzz of voices swirls around me in the cafeteria.

"Both of you! Now!" Mastro shouts as he releases my wrists from his G.I. Joe super grip. He drags us out of the cafeteria by our shirts like he's the secret spawn of Wonder Woman and the freaking Terminator. Geez, who knew Mastro's the real badass around here? I mean, I thought he just sat around reading poems and feeling emotional all day. I never expected him to have the heart of a drill sergeant and the strength of King Kong, but trust me, John and I didn't get tossed into the hallway by a brisk wind.

Mastro corners us in front of a bay of lockers. His hair hangs down in tangled strings and his dress shirt is half untucked from breaking up the skirmish.

"Excuse the language, gentlemen, but what the hell is going on with you two?"

Neither John nor I utter a sound. We don't even look at each other. Mastro waits for a response, hopes the awkwardness of the silence will be enough to get us talking. It has no such effect.

"Okay," Mastro continues, "have it your way. Principal Gechkardt will want to hear about this." That's all John and his stupid, perfect, little permanent record needs to hear.

"He's an ass," John says. There' a part of me that wants to tackle him again and finish what I started, but I don't want to engage in another tangle with Mastro so I let it go.

"He's the one that bullies girls," I say.

"She's a girl? I always thought she was a parrot."

I take a small, threatening step forward and Mastro gives me a look.

"He insulted my girlfriend," I say to Mastro—figured I'd cut out the middleman. But John doesn't get cut out of anything. Ever. Probably learned that from the best: Lily Chen.

"Your *girlfriend*? Is that what—"

"Hey! I wasn't talking to you," I say, "and it's none of your business. I know you're pretty freaking terrible at staying out of people's lives, but this is ridicul—"

"That's unfair, Gabe. You know we were just trying—"

"I don't care what you were trying to do. I never asked for—"

"Enough!" Mastro's booming voice echoes through the hallways and shuts us down in an instant. "I don't know what's at stake between you two, but you need to clear this whole thing up. You guys are supposed to be friends."

Neither one of us respond. John lets a whistling rush of air escape through his nose. He smacks his lips and tongue against his gums in one, loud click. Then he turns on his heels and walks off, leaving Mastro and I alone in the hallway.

"You need to fix this, Gabe," Mastro says in his usual, soothing, non-badass voice.

"Screw that," I say. I shake my head. How do you fix something that's been blown to smithereens?

Gabe LoScuda
English 4A – Personal Essay #8
Mr. Mastrocola
February 12

A Blameless Wight

It's weird not having your best friend around after years and years of Siamese-twinning it. But that's how it is for my buddy John and I, though I can hardly call him that now. Not since he betrayed me . . . or I betrayed him. Who knows? I can barely remember anymore.

It hasn't been that long since we parted ways, but I see him at school and I know he sees me. We don't talk. Not ever. It reminds me of a few lines from Henry David Thoreau's "I Knew a Man By Sight."

> I knew a man by sight
> A blameless wight
> Who, for a year or more,
> Had daily passed my door
> Yet converse none had had with him.

And I think: Why?

Why the hell am I punishing myself and my friend—a friend who happens to be the original blameless wight, I might add? In fact, when I really try to sit and pinpoint all the times John has betrayed me since we were kids, nothing comes to mind. Not unless you count opposing thoughts—that is, all the times the kid's saved my ass and been solid as a freaking rock. I mean, here's a wight—totally and completely blameless—who's never been the cause of any of my troubles and has more often than not provided me with solutions. Covering foolish lies I decided to tell my parents, my teachers; tutoring me through algebra, even dancing like Michael Jackson to help me woo love interests that were, at the time, completely out of my league. The kid has done it all. But nothing compares to how John helped me navigate my very first day of school at Schuylkill High.

> In a more distant place
> I glimpsed his face,
> And bowed instinctively;
> Starting he bowed to me,
> Bowed simultaneously, and passed along.

We were at the township pool, a place where toddlers apparently flocked for the soul purpose of filling the kiddie pond with their own urine, and where teens met in a frantic attempt to bolster their social statuses before the start of a new school year. Under a blistering August sun, rising senior boys tugged at the bikini straps of their female counterparts while rising freshman, like John and I, played Marco Polo and tried to stay out of their way.

Around noon, John and I embarked on our traditional poolside lunch journey, which consisted of a methodical walk between seven-year-old, living obstacles that ran and jumped and weaved their way between Mommy's beach chair, the wet cement pathway, and the pool itself. Lifeguard whistles blared and were followed by the usual calls for "No running!"

We dodged and tripped and stepped on little ones until we reached our lofty destination: the snack bar. John would order a hot dog, a Coke, and two ice cream sandwiches (as always), and I'd have my usual slice of pizza, Sprite, and a Flintstones push-up pop. We never strayed from the path.

Only this day was a little different. Instead of holing ourselves up at the last picnic table between the dense woods and a rusty, chain-link fence where our hideous, pimply, scrawny, pubescent forms would be hidden from public view, we found ourselves lost and abandoned. Homeless, in a way. The table was already occupied, and the worst part was the occupants were all members of Schuylkill's incoming senior class. We recognized them all because, to us, they were freaking legends.

There was Zach Holt, linebacker extraordinaire from the mighty Schuylkill football team; the Ballinger twins, who'd never lost a fight in their lives (I guess two against one gave them pretty good odds); and Sammy Spieth, the guy who'd been with basically every girl at Schuylkill and more than likely all of their sisters and mothers as well.

John and I grabbed our food and looked at each other. We didn't need to say anything because both of us knew there was a better chance of us each sprouting chest hair and full beards right there on the spot than there was of us asking the senior crew to vacate our regular seats. I motioned to the safety of our beach blankets laid out on the other side of the pool and John nodded. We turned to walk, but safety, security, and a clean set of drawers were apparently not in our fate.

"Well . . . looky what we have here," Zach said as if he was singing some cheesy Broadway show tune. "Coupla incoming frosh."

There was a general clatter among the boys who all seemed to be sharing some kind of secret Neanderthal language that even Neanderthals would have had trouble understanding. Then Zach continued. "Those were the days, boys. Those were the days. Why don't you two come and have a seat with us?"

Zach stood and patted the palm of his hand on the picnic bench. "I kept it warm for you."

John and I looked at each other again. He shrugged, I followed suit, and the decision was made—as if there was any other decision we could make. I mean, you don't just turn your back on three bruisers and a ladies man—especially if they're seniors at your high school—unless, of course, you're sick and twisted and interested in one hundred and eighty days worth of ass beatings. John and I were not, so we walked over with our food and squeezed both of our asses on a section of the bench meant for a single ass. It was awkward, but so is hanging from a locker hook on the first day of school—something we were desperately trying to avoid.

"So, you boys are the new fresh meat?" Sammy asks.

John and I kept eating, too scared to respond.

"Hey! Sammy asked you a question," one of the twins said, and he looked all menacing, gnashing his molars together and clenching his fists. "Answer the gentleman!"

"Yeah," I said. "We're fresh meat alright."

I half expected to have all the actual meat stripped directly off my face at that moment so that I'd be sitting there shoving pizza through the jaws of a skeleton head. But it didn't happen like that. Turned out those guys weren't as rough and tumble as they let on. They were actually kind of cool to us—or so I had thought at the moment.

"You're in for some good times," Zach said to us. "I'd do anything to go back and live it all over again."

"Me too," said Sammy, "but that'd probably be a serious hazard to my health."

I didn't get it (neither did John), but all the older guys started cracking up and slapping high-fives with Sammy for some reason. Seniors.

"You guys are about to be a part of so many traditions at Schuylkill," Zach continued. "I'm sure you've already planned your attack for the first day of school, but we can keep you in the know after that."

"First day of school?" I asked. "What happens on the first day of school?"

Zach twisted and contorted his face into shapes you thought were only possible for cartoon characters. "You mean, you don't now about Freshman Formal Day?" He slapped his palm against his forehead as if to say, "God damn freshman," and then he started pacing back and forth at the head of the table like my ignorance of the Schuylkill High School unwritten laws of tradition had insulted every one of his ancestors and threatened his very way of life. "Did you hear that, guys? They've never heard of Freshman Formal Day. Never freaking *heard* of it!"

The Ballinger twins and Sammy Spieth made eye contact. They looked a bit confused for a second, but then they each offered Neanderthalic grunts of disapproval in turn. I looked at John. His head was pointed downward and his eyes were locked-in on his hot dog. Maybe he was so concentrated on not pissing his pants that he had nothing to add to the conversation. Maybe that's just how I felt. But I spoke anyway, because that's the kind of stupid thing I do when I'm nervous as hell.

"So, what is it?" I asked. I was kind of afraid to find out to tell you the truth, but I figured there might never be another opportunity to receive spot-on advice from guys who'd spent the last three years transforming from idiot pencil necks like John and I into freaking high school superheroes.

"What is Freshman Formal Day?" he asks me. "Did you hear that guys? Unbelievable." Zach was really starting to worry me. Like everyone at Schuylkill High knew the score but John and me. Like we were destined to be losers for the next four years in the same way we had been for the past eight.

"Well, I'll tell you what it is," Zach continued. "First day of school, it's a tradition for all the freshman guys to wear a suit." It didn't seem all that bad. Not like walking on hot coals or bobbing for brown, smelly toilet apples or anything. But wearing a tie? Man, I wasn't in to that part of the deal.

"What happens if we don't?" I asked. I immediately knew I'd made a bad choice. The seniors got deadly silent. They moved in closer like those imposing, spiked walls that threatened to crush Han Solo and Princess Leia in *Star Wars*. I felt one of the Ballingers' hot breath burn at the back of my neck.

Zach chuckled—one of those snide, weasely laughs you expect to hear from a tax collector, a mad scientist, or a sea otter. "Gentlemen, what happens if our fresh meat here doesn't look absolutely dapper?"

I heard a knuckle pop right behind my ear, and the twin shadows of the Ballinger boys grew darker and heavier on the surface of the picnic table. Sammy Spieth stood there with his cold, blank stare on me just chewing on a Popsicle stick, mashing it into tiny smithereens like he probably wanted to do to every bone in my body. And who could stop him? Not me.

But John? Well, he didn't even break a sweat. As Zach clamped his robotic gorilla hands down on my shoulders, and I struggled to retain the half a cup of Sprite resting in my bladder, John popped the last bite of hot dog in his mouth and looked up from his paper plate, like he'd awakened from some ancient and mystic form of poolside meditation.

"Gabe, stop messing with these guys," he said. He took a sip of Coke and chewed on an ice cube. Then he looked directly at Zach. "He likes to screw with people. We picked up our suits from the cleaners last week. Got it covered, fellas." Then he patted Zach on one of his massive biceps like they were old chums.

I was stunned.

The terrifying posse of murderous seniors was stunned.

The freaking squirrels plucking old popcorn kernels off the cement were stunned.

John bottomed out his Coke and munched a few more ice cubes. And Zach Holt and the Ballinger twins and freaking Sammy Spieth, they had no choice. The only thing they could do—the only respectable thing—was to burst out laughing. And I mean gut-blasting, belly bursting stuff.

And, just like that, with a little Jedi mind-trickery on John's part, we would survive the day with all of our limbs intact.

For he had hardships seen,
And I a wanderer been;
He was my bosom friend, and I was his.

Things would have ended there—they really would have—if Zach Holt didn't turn around as the boys left our table and say even one more dreaded thing. "Oh, and the suits? Yeah. We weren't kidding about that."

So began my two-week obsession with pocket squares and Windsor knots and shoe polish. I must have spent every moment of those two weeks—the last few glorious drops of summer—trying to figure out how I'd fit five foot nine inches of me into the five foot five inch accommodations of my confirmation suit. Thank you, sudden growth spurt.

The whole time John's telling me, "You're an idiot, Gabe. Those guys were just messing with us, Gabe. Please don't wear that purple suit on the first day of high school, Gabe. You're ridiculous. Idiotic. Ben dan,"—and all sorts of other sage warnings I decided to ignore.

I told him, "I'd rather look like a fool than look like a human cow patty that the Ballinger brothers track in on the heels of their combat boots."

John shook his head.

On the morning of the first day of school I don my suit, slick back my hair, and slap on some Aqua Velva from the trial-sized bottle I'd snaked from Gramps. I looked in the mirror. The cuffs on my jacket were at least four inches shy of the wrist. The pants would have been perfect if a hurricane suddenly ransacked the area and I had to wade through a foot of water to get to class. The shoes looked like they'd been stolen off the set of a 70s-era gangster movie—and they may well have been. I *did* take them from Dad's closet.

I had to face it. I was a plum-colored nightmare. But at least I wouldn't get my ass kicked. Or so I thought, until I arrived at the bus stop. I could hear a group of sophomore boys from the neighborhood laughing at me from half a block away.

"Nice freaking suit, LoScuda," one of them said as I approached. "Makes you look like you have gigantism." I didn't bite. Because it was tradition, right? Because these sophomores had been in the same position the year before, right? Because I was part of something larger than myself, right?

But then I saw Chad Jarvis, one of my classmates from eighth grade, and he was wearing a plain, black t-shirt and jeans. No suit. No tie. No freaking gangster shoes. Maybe he didn't get the memo.

Then I got on the bus. More laughter. More pointing. More freshman classmates. Not a single suit in sight. I took a seat in the front behind the bus driver and tried to hide behind my backpack. I leaned my head against the window and squeezed myself into the farthest possible corner crevice in the row. The vibration of the road against my ear through the warm Plexiglas partially muffled out the sounds inside the bus, but I could still catch a phrase here and there. Things like, "Did you *see* what he's wearing?" and "I didn't know he was in the circus," and "He's *such* a loser," stood out above the rest.

The bus pulled up to the next stop with a banshee-like squeal, and the driver folded the door open with the mechanical arm. I didn't bother to raise my head from behind my book bag. Then a whole new chorus of laughter and shouting overtook the cabin. There were some whistles, even a few hoots and hollers. I couldn't resist popping my head out, like one of those crooks in grainy Westerns who sticks his neck out from behind the old, swinging saloon door just in time to catch a bullet. But there was no bullet waiting for me—only John. In a bright teal suit with a purple tie that was straight off the set of *Miami Vice*. The dude was strutting up and down the aisle like it was a runway at Fashion Week. He stopped here and there to strike a pose, and received cheers and laughter in return. The kid could always work a room, even when that room was the inside chamber of a sweaty school bus.

He sat down in the seat next to me and pulled a copy of Chaim Potok's *The Chosen* out of his bag. I didn't say anything.

"Summer reading," he said. "Got to refresh my memory before English class today. Read this way back in June." He raised his eyes from the pages for a moment to notice my deflated posture in the seat. "Oh, and you're an idiot," he continued. "I told you Freshman Formal Day wasn't a thing."

"Well, thanks for dressing up," I said.

"Here," John replied. He reached in his bag and pulled out two sets of Schuylkill High PE uniforms—brand new and freshly washed. "Thought you might want to change into something more comfortable."

I nodded, and we both spent our first day of high school in a perpetual state of gym class—and I was happy (and thankful) to do it.

And as, methinks, shall all,
Both great and small
That ever lived on Earth
Early or late their birth,
Stranger or foe, can one day each other know.

20

THE MAN IN THE MIRROR

I miss Gramps. I only get to visit him about once a week since the Crypt Keeper ordered him banished to the funny farm for the rest of his brain-addled life. I hate thinking about him alone in a white room that smells like burnt toast all the time. And I hate theorizing about what Dad must think of me now. I don't know where he is, but I can feel him watching over me sometimes. And I can tell he's pissed. I'd be. Scratch that. I still am. Probably always will be to some extent. But there's not much I can do about it now, other than try to get back to life as Gabe LoScuda.

Once I look past all of my failings and the total abandonment of my own blood and the disgrace of having my very public lie exposed to the whole community, I can sit back and maybe even enjoy the relief that comes with not having to play nursemaid to a crazy, old man. I might even be able to start figuring out what I want to do with my life. I mean, once I lost Mom and Dad and had Grandpa and Nick to worry about, I really started to believe I had no future. I kind of forgot that I'm a person that can have dreams, too. I don't have any right now or anything. I'm not like John, sitting around polishing his American Medical Association-approved stethoscope that Mrs. Chen bought him when he decided—at age four—he would be going into medicine, like he was Doogie Howser or something—which actually might not be too far off.

I never had a clear direction to follow like that. The only things I ever feel comfortable doing are playing baseball and reading poetry, but it's not like I can hit like Tony Gwynn and Dad once told me, "son, all poets are unemployed." So it looks like I'm stuck. But at least now that I have some time to think my own thoughts and not have to supply all of my brainpower to another human being, the fog is lifting away. Things are starting to become more clear. Like, I'm realizing some stuff that wasn't so obvious to me when I was forced to cram my life in between Grandpa's doctor's visits and his outbursts.

Take today, for instance. I'm in the bathroom taking my sweet ass time—no worry in the world about drugging pudding snacks or wiping drool off grey-stubbled chins. Dad's old radio is in here with me and I'm jamming out to Power 99, Philly's favorite R&B station, of all things. I actually have time to stand in front of the mirror and shave with an actual razor that I bought from the actual pharmacy—because I finally had time to stop. It's, like, total luxury when you think about how I'd been shaving with the cracked, disposable Lady's Schick I found inside Dad's shaving kit. Don't ask me why it was in there, but the thing looked like it was produced during the Nixon administration, and I'm rubbing it up and down my face each day for, like, four months straight. The razor bumps started to look like freaking goiters.

A Michael Jackson song comes on the radio and I crank up the volume to full blast. Nick's still asleep—he moved into Grandpa's old room—but the dude seems to go into hibernation mode each night, so I'm not worried I'll wake him. The King of Pop is belting out the lyrics to "Man in the Mirror." It's not my favorite Michael song—that would be "Billie Jean"—but it's one of those songs you hear where you definitely don't change the dial.

I start bobbing my head to the beat. I think back to my early childhood obsession with the Jackson 5 and Michael's *Thriller* album—both things I'd never admit in front of anyone at Schuylkill High, by the way—but they still get my feet moving. I sing along, using the can of Barbasol like one of those giant, old school microphones you'd see on a black and white variety show from the 50s.

I shave the last strip of stubble off my chin and let Michael carry me through the refrain. Then the beat picks up and my body feels lighter—like I'm bound to pull off a few twists and spins; maybe moonwalk across the tiles like I might have done when I was five. I can't hold it back anymore. I pop up on my toes, swing my lower leg around a few times as if it were made of rubber, and finish with the ultimate crescendo: a trademark screech and a crotch grab.

For a few moments, I'm totally free. Liberated. Ready to take on the world as the new, improved Gabe LoScuda—or at least a man who more closely resembles the Gabe LoScuda of old. I think of John. I think about how he would have shredded the dance floor with this song playing in the background. About how he'd lose himself in the moment in a way I always wished I could.

I think about what happened that day, when I returned to the lunch table after John and I performed our Rock 'em, Sock 'em robots routine and after Mastro wrestled us apart. I think about how Marlie said, "What was *that* all about?" and how I was like, "He'll be alright. He just needs to cool off." And then I think about how she said something ridiculous like, "No. I mean, how do you even know that guy? What. A. Lo-ser!" And how I just picked up my books and said, "Marlie. He's my best friend." I walked to class alone that day.

I think about how, ever since that moment, my lunch dates with Marlie seem to pass without many actual words being exchanged between the two of us. I guess that's kind of normal when you're in a relationship. At least, I think.

And I think about the essay I wrote that was basically dedicated to John, and about how much I miss having the kid around — maybe even more than I miss Gramps. I look at my reflection in the mirror and barely recognize the guy looking back. What happened? What in the hell had I been thinking?

And that's when I make a decision.

Even though I still have plenty of time to loaf around the house this morning watching *Sports Center* and eating Cheerios out of coffee mugs and taking twenty-minute showers — all the general luxuries I've enjoyed since my captivity by Gramps ended — I realize my time might be best spent elsewhere.

I'm in and out of the shower in under two minutes, and I'm dressed in even less time. Quick-change artistry became somewhat of a specialty when I was taking care of Grandpa. I hop in the Trans-Am without eating a single Cheerio, and guide her around the block. I pull up in John's driveway just like old times — only I'm early for once. The screen door on John's porch opens and John shuffles out with his four-hundred pound backpack. It's loaded down with even more books than usual today.

He glances at me as he traverses the walkway in front of his house and, for a second, I think he's going to just step right over to the passenger side and hop in like our normal morning routine. But then his eyes glaze over and he looks off into the distance, far beyond me and the Trans-Am. Far, far beyond the limits of our friendship. And he keeps walking. Right past me and down the driveway. He turns on the sidewalk and heads in the direction of school. On foot.

I pop the Trans-Am in reverse and inch up along side him and roll the window down. "John!" He keeps walking, so I trail him in my car at a snail's pace. "Come on, man. Let me at least talk to you for a minute. Just give me one stinking minute."

He stops. He doesn't bother to look at me, but he dismounts from his backpack and lays it down on the sidewalk, which is John-speak for "I'm listening. You have sixty seconds."

"Look," I say, "I don't know what's going on between us. But it's stupid, man. We don't need to go on this way."

I'm silent for a second, waiting for John to respond — to say everything's alright and hop in the car and go to school like nothing ever happened between us in the first place. But he doesn't say anything. He just stands there with his bag on the ground and his arms folded across his chest. The silence is killing me so, against my will, I let words continue to tumble out of my stupid mouth. I just wish they'd been the right freaking words. They were not.

"We're both sorry," I say. "We both messed up. But things worked out, didn't they? I'm not it jail. I'm with Marlie now. I — "

Suddenly John's face goes blood red and his nostrils flare like he's a raging bull and I'm a giant red blanket.

"I'm so happy for you, Gabe. I really am, you know that? It's great that you're Mr. Freaking Schuylkill High all of a sudden. Good for you. But would it kill you to say *thanks* once in a while?"

"*Thanks?* What the hell are you talking about?"

"Exactly," he says. "You've changed, man. And not for the better. Maybe Sofia was right about you. You're just a poseur, Gabe. You and Marlie deserve each other."

I'm speechless. Not because he insulted Marlie for the second time, because I have to say: each lunch period I spend with her seems to nudge me ever-closer to John's perspective. No. I'm speechless because in all the time I'd known my best friend and after all the stupid and selfish things I'd done, John Chen had never lost faith in me. He knew I wasn't perfect, but at least he knew who I was. But something had changed, and now John seemed pretty confident we were destined to become nothing more than strangers.

John picks up his bag, slings it over his shoulder, and continues the long walk to school. He doesn't look back. He can't bear to see the stupid face of a rotten, unappreciative poseur. Not even for one more second.

And maybe, just maybe, if I actually look in the mirror long enough and hard enough, I might be able to see the same thing.

21

EXODUS

"Let's park in the lot today," Nick says.

"The paid lot?" I ask, which for Nick was like asking him if he wanted me to drive the car off a cliff.

"Yeah, he says. "My treat."

The light turns green but I don't push the gas pedal. My foot won't respond to the shock.

"What's the occasion?" I ask as an impatient driver behind me lays on the horn.

"Besides not wanting to waste half of our visiting hours?"

"Yeah, because combing the streets for a spot never forced a spare nickel out of your pocket before."

"It's not *before* anymore," he says, which ranks up there as maybe the deepest statement that has ever left Nick's mouth. "Besides, I owe you."

I inch the Trans-Am over a series of speed bumps, the way Dad taught me how to take them at an angle. I snatch the little ticket out of the mechanized attendant and begin a spiraling ascent to the summit of the parking garage.

"You don't owe me anything," I say, and I'm a bit confused by his statement.

"I do," Nick says. "For so many things. I can't even list them all. But the most important thing was that you *inspired* me, Gabe. I watched you with Gramps every day. I know you may not be able to see it now with all the old age and depression in that place."

I nod. I can't stand seeing Gramps holed up in the assisted living wing at the veteran's hospital. He gets to keep Doc Weston as a protector in exchange for anything that resembles freedom. I'm not sure my grandfather got the best end of the deal, but at least it's the safest one—for him, for the neighborhood, and maybe even for Nick and me. But no matter how many times I tell myself this is what's best for Gramps, I can't help but picture Dad's face all sour and twisted, just shaking back and forth and saying something like, "Moron!" I guess it's something I'll have to learn to live with.

"But Gabe," Nick continues, "I don't know where Gramps and me would be without you. Not getting treatment, like Gramps, I can tell you that. And definitely not putting registration materials together for the Bar exam, like me."

"You're gonna take the test again?"

"I have to finish, Gabe. I owe that to a lot of people."

I pull the car into an empty space on the top tier of the lot, flick off the ignition, and hold out my right hand to Nick. He grabs it and shakes it. "I'm proud of you, Uncle Nick," I say. And this time, when the words leave my mouth, they don't surprise me in the least. A pinkish hue rises on Nick's cheeks.

"And just think," he says, "all it took was the threat of my nephew's jail time on my shoulders."

We laugh, and without either one of us being conscious of it, our handshake turns into a bear hug. I feel one of Nick's hot tears slip off his cheek and roll down the back of my shirt. It makes me jump, and then the whole thing starts to feel awkward, so we gather the last of Grandpa's things and head for the entrance to the hospital. But as we reach the door, Nick throws one of his mutant-sized arms out in front of me and turns to speak. I can tell the words weigh heavily on his tongue. He measures them with his teeth before he dispenses.

"You do know that none of this is your fault, right?"

"Yeah, I know, Nick."

I try to side step him and head for the door—anything to avoid hearing this load of crap I'm not prepared to accept; will never be able to accept—but he's massive, like a blubber-encapsulated boulder. And he's right in my path.

"I'm serious," he says. "You cared for Gramps better than you cared for yourself. I saw it. And I sat there on the couch for most of it, as if you guys were some comedy routine just there for my entertainment. But it's not funny. None of it is funny . . . but . . . but I want you to be able to laugh again, Gabe. Some day. Maybe not today. But some day I want you to remember there was nothing and nobody in the world who could have prevented this. Not you, not me, not Doc Weston or the judge. Not even your father, Gabe. Not even him."

Nick reaches in his jacket pocket and pulls out a handkerchief. He gives it to me and I wipe away tears I didn't know were there. I feel this weird, constricted feeling in the back of my throat that tells me there's nothing I could say right now even if it were possible to find the words.

"Tell me you'll laugh again, Gabe. Promise me, OK?"

I nod and wipe a few more tears away. Nick slaps me on the back and leads me through the door. "I needed to know that," he says.

We sign in at the reception kiosk and head down the hall to Room 706. The hallway is bustling with activity as usual—probably my least favorite part of the visit. A fat, red-faced orderly pushes a cart loaded down with jiggling, green Jell-O in plastic cups. He nods to a nurse as she strains to lift an old woman in a stained nightgown from one wheelchair to another. The lady shrieks as if the nurse were throwing her in the stockade and the nurse tries to diffuse the bomb by making cooing noises and by stroking the lady's silver hair. It seems to work. Two old men sit in folding chairs outside their rooms. They toss ragged playing cards in a pile from opposite sides of the hallway to complete the objectives of a game that probably doesn't exist and never will. One of them screams, "Yaaaahtzeee!" out of the blue and at a moment where no action from either man should have warranted such a reaction. One of the fluorescent light bulbs overhead flickers and flashes every minute or so, just like it did on our last two visits.

This is apparently all you're afforded after serving your country and dodging bullets for years in a freaking trench in France. Your reward for survival. Not like the kinds of places Nick and I looked at in the Crypt Keeper's brochures, where rooms were furnished by freaking Waverly; where tennis pros taught forehands and backhands to geriatric cases; where you could dial *9 on your phone and order room service at any time of day. No, those places are only made available to people who spend their lives lying and cheating people out of their money. Stockbrokers and bankers and other assorted a-holes of the socio-economic breed. Not war heroes. War heroes get to spend their final days in places that aren't even fit to be bomb shelters.

But we get to Room 706 and I wipe the scowl off my face for Grandpa's sake, because no one likes to hear that their new place is a dumpster fire.

Doc Weston and two hefty nurses—who looked like they may have moonlighted on a local roller derby team—surround Grandpa's bed and move in on him like they've cornered a rabid raccoon. Gramps sits in a pile of his robes and socks in the middle of the bed with both hands clamped over his mouth. I can barely understand the muffled noises forcing their way through tiny gaps between his fingers, but I think he says something like, "I won't swallow them!"

Doc stands at the foot of the bed with a tiny cup filled with various pills. "They will help you, Mr. LoScuda. You need to take them."

Doc jumps a little when he notices Nick and I hovering at the back of the room. He glances at his nurses who gradually inch toward Gramps with his twin talons clutching at the acrid, hospital air. I can't bear to watch any more of this.

"Let me try," I say to Doc. "See if I still have the touch."

I yank the plastic cup out of Doc's hand before he can protest, and I approach the bed. Gramps sees me, and the glaze of ice over his eyes melts away. He lowers his hands from his mouth and there's a smile full of ragged, yellow teeth behind it. "Keep your nose clean," he says. "Keep your nose clean." He's excited, and who can blame him after being holed up in this room all week.

"I'll keep it clean, Grandpa," I say to him, and I hold up the cup of pills to show him what I plan to do. No need to fool the old man anymore.

"No pudding today," I tell him. "The whole town ran out. Must be a shortage."

I hear Nick and one of the nurses fighting back a snicker. I sit down on the edge of the bed. Gramps reaches for a pair of rolled up socks and glares at Doc Weston. I can see the old man's thoughts register, like a mental news ticker, across his forehead.

"No grenades today," I say. "They've already surrendered, soldier. Now stand down."

Gramps looks at me, then at his sock grenade, then at the glass of water. I hold it out to him. He takes it. Drops the socks on the mattress. I slip the pills in his outstretched palm and he gobbles them up like a bunch of Tic-Tacs and then washes them down with a few hearty gulps of water.

"You're a fine soldier, lieutenant," I say, and we salute each other before I dismount the bed and file back into the ranks. Gramps goes back to unfolding and refolding his dirty laundry—one of the perpetual rigors of a man in assisted living.

I feel Doc's hand on my shoulder, patting out the universal rhythm that says, "Good job, kid." But I feel this urge to slap his hand off my shoulder and tell him to go to hell. That if he ever treats my grandfather like he's some kind of hopeless case, some deranged mental patient, I'll fire him out through the grimy windows of Room 706. But then I remember: Gramps is a hopeless case. He'll never get better. Never rise up out of that bed and recite the state capitals. So I let Doc have his moment—let him think he's turned out to be some great mentor to me or something. Adults seem to love that crap. Mostly I keep my mouth shut because I don't want to upset Gramps on our only day together.

After we're all settled, Doc sits us down in the back of the room and updates us on Grandpa's condition. "It's pretty much status quo," he tells us. "He's eating, taking his medication with some prodding, and he seems to be sleeping rather consistently."

"That's good," I say. "But does he seem happy?" Doc looks at me funny, like I'd just asked him to explain the theory of relativity to a classroom full of third graders.

"Well, he seems comfortable," Doc says.

"That's not what I asked. I asked if he's happy."

Doc exhales and taps his pen on the corner of his clipboard.

"Are *you* happy, Gabe?" he asks. "I would say, in looking at you, that you are a generally happy person—but is that truly the case?"

I don't respond because I don't know what the hell he's talking about. Doc takes the silence as a cue to continue his Psych 101 lesson.

"You see, we're the only ones who can truly say whether or not we're happy. You don't have to be a patient in an assisted living facility to fall in that category. Does your grandfather appear to be happy? At times, yes. But if you want an honest answer, Gabe, I can't provide it for you. The research on patients like your grandfather hasn't reached levels where we can predict with any reliability what the experience is like from a mental standpoint."

"Is he suffering?" Nick asks.

"Not at the moment," Doc says. "He's just as strong as any healthy man his age, but you can never predict how the body will react to changes in the brain. We'll have to monitor him and cross bridges as we come to them."

"I'm not," I say. And that puzzled look rises on Doc's face again.

"Not what?" he asks.

"*Happy.* This whole situation sucks for all of us."

"Yes, but—"

"But I'm not incapable of being happy again," I say, "and I guess I can accept what's ahead of us—because what choice do we have?"

"Well, that's a start," Doc says, and he pats me on the shoulder.

This time I don't have the urge to put him in a headlock.

"We changed dosages on some of your grandfather's meds. Nothing major, but you'll need to sign off on a few documents for insurance purposes. Don't forget to do so at the front desk before visiting hours are over."

I thank Doc and tell Nick to enjoy some time with his father while I get all the paperwork out of the way. I hop on the elevator and press the button with a big star on it to go to the lobby. There's some lame elevator version of Lionel Richie's "Dancing on the Ceiling" playing—as if the original wasn't lame enough. The elevator lurches and begins its slow, shaky descent to the lobby. After it passes the fifth floor, I feel the cable tighten and the floor push up against my feet. The bell chimes as the number four pops up on the overhead indicator. The doors rattle and open and, standing in front of me, is a splattered nightmare of ink and mascara holding a cup of coffee.

The dark circles around her eyes make the sockets look bottomless, and they clash against the redness of her lids. Streaks of makeup slash across her face like war paint, and her shoulders hunch forward like she's bearing the weight of eternity on her back.

Her eyes flash when they meet mine. She recovers and plods forward to join me in the elevator car. She pushes the button for the second floor—the cancer unit—and stands on the opposite side of the car, as far away from me as possible.

"You can talk to me, you know," I say as the doors slide shut.

"I know," she says, and her voice sounds all distant and empty.

"You okay?"

And that's all it takes for Sofia to drop her cup of scalding coffee on the floor and to bury her face in the sleeve of her flannel shirt. Sobs take over her body and wrack at her ribs and back until my arms are around her and her tears stain the shoulder of my t-shirt.

"She's not gonna make it," she squeezes through the tears and the sobs and the sniffles. "My mom. She's not gonna make it."

She says it over and over again as I press her to my chest and rub little circles on her shoulder blades. The doors open on the second floor and I lead Sofia to a pair of folding chairs outside of her mother's room. I grab a box of tissues off the nurse's station and wipe the tears from Sofia's face the way my mother used to do when I'd fall off my bike.

"What's happening?" I ask when it seems I have her calmed down.

"It spread," she says with a sniffle, "to her lungs and her lymph nodes. It'll be any day now." And that instigates a whole new round of sobbing and embracing and tear wiping. The whole time I feel like this wimpy little alien who landed on a new planet where there's no chance for survival. And here's this girl who'd literally make me piss my pants if I didn't know her and happened upon her up some dark alleyway—and even *she* can't seem to stand up to this freaking bully we call life. And it's weird because, in those moments of grief and strife, I see the frightened little girl under all of those tattoos and the dyed hair and the ripped clothing and the punk rock. I see that, under it all, she's just Gabe LoScuda like the rest of us— just in a meaner and cooler package.

"I'm so sorry," I tell her. "I really am sorry."

"I know," she says.

"And you might not want to hear this, but you were right."

"About what?"

"Grandpa. You and John did the right thing. I didn't see it at the time, but it was what I needed."

"I know," she says.

"And, even though we've been kind of like strangers lately, I need you to know that I'll be there for you because I'm not a poseur. Not even as a friend."

"I know," she says. "I've always known. From the first time we talked, Gabe, I've been all ears. See?" She unbuttons a tiny pocket on the sleeve of her flannel and pulls out a small piece of flesh-colored plastic. She hands it to me.

"It's a freaking ear," I say. "Don't tell me you're going all Van Gogh on me. I mean, you're a pretty good artist but—"

"You don't remember?" I flip the plastic ear up in the air like a coin and catch it on the back of my hand.

"Of course I remember. Mr. Potato Head! The dude wouldn't shut the hell up that day in the waiting room."

Sofia laughs and tries to mask her smile, but she can't. When I see the tension lift from her face, I can't help myself. I laugh. And then I think about what Nick had said to me back in the parking lot about finding the laughter again. The good times. And I look at Sofia's face. There's so much in it. So much character. So much pain. So many years of caring for her mother that I doubt she'll understand life when she's not bound by her servitude any longer. She'll barely recognize it—like a wimpy, little alien on a foreign planet filled with pain at every turn.

"Keep it," she says.

"No, no. You have to keep it," I tell her. "You were smart enough to save it so—"

"I already have my own," she says, and she pulls down the front of her shirt a few inches to reveal a new work of art. "I did it myself. Had to use a few different mirror angles to get it right."

I'm amazed. On her chest, just a few inches above her heart, is a tattoo of a Mr. Potato Head ear. There's a dangly earing hanging from the lobe— one like you might have seen worn by Giants legend Lawrence Taylor— with a diamond-encrusted cross hanging from the end of a chain. Only Sofia could have dreamed up something like that.

"As usual, mine's a little cooler than yours," she says.

I laugh. Again.

"I love it," I say. "It's perfect." And before I can make a protest to my body, I feel my face move closer to Sofia's. She doesn't look away, just stares at me through midnight eyes. The warmth of her lips meets mine, and our fingers instinctively lace around each other and, for a few moments, we're lifted far, far away from the antiseptic din of the hospital; far away from court rooms and assisted living facilities and funeral homes; far away from all that makes the act of living on this planet feel like living. And then our lips part and Sofia rests her head down on my shoulder.

We sit in folding chairs outside her mom's room without saying a word and listen to the squeaky wheels of a portable IV unit call to us from a distant hallway. And everything feels all right. For once.

"So what are you gonna tell Marlie?"

"Oh God," I say, "you know about that?"

"John and I have kept in touch. You didn't think I'd stop spying on you, did you?"

"Boy, am I screwed with her."

We burst out laughing and raise the eyebrows of a stern nurse who'd just returned to her medical station. But we don't care because, at least for now, the laughter has us insulated from the worst—lying only a few yards behind us through the hospital-white threshold. We know we can't stop it from coming.

22

LAUGHTER

Uncle Nick must have grown tired of looking at the stupid grin I had plastered on my face all the way from the hospital to our driveway. I didn't talk. Just smiled and kept my foot on the pedal.

"You didn't happen to swallow some of Grandpa's pills, did you?"

"What?" I ask, with the same stupid grin still stuck on my face.

"Pills . . . grandpa's pills," he repeats. "Maybe one of the little, pink ones?"

He was talking about Razadyne. Happy pills. They give them to building jumpers and people like Gramps, so even if we can't tell if they're happy or not, at least it looks that way on the outside. Makes us feel better. Also makes me wonder whom the pills are really meant to serve.

"No. You're kidding, right?"

"Well, we go to a hospital and you come home with a face that looks like it should be floating over the Thanksgiving Day parade. What am I supposed to think?"

"I'm fine, Nick." Shitty grin still hanging strong. "No. I'm not fine. I'm *great*, actually. Really freaking great!"

I lean back against the grey cloth of my faithful car's interior. Take a breath. If I inhale just right and think hard enough, I can still smell the new car scent from the day Dad first rumbled into the driveway with it. It would have been nice to make him proud. To stand up in the face of the improbable—maybe even the impossible—and flick it away like some annoying fly.

But today, after seeing Sofia transform from the model of Athena into a puddle under Athena, and seeing how even *she* is nowhere near indestructible, it made me think: maybe Dad isn't so disappointed in me wherever he may be. That maybe somewhere, stuffed deep inside the hard shell that has cooled around Grandpa's surface, the old man *is* happy. He's taking Sunday drives down wooded roads and there are no squirrels in sight.

And hey, at least I have Nick. And at least I have *time*. And at least I have *friends*. And that's about when I feel the grin vanish from my face like it'd never been there in the first place—because something very big was missing.

"Nick. Can you get out of the car? Now. Please," I say. Nick looks at me like maybe he was the one that swallowed half a bottle of pills.

"You alright?"

"Yep. I'm fine. But there's somewhere I need to be."

Nick steps out on the driveway, pushes the door closed, and leans in like he's about to say something. Probably something like, "Dude, did you catch something from Grandpa?" But I'm already halfway down the driveway, maybe even nipped the poor guy's foot with my front tire. I couldn't tell. But I'm too locked in on necessity to worry, so I spin the Trans-Am around and race off down the street.

I ring the doorbell and listen to footsteps scatter across the wooden floor inside. John and I used to pretend we were Olympic speed skaters and glide around on the same sheet of pine in our socks on days after Lily had waxed it to a shine. She was like a tiny Zamboni filled with fury instead of water—especially after a few rounds on the "rink" wiped away her shine.

The door swings open and Lily Chen stands there expressionless.

"Hello, Gabe."

"Hi, Mrs. Chen. I was—"

"John's not here."

"Oh, I see. I was—"

"I gave up my secretary job long ago. If you have a message you can tell him yourself."

"He won't talk to me."

"Me neither."

It's weird. For a second, I think I see a muscle twitch in her face as she says it. Probably just my imagination.

"He won't?" I say, trying to sound as surprised as possible. "That's weird."

"Not weird, Gabe. It says so in this book."

She holds up a copy of some text-booky looking thing with a picture of these two lanky teenagers in cutoff jean shorts walking down a wooded path. Their backs are turned and they both have 70s-style afros, so you can't really tell which one is the guy and which one is the girl—or if that's even the combination of genders at all. "It says here that teenagers rebel. They try to leave the nest. Avoid responsibility. Get pimples."

"I'm sure it's just a—"

"It says it, Gabe. In this book. Right here. You see it?"

She spins a few pages and shoves it about two inches in front of my face. I push it away.

"It's just a book. And it can't account for people like John. He's a good son, Mrs. Chen. He works harder than anyone I've ever met. He's always on time. He holds doors—all the stuff you're always ragging on him about."

I take a breath and notice Lily's eyes are wild with fire, but I'm on a roll so I jump right back in the ring. "He does his homework, has perfect freaking attendance—*and he's my friend.* And that's not an easy thing to be, Mrs. Chen. I mean, have you seen me? My Uncle Nick and my crazy, robotic grandfather? We're borderline psychopaths, us LoScudas. If it wasn't for your son we'd all be in straitjackets by now. He's a great kid, Mrs. Chen. The best that I know of, and no book is ever gonna tell you that. You have to look. With your own eyes. And you'll definitely see it." Then I notice it again. A muscle twitches and then an eyelid budges, and then a single, perfect tear rolls down Lily Chen's face, extinguishing the flames.

"And one more thing—please, *get that kid a car!* Don't you think he deserves some freedom?"

But Mrs. Chen never gets a chance to respond because the door swings back a little further and from behind it springs the Asian Michael Jackson. My best friend.

"The car thing was a nice touch," he says, "but don't count on it."

"John!" I say. "So I should keep picking you up late every morning?"

"How do you think I'll get to school? Walk?"

And for the second, maybe third, time that day I find myself laughing.

Gabe LoScuda
English 4A – Personal Essay #9
Mr. Mastrocola
March 17

No Sad Songs

Life is a series of your best and worst moments. It's like pizza—and hear me out on this. Because, one day, you might find yourself sinking your teeth into the cheesiest, crustiest, most pepperoni-laden slice of pizza you've ever experienced. It could be, in the moment, the greatest slice you've ever encountered—the grand, motherload of all of pizza's past, present, and future. But inevitably, that moment passes and you find yourself—at another date in the not-so-distant future—nibbling at the edges of a slice of pizza with a cheese-to-crust-to-pepperoni ratio that makes your current favorite taste like an old dishrag.

My point is that living life, like being a self-proclaimed pizza connoisseur, takes a certain understanding of how to cope with rising temperatures— because you always have to be prepared for the next in a series of escalating degrees. You have to be prepared at all times for something far better or something far worse than you've ever imagined to swoop in and steal the title of "best or worst thing ever." Whatever that thing may be.

Take me, for example. I thought the hardest thing I'd ever face was losing my parents on some random night in August. I figured I'd binge out on some video games, go to sleep, and see them in the morning. The next thing I know, a crowd of officers flanks me and they're asking me if the two lifeless shells on the metal gurneys in front of me are the same people who raised me. It was hard. Shocking. Life shattering.

But then I became a parent. At the ripe old age of eighteen, I became the world's first teenage male to give birth to an eighty-year-old man. And it happened at the precise moment Dad's Volvo flipped over the guardrail and passed beyond this world forever.

And if it wasn't enough, at that point, to clean dribble off an old guy's chin, and bathe the man who used to bounce you around on his knee, and to run back and forth from doctor's appointments to work to school and back again, enter my Uncle Nick—the only man in history too invisible to be named as the black sheep of his own family—with a half a pint of scotch and two smokes in his pocket. Suddenly, I'm a single parent of two. As if I hadn't already been striking out with Marlie—and any other girl within a fifty-mile radius—at a rate that made Pete Incaviglia look like Ted Williams. I was about one disorderly conduct charge away from a Jerry Springer episode.

But then, one solemn morning, I awoke to a quiet house. Gramps was cuddled up and expertly medicated in his room at the veteran's hospital; Nick was on his customary loop to the library and then the coffee shop, where he'd cram any last minute legal jargon into his already teeming mind.

I reached deep into the old shaving kit on this morning. I pulled out Dad's ratty, disposable razor, which I hadn't used in months. I figured that on this day, I could use all the help I could get. I shaved, showered, and squeezed myself into the gently-used suit I'd picked up at a thrift store along Main Street.

I folded up the piece of notebook paper with the frayed spiral edges and tucked it inside the breast pocket of my jacket. I'd been bent over that page and chewing on my pencil for the majority of the previous night. I hadn't slept, but something told me Sofia's night had been much worse than mine. That thought kept me going. Sofia and I had only spoken one time on the phone over the few days prior, but she'd asked me to say a few words the last time we'd been together—at the hospital.

I wanted to say "no." Lord knows the fear locked up in my throat wouldn't allow me to utter a word or I probably would have. I nodded instead, and then Sofia buried her face in my sweater and I held her so tightly I thought she would crumble.

But she didn't—and neither did I. I rose in the pulpit that morning and took the two steps up to the peak of the podium. I stood in front of the microphone, in front of a sea of black-clothed observers I'd never met and would never know, and I took a deep breath. I looked at Sofia's chocolate eyes, rimmed in red and swirling in grief. They were dry, but tears seemed heaped just at the edges, ready to overflow. The thought of it brought the same, unmistakable sting to the backs of my pupils. I unfolded the wrinkled piece of loose leaf and cleared my throat.

Then I touched on the words of Christina Rossetti.

She wrote:

When I am dead, my dearest
Sing no sad songs for me
Plant no roses at my head
Nor shady Cypress tree.

And I talked about the beauty of Lola Flores and that, even though I only knew her as a woman in a hospital bed, it was clear how much she valued life and how much she loved the one thing she could always count on—her daughter Sofia. I told of the only real conversation I'd ever had with Ms. Flores on a rainy evening when Sofia had left the room to fetch ice chips or broth or a nurse. She told me I reminded her of her brother, Javier, who was the first in her family to leave Mexico City and come to the United States to seek a better life. She said he was a good man. An honorable man. That he left his home but never truly left his family. Even so, she missed him, and her longing eventually turned to anger towards the big brother she felt had left her behind. She never had the chance to forgive him; but she would not allow the experience—nor any of her experiences—to escape her.

She told me, "Gabe, do not mourn the past. That is the devil's keenest trap. But don't forget it either. Because it is not garbage. It is gold. You should treasure it, learn from it, celebrate it—in that order—and then use it to harness the present and adapt for the future."

And so, please—I beg you—sing no sad songs for me. Do not grimace or fret or lose a second of sleep wondering if I'll make it without Mom and Dad. Because I've got Nick and Sofia and John to be what Rossetti called the "green grass above me." Freaking John. An ever-present strip of brilliant, green sod—even through the coldest days of January. Rossetti would like my best friend. She most certainly would.

And don't drop your jaw in horror and run all the devilish possibilities of how my relationships with Gramps or Sofia or even my Uncle Nick could morph and twist and coagulate in any number of negative directions. I used to think I could control stuff like that. Now I know it's not possible.

No, for me, it's all about taking the hardest moments as they come—dealing with them one by one—each instance a personalized preparation for the next impending challenge—and dwelling only long enough to remember the good without getting sullied by the bad.

Or, as Rossetti would say, "And if thy wilt, remember. And if thy wilt, forget."

When I think about it that way, I realize that I didn't break my promise to Dad after all. Maybe he's smiling, watching over Gramps in his hospital room, and thinking "Ah, my son, Gabe. He may not have followed the blueprint, but he sure as hell gave it his best shot."

Maybe he's even proud of me.

Yes, I think he is.

And as I watch my grandfather fade away a little more each day, I'll refuse to see him with a string of saliva hanging from his lip, or with a clenched-fist raised to an invasive nurse. No. I'll see him behind the wheel of his Cadillac; with the sugary remnants of vanilla ice cream trapped in his beard; with a tiny bundle of Gabe lifted high over his head; and with the soft gruffness of his voice as my tired eyes trail off to sleep.

"Haply may I remember (Grandpa)
And haply may I forget."

Haply may we all forget.

23

ELYSIAN FIELDS

No matter how long I play this game, no matter how many times I hear the trademark ping of aluminum collide with rawhide, I'm convinced baseball is not a sport meant to take place in March in places like Philadelphia. I mean, isn't that why God created freaking spring training and Clearwater, Florida and giant mesh bags filled with grapefruits? Isn't that why a human hand reacts with such disdain to the sting of a long throw from centerfield caught in the center of the palm?

But today is somehow different. Cold, yes. But different.

Today, instead of pressing my poor butt cheeks against a metal bench and praying I'll win my personal battle against frostbite on the unmentionable parts of my body, I take two steps off the grass and feel my spikes crunch through the frozen, orange clay of the infield. Today, I force my heart down out of my throat and take a few suppressed breaths and watch the steam spout out of my mouth and nostrils. Today, I watch Coach Foley swing the fungo and direct ground balls through the infield grass and out to second base. Today, I open my hips just like Dad taught me and pivot towards the hole close to first base. I squeeze the ball in my forehand, set my feet like I've practiced since the days of my training sessions with Carter, and I fire it over to Billy Barfield, our first baseman. See today, I'm just an anxious, nervous, ready-to-puke, butterflies-in-my-stomach kind of player. Because today, like no other day in the history of the sport, the lineup card that hangs in the Schuylkill High locker room looks something like this:

1. Clint MacGlinchy – SS
2. Foster Cunningham – CF
3. Richie Johnston – 3B
4. Billy Barfield – 1B
5. Brent Holidell – LF

6. Jerry Skinner – C
7. Khan Phiathep – RF
8. GABE LOSCUDA – 2B
9. Bradley Beyring – P

Yes, you read that correctly: a freaking starter!

Even I have to stand here at my position for a moment and let it all sink in. I breathe in the cold, crystalline air. Let it burn my lungs as Coach shoots a grounder over to Johnston at third and he completes the play with a bullet across the diamond. I reach down and scoop up a handful of loose gravel, put a few pebbles in my back pocket for the memories, and rough up the palms of my hands with the rest of it. I stare off into the stands, filled with Schuylkill High students of every shape, size, color, and social standing. And then I see a pair of stragglers walking in through the front gates of the ball field. They are different from the crowd, because it's not every day you see the Asian Michael Jackson and Johnny Rotten's long lost niece stroll in to watch a high school baseball game—even if it's the season opener and the famous Gabriel "Freaking" LoScuda is creating magic at second base.

I tip my cap to them as I hear "LoScuda!" ring out in Coach's gruff voice. Then the trademark PING! And I'm half out of my shoes and my legs are all tangled up on each other, and then the ball takes a short hop a few feet in front of my glove . . . and then it's past me and into the outfield. Freaking booted. I look over to the stands where John and Sofia are about to take a seat in the third row. Sofia nudges John with her elbow and points in my direction. There's a fat, caterpillar-shaped smirk on her mouth, while John pulls a tiny golf pencil out of his pocket and makes a quick tic mark on his clipboard. Sheesh, some things never change.

"One more!" I shout to Coach. And this time I keep my eyes away from the stands, away from the pebbles on the infield, away from anything other than the white globe that skitters towards me through the yellow grass. I charge it, get my legs wide and low to the ground, and caress the ball in my glove as if it were the most fragile egg on the planet. Then I pivot, drop to one knee, and fire a strike to second base, where Clint McGlinchy swipes the corner of the bag and fires a laser to first to complete a sweet double play. "Atta-boy, LoScuda!" Coach shouts, and at that moment all of the butterflies lift away. I glance over to the stands and see Sofia with two thumbs in the air and John scribbling notes on the clipboard—but he's smiling, so I know that must mean I'm ready.

I trot off the field, grab my bat, and head to the cage along the third base line for a few practice swings. As I squeeze a helmet onto my huge melon, I notice Sofia and John make their way from the stands—which is cool because they know they're the only ones with the power to keep me from thinking too much. Without them I'm liable to turn into a freaking basket case before they even play the "Star-Spangled Banner." They're special like that. Kind of like the poet John Donne, who will forever be famous for writing, "No man is an island, entire of itself, every man is a piece of the continent, a part of the main."

It's easy to forget that point when you're wiping dribble from an old man's lip, or watching a family member drown in a bottle of whiskey, or sitting alone on a witness stand hoping to salvage what's left of a life you barely own. But when you have a smooth-dancing pseudo-pop star and a sexy, tattooed nightmare as your closest friends, the continental divide doesn't seem so divided anymore.

I smile and step into the batter's box as John and Sofia find a secret perch behind a neighbor's privacy fence and adjacent to the batting cage—a good place to hide from the watchful eyes of Coach Foley, who is absolute in his desire to keep his players separated from the fans, or what he calls "the riff-raff."

"Fifty-percent aint gonna cut it, Meat," John says from over my shoulder. The first pitch rings off my bat and sails on a line over the L-shaped pitching screen. I glance back at John. His eyes are wide and Sofia has this look of contentment on her face—even though I'm pretty sure she basically hates anything even resembling a sport.

"If I keep doing that," I say, "Coach won't care if I field a damn thing all day."

"Yeah, yeah," John says. "Lucky swing." But then I rip another liner off the left-side netting of the cage. And then another. And then two more.

"The kid's alright," Sofia says in the voice of some old-timey, Knute Rockne kind of coach from the forties or fifties. "Don't know how he'll run with that enormous head of his, but, hey, the kid's alright."

"Hey," I say between swings, "this enormous head of mine is where I get my power. I'm like Samson, with the hair and all."

"Yeah?" John says. "If we cut it off, will that weaken the sound of your stupid voice?"

"You mean the hair?"

"No," he says, "the head."

"Man, you play way too many video games." I say. Then I smash another liner, this time directly off the L-screen. It wobbles back and forth a few times and I let that sink in a little before I look back at John and Sofia.

"You're ready," John says, and I notice his pencil is packed away in his pocket and the clipboard hangs loosely at his side.

"Yeah," Sofia says, "you might just not make a complete ass of yourself out there. I'm impressed."

I feel my face get all hot and I grab the brim of the helmet and pretend to adjust it on my head so nobody—especially Sofia—notices the red splotches rise on my cheeks. I step out of the cage and drop my bat against the fence. Then I prepare to step onto the field for my first time as a starter on the Schuylkill High School Varsity Baseball team. Man, I like the sound of that. Dad would have appreciated it, too.

I grab my glove off the bench and start to take my first step over the chalk line, but then I stop. I look over my shoulder at Sofia and John—my sister islands. We're all floating on the tide together, striving to form the world's most impenetrable archipelago.

"Thanks," I mouth to them, and they understand perfectly. Neither of them feel the need to say a word in return—well, except for John.

"Gabe," I hear him shout over the crowd as I trot out to second base, "Can I get a ride home?"

"Christ," I mutter. But then I turn and tip my cap to him—one of those famously esoteric baseball signs that means "sure, buddy, I'll meet you at the Trans-Am, you driver's-licenseless bastard!"

About Alzheimer's and Dementia

The Alzheimer's Association estimates almost a quarter of a million people will be diagnosed with Alzheimer's or another form of dementia in the next year alone. Currently, more than five million people are living with Alzheimer's and, by 2050, this number could grow to over sixteen million. Alzheimer's disease is actually the sixth-leading cause of death in the United States. But it's the only cause of death among the top ten in the United States that cannot be prevented, cured or even slowed. In fact, one out of every three seniors dies with some form Alzheimer's or dementia.

What many fail to recognize is how their family members (the caretakers) may also have their lives derailed by the disease. Right now, more than fifteen million Americans provide unpaid care for people with Alzheimer's or other dementias.

It is my hope that young readers will finish *No Sad Songs* with a new respect for what it takes to be a caregiver, and an understanding of how intertwined these duties become in the lives of people fighting on the front lines of a growing health dilemma that is rapidly approaching epidemic levels. And I want them to be inspired to become champions in the fight against this terrible disease so that future generations will never have to watch their loved ones disappear right before their eyes.

Alzheimer's Association. "2017 Alzheimer's disease facts and figures."
Alzheimer's & Dementia 13.4 (2017): 325-373.

FRANK MORELLI has been a teacher, a coach, a bagel builder, a stock boy, a pretzel salesman, a bus driver, a postal employee, a JC Penney model (see: *clerk*), an actual clerk (*like in the movie of the same name*), a camp counselor, a roving sports reporter, and a nuclear physicist (*okay, that's not true*). At heart, he's a writer, and that's all he's ever been. His fiction and essays have appeared in more than thirty publications, including *The Saturday Evening Post, Cobalt Review, Philadelphia Stories, Jersey Devil Press,* and *Indiana Voice Journal.* His sports-themed column, Peanuts & Crackerjacks, appears monthly at *Change Seven Magazine.*

A Philadelphia native, Frank now lives near Greensboro, NC in a tiny house under the trees with his best friend and muse, their obnoxious alley cats, and two hundred pounds worth of dog.

Connect with Frank at www.frankmorelliwrites.com, on Facebook, or on Twitter @frankmoewriter.